THE POISON PEN

ALSO BY PAIGE SHELTON

SCOTTISH BOOKSHOP MYSTERY SERIES

The Cracked Spine

Of Books and Bagpipes

*A Christmas Tartan
(a mini-mystery)*

Lost Books and Old Bones

The Loch Ness Papers

The Stolen Letter

Deadly Editions

The Burning Pages

Fateful Words

ALASKA WILD SERIES

Thin Ice

Cold Wind

Winter's End

Lost Hours

Dark Night

COUNTRY COOKING SCHOOL MYSTERY SERIES

If Fried Chicken Could Fly

*If Mashed Potatoes
Could Dance*

*If Bread Could Rise
to the Occasion*

If Catfish Had Nine Lives

If Onions Could Spring Leeks

FARMERS' MARKET MYSTERY SERIES

Farm Fresh Murder

Fruit of All Evil

Crops and Robbers

A Killer Maize

*Red Hot Deadly Peppers
(a mini-mystery)*

Merry Market Murder

Bushel Full of Murder

DANGEROUS TYPE MYSTERY SERIES

To Helvetica and Back

Bookman Dead Style

Comic Sans Murder

THE POISON PEN

A SCOTTISH BOOKSHOP MYSTERY

Paige Shelton

MINOTAUR
BOOKS
NEW YORK

First published in the United States by Minotaur Books, an imprint of St. Martin's Publishing Group

THE POISON PEN. Copyright © 2024 by Penelope Publishing, LLC. All rights reserved. Printed in the United States of America. For information, address St. Martin's Publishing Group, 120 Broadway, New York, NY 10271.

www.minotaurbooks.com

Library of Congress Cataloging-in-Publication Data

Names: Shelton, Paige, author.
Title: The poison pen / Paige Shelton.
Description: First edition. | New York : Minotaur Books, 2024. |
 Series: A Scottish bookshop mystery ; 9
Identifiers: LCCN 2023051645 | ISBN 9781250890603 (hardcover) |
 ISBN 9781250890610 (ebook)
Subjects: LCSH: Booksellers and bookselling—Fiction. | LCGFT:
 Cozy mysteries. | Novels.
Classification: LCC PS3619.H45345 P65 2024 | DDC 813/.6—dc23/
 eng/20231103
LC record available at https://lccn.loc.gov/2023051645

Our books may be purchased in bulk for promotional, educational, or business use. Please contact your local bookseller or the Macmillan Corporate and Premium Sales Department at 1-800-221-7945, extension 5442, or by email at MacmillanSpecialMarkets@macmillan.com.

First Edition: 2024

10 9 8 7 6 5 4 3 2 1

To: Josh, Sam, Leslie, Ranie,
Jan, Bob H., and Rubi: Gratias tibi.

THE POISON PEN

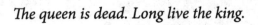

The queen is dead. Long live the king.

CHAPTER ONE

"I know of no single formula for success. But over the years I have observed that some attributes of leadership are universal and are often about finding ways of encouraging people to combine their efforts, their talents, their insights, their enthusiasm." The familiar voice came through the taxi's radio speakers.

I sniffed and then grabbed another tissue from my bag.

"Lass, are you all right?" Elias glanced at me as I sat in the passenger seat.

I smiled sadly and dabbed my eyes. "I'm fine."

Elias and his wife Aggie had shed plenty of tears too. They'd been at my and Tom's blue house by the sea when we heard the news of the queen's passing.

Queen Elizabeth II had died, right here in Scotland, in fact.

Though it hadn't been a surprise, it had most definitely been a shock. Her death would have made me sad had I still been in Kansas, but here in my new home in Scotland, I thought it probably hit me even harder. In one way or another, she'd been a part of my everyday life since I'd answered the online ad for my job and traveled across the sea, chasing the promise of an adventure. The promise had been more than fulfilled, and the queen had been a part of it, even so far as surprising us all one day by making an appearance on behalf of my boss, Edwin MacAlister. If she hadn't been endeared in my heart already, she certainly would have been then.

Edwin was more upset than the rest of us, unable to discuss her death without breaking down into sobs. Edwin's sobs were executed in a more sophisticated way than mine would be, but they were sobs nonetheless.

I'd asked him, as well as my coworkers, how well he'd known her, and he said that his sadness was wrapped around what a lovely woman and public servant she'd been. Both Rosie, my grandmotherly coworker, and Hamlet, my other coworker who had become like a younger brother to me, claimed that Edwin had never told them any more about his relationship with any of the royals than that he'd simply had the opportunity to meet the queen a long time ago and had been fiercely loyal to her since.

Rosie did confide in me that the queen was their favorite royal, and she would always be close to the hearts of the people I cared for. I understood completely.

Though she had passed a week ago now, tributes were still resounding from all media outlets. Elias had tuned his taxi's radio to a station that had been playing snippets of her speeches throughout the years, and we had just listened to an inspirational moment.

My bookish inner voices seemed to be on respite, making way in my head for only her voice. I kept hearing her words, via the radio and television, as well as when all else was silent and my mind worked to conjure what I'd heard earlier in the day. In fact, I felt somewhat distracted. We'd all been having trouble focusing.

As if knowing I needed a distraction from all the distraction, Edwin had called me the night before, telling me he had a project specifically for me, something different than I'd ever done.

I'd been excited to hear all about it, a new endeavor to sink my teeth into was exactly what the doctor ordered.

After I'd spoken with Edwin and told Tom about my new assignment, I'd called Elias, asking if he would be willing to drive me to a destination, at least on the first day of my new project. After that, I'd borrow Tom's car and drive myself.

I was a capable driver. At least I had been, back when I'd driven on the right side of the roads and the steering wheels were on the left sides of the cars. The differences in Scotland, along with so many narrow two-lane thoroughfares, had been a dizzying change from Kansas roadways. Wichita had its fair share of heavy traffic, but Edinburgh congestion had been a new and sometimes terrifying experience.

Nevertheless, I'd adjusted—mostly. But this trip was a little south of Edinburgh, in a village called Roslin, known for many wonderful and historic things, not the least of which was its big role in *The Da Vinci Code*, popular back in the early 2000s. The Rosslyn Cathedral had been a key location for the main characters' hunt in the book as well as the movie.

Another of its claims to fame was the Roslin Institute, where Dolly had become the first cloned sheep. The institute was still there, its mission to make the world a better place for animals and humans.

But my new project had nothing to do with the institute or any sort of treasure hunt—though treasure might be involved.

Roslin was seven miles south of the city, but I'd never been in that direction before. Since it wasn't too far away, Elias would drive me and then pick me up later. He'd been more than happy to do it. In fact, as I'd gauged his excitement, I'd realized that I probably should have been asking him to drive me more often. Today's ride might be melancholy, but we still had a chance to catch up with each other's lives.

We were on our way to an estate that belonged to a woman named Jolie Lannister, a "grand old broad" according to Edwin. I'd been startled by my buttoned-up boss's words. "Broad" wasn't something I thought he'd ever used to describe a woman. He'd chuckled then and said, "Her words, not mine."

I couldn't wait to meet her.

I was excited about the project that I was being sent to explore, retrieve if at all possible, and keep to myself at all costs. At least for now. Edwin had asked me not to give Elias any details. He'd suggested I might not even want to tell Tom quite yet, though he would never ask me to keep any secrets from my husband. I'd gone ahead and told Tom everything, and he'd been mightily intrigued.

Jolie Lannister had found something she was sure was rare and valuable, and had immediately thought of Edwin. She'd called to ask him if he wanted to take a look at it, maybe buy it or sell it in those auctions she knew he was a part of. That was the story he'd given me, though I sensed he'd left out things he didn't want *me* to know yet. I was too intrigued by all of it to push him for more information. I'd learn everything I needed to eventually.

Fleshmarket Batch, the auction group, was, at its most intrinsic level, a group of rich people who got together secretly (mostly) so they could buy and sell thing things for more money than most of us could understand. During his call, Edwin shared with me that a long time ago the group had invited Jolie to join but she'd declined, telling Edwin that she was unable to part with anything, ever. She liked her *things* and wanted to live her life and die with them surrounding her.

Edwin had also told me that in setting up this meeting, Jolie had surprised him by stating that she was now "ready to throw it all in a bin."

But before she did that, though, she wondered if Edwin wanted any of it, particularly the secret item that had recently been found on the grounds of her home. Edwin had told me that he'd been willing to take a look at everything himself but preferred that I do it instead, or at least first. This sort of thing was my job now, or it should be. He hadn't loosened his grip on the reins enough, he claimed, but he wanted to now. This was going to be my project until I thought he should become involved.

And I was grateful to have this new distraction.

Though I felt like I knew him and knew how he would want me to handle most things, I had asked if maybe he should come along on the first visit, and then I could take it from there.

"You will do fine, Delaney," he'd said. "In fact, I would guess you would do better than I've ever done. You have my blessing to make whatever decisions you deem appropriate." He'd paused. "Honestly, I'm not sure Jolie has what she thinks she has. You and I will discuss later, but, aye, give it a go."

So here I was, giving it a go, and very excited about it too.

The assignment had accomplished one thing already—I hadn't been quite as sad after the call with him as I had been before. Hearing the snippet of the queen's speech on the radio had brought more tears to the surface, but I was able to wipe them away for now so I might focus on the job. I would be sad about the queen's death for a long time, and I was okay with that. She was worth being sad over.

Jolie's estate, named West Rosebud House, was a mansion that had been in her family for a hundred years. According to Edwin, the family had always been populated with "lively characters," though he didn't go into more detail, telling me I'd enjoy learning about them on my own.

"Here we are." Elias nodded to his left.

I leaned forward and looked out the windshield toward the mansion. "Oh."

"Not what you expected?"

"Not even a little bit. It's . . . it looks like it could fall down any minute."

"Aye. It does."

The house belonged in a horror film. The wide, dark-brick structure was two gothically tall stories in height. Windows that were probably a normal size reminded me of castle windows that always seemed too narrow for the building, made more for shooting arrows out through than letting in the light. The tall façade overpowered the windows.

Nothing appeared plumb. None of the edges were without imperfection. A cobblestone circular drive appeared neither welcoming nor all that utilitarian—potholes throughout, even though two vehicles—a bright yellow van with illegible and faded red letters and a boring blue car—had already parked on it, one directly behind the next. A partially broken cherub sculpture sat atop a fountain in the middle of driveway, but no water ran through.

"More cars? Did you expect anyone other than Ms. Lannister?" Elias asked.

"I didn't know what to expect."

"Aye, and maybe they belong to her."

Elias pulled the taxi to the available spot behind the second vehicle.

"I'll be coming in with you," he said.

"Elias, I'll be fine."

"Aye, I'm sure. But I willnae drive away from here without checking things out inside. I'm sorry if that makes you uncomfortable or breaks Edwin's rules." He slipped the taxi into park.

I nodded. Edwin would never send me someplace unsafe, but he might not have known about possible other visitors or the state of the house and the impression of danger that it presented.

Tom and I had visited my family in Chicago a few months ago. It had been a wonderful trip, and moments with my own father had reminded me again how alike Elias was to him. He'd been the one I'd gravitated to that day I'd arrived in Edinburgh, stepping out of the airport in search of a ride.

I'd been lucky to have so many good men in my life, even when I'd just been looking for a taxi.

Carefully, Elias drove over the cobblestones, or what was left of them, and toward the three stairs that led up to the front stoop.

As we stepped out of the taxi, a man came around the side of the house. His head was down, and he appeared to be deep in thought.

"Aye?" Elias said as he cocked his head and looked hard at the man. "Homer, is that you, auldjin?"

The man stutter-stopped and looked up. He squinted one eye as he looked at Elias. Another moment later, a smile, with one missing front tooth, lit up his wrinkled and age-spotted face.

"Elias?"

"Aye!"

The two men came together and hugged and patted each other's back heartily, lifting a cloud of dust from Homer's jacket.

"'Tis so good to see you," Homer said as they pulled away. His accent was just as strong, if not even stronger, than Elias's. "I'd've ken you anywhere."

"Same." Elias laughed. "I ken you by yer walk, lad."

I thought I saw tears in their eyes. It took another beat for Elias to remember I was there.

"Och, apologies. Lass, this is an old friend from a long time ago, Homer Vanton. We worked the docks together a hundred years ago. Homer, this is Delaney, a lass I've come to think of as my own kin."

Homer extended his hand. "A pleasure."

We shook. "Nice to meet you."

"Are you on here?" Elias asked.

"Aye. I've been the groundskeeper for nigh on thirty years now. Ms. Lannister's parents hired me, and here I've been."

I hadn't taken the time to look at the grounds, but I did now, at least the parts I could see—the front and a downward slope on the side. They were green and well-groomed, in far better shape than the house. I knew the main item I'd come to investigate had been found somewhere on the grounds—had Homer been the one to find it? I didn't ask that question. "How much land do you care for?"

"Near a hundred Cunninghams," Homer said.

Elias, catching the question in my eyes, clarified. "A Cunningham is a wee bit more than your American acre."

"Wow, that's a lot of land," I said.

"Aye. Much of it is untended woods, but I'm still able to manage the parts that arenae."

Elias was still strong—he was the type of man I thought had probably always looked that way, with wide shoulders and a barrel chest, not sunken yet with age. I could tell Homer's arms were thin, though, underneath the worn jacket.

"Of course you are," Elias said as he patted his friend on the shoulder again.

"Are you here to visit the miss?" Homer asked.

Elias looked at me. "Yes. Delaney has an appointment with Ms. Lannister. I came along for the ride."

I nodded at the other vehicles. "It appears we aren't the only ones."

"Aye. She rarely welcomes guests, and it's been a busy day." Homer frowned.

A beat later, Elias asked, "Everything okay in there?"

Homer shook his head. "I'm sure everything is fine. I'm protective is all, and . . . well, none of us are getting younger." He smiled. "My heart is glad you are one of her visitors. She will be fine with you."

"Aye. Of course." Elias rubbed his chin. "Homer, you must come for dinner some night soon."

"Aye? Please tell me you are still with the most beautiful lass of all time."

Elias laughed. "Aye. Aggie's still keeping me in line. Join us this week. Let's exchange mobiles."

I stepped away as they exchanged numbers and hugged again.

"Nice to meet you, lass," Homer said as he continued on his way around to the other side of the house.

"A pleasure, Homer. See you again, I hope."

"Aye."

"That had to be a surprise," I said as Elias came up next to me.

"A pleasant one. We have a history together made of hard work followed by tired nights in pubs."

"Sounds like a good history."

"Aye." Elias smiled into the past a moment. He looked at me. "Come along, lass. Now I'm even more curious to see what's going on in there."

It had been a pleasant reunion, no doubt. But I could see in his eyes the melancholy that comes with running into an old friend. It would give us something to talk about on the trip home.

"Let's do this." I led the way to the door.

CHAPTER TWO

The peaked and ornately arched, though dilapidated, entryway led to two front doors, both made of wood and chipped varnish. I was now even more aware of the stark differences between the conditions of the house and the grounds. That said, there was a lot of land we hadn't seen yet. I wondered how much we might get to explore.

As we stepped closer to the doors, the distinct sound of raised voices came from inside. It wasn't easy to discern if we were hearing anger or excitement.

I looked around for a bell, but had to settle for a large, tarnished knocker in the shape of a dragon's head, a fabulous piece of art that we didn't have time to contemplate. I lifted it by the beast's tongue and let it drop. The voices inside stopped with the first heavy blow.

Elias and I shared raised eyebrows as we waited.

Just as I was about to try again, the door opened slowly with a lingering squeak. A small woman with a crown of gray hair peered through the opening.

"Jolie?" I said. "I'm Delaney from The Cracked Spine."

"You're who?"

I cleared my throat. "I work with Edwin MacAlister."

"Och, Edwin. Aye. One moment please." The door closed.

Elias and I shared another look, and just when I was about to try again, the door pulled wide.

Another gray-haired woman greeted us, but this one was tall, with wide shoulders. She was dressed in a long, purple velvet gown.

"Greetings, Delaney. I'm Jolie. Welcome to my home."

"Thank you."

She didn't move or extend her hand for a shake but stood there a long minute, looking over both Elias and me.

"This is my friend—and Edwin's too—Elias," I said.

Elias stepped up and extended his hand as he smiled in his sweet way. "Nice to meet you."

Elias was always charming. Jolie's tall stature had been stiff, but it softened as she smiled and shook his hand.

"A pleasure to meet you both. Please come inside. Forgive the mess as well as all the people. I've been trying to get rid of them, but they don't seem to want to leave. Well, the mess can stay. I'd like the other people to leave though."

We stepped into the capacious entryway. It wasn't exactly like the castle great halls I'd seen, but it wasn't too far off. On the second-story roof was a stained-glass skylight. Though it was mostly cloudy outside, different colored rays came through the glass. The kaleidoscope effect only added to what felt like confusion inside.

There were other people, but it was mostly the stuff every-where that made the space, which should have felt voluminous, give me a sensation of claustrophobia.

The entry extended all the way to the back wall, which was made of paned floor-to-ceiling windows—much larger than the home's front windows. The ceiling topped off at the first level back there, under a second-level balcony that could be reached by two curving stairways on each side.

There were so many things stacked everywhere that I couldn't digest them quickly, though it was easy to tell that we'd walked into the home of a hoarder. If there were degrees of that affliction, I would immediately guess that Jolie's would be somewhere in the middle of the spectrum. I neither smelled nor saw any garbage, and there was still space to walk up the stairs and across all the floors, if you stayed in what seemed like designated paths.

I counted five people other than Elias and myself. They were spread throughout the great room, all of them in a pose that indicated irritation. And their attention was currently directed toward Elias and me.

I wondered if we'd come at the wrong time, but I'd confirmed the meeting time with Edwin more than once.

I felt the need to apologize for the intrusion, but Jolie beat me to the punch with a heavy sigh.

"Well, as you can see, our tête-à-tête has been invaded by opposing forces," she said to me as she waved an arm toward the others.

"Jolie," a woman in a suit began. Her arms were crossed in front of herself as she leaned against the right stairway railing. "We aren't invading, and we are far from opposing forces."

"I don't know what else to call all of this then," Jolie said.

The suited woman frowned. "We are here to help. That is all."

Suddenly, everyone looked right at me.

"I . . . uh." I was speechless.

I turned to Elias, thinking he might just want us to get out of there, but he was making no move to leave. Instead, he stuck his hands in his pockets and sent me some raised eyebrows. He was more curious than anxious that we might have come at a bad time.

"I know why you're here, Delaney," Jolie said. "You've come to look at the books. I've been expecting you and I look forward to taking you through the library . . ."

The suited woman bounced herself off the railing but didn't try to walk around the stacks of newspapers near her feet.

"Bowie Berry." She waved in my direction. "I'm Ms. Lannister's legal counsel."

"Bowie is an attorney I hired a number of years ago. However, she is currently overstepping her bounds," Jolie said.

Bowie cringed. "Not at all, Jolie. I just want to make sure the best thing is done for you, my client."

"Oh, pishposh." Jolie's hands went to her hips. She frowned at the other two men in the room, who stood next to each other, close to the front wall, appearing to me as if they'd been trapped there. "The men are people from an auction house Bowie hired to take away all my things."

"I didn't hire them to take anything away. I hired them to take an inventory." Bowie looked at me. "Gilles Haig is the best in the business. His assistant, Alban Dunning, joined him today." She gestured toward them with her arm.

The two men smiled awkwardly, the younger one wearing the brightest orange sweater I'd ever seen—though he'd call it a "jumper." Whatever this confab was, it wasn't what they'd signed up for, I could tell that much.

"Mr. Haig," I said. "I spoke with you," I nodded at the younger man next to him, "My name is Delaney Nichols. I was inquiring about a carriage that has been kept in my boss's old stables. His name is Edwin MacAlister."

"Aye. I remember. Did it get sorted?" Haig asked.

"Edwin is still considering what to do. Thank you for your patience," I said.

"Aye, and we're Gilles and Alban. No mister needed," Gilles said.

Before I'd spoken to him, I'd heard of Gilles Haig. Considering the circumstances of Edwin's business, the warehouse in the back of the bookshop, and the auctions, Haig's name had come up many times over the last few years, and always with a positive endorsement. I'd only spoken briefly with him and remembered nothing but a good experience.

"Aye, he's a fine reputation. But I do not want him here," Jolie said, as she looked directly at Haig. "Not yet."

Bowie bit her top lip. "Okay, Jolie. Okay. One more day wouldn't hurt. We'll give you today to talk to . . . Delaney Nichols and her associate, but we'll be back tomorrow."

Bowie stepped around the newspapers and toward me. "I am Jolie's legal counsel," she repeated with vigor, "and I have a right to know what's going on here. Oh." I looked at Elias who was frowning at Bowie. I looked at Jolie, who sent me a quick, almost imperceptible nod. "I am here to look through Jolie's library as a representative for Mr. Edwin MacAlister."

That was kind of the truth, but I figured that Jolie had set the lie in motion when she'd mentioned the library. I'd just hitched a ride upon it. I wasn't exactly here to look at her library, at least not solely. I wasn't about to spill the beans on the real deal though, legal counsel or not.

"Fine. That's fine, but you will not take anything out of this house without my approval," Bowie said.

I smiled wearily. "Ms. Berry, you might work for Jolie, but I work for Edwin, and no one has served me with any sort of cease and desist here. I will work with Jolie to her satisfaction. If you know anything at all about Edwin MacAlister, it is that he is a fair man, one who only does business on the up and up." I held my chin firm.

"I will be back tomorrow with the proper paperwork, Ms. Nichols, but I would highly recommend that you do as I ask and not take a thing."

"I will take your instructions under advisement," I said.

The withering look she directed my way caused Elias to chuckle once.

"Sorry," he said when Bowie glared at him, though he wasn't.

Bowie looked at Gilles and Alban. "Let's go. For now."

Bowie, Gilles, and Alban filed out, Bowie the last one through the doorway. She closed it lightly, as if she was forcing herself to not to slam it but wanted everyone to know that she could have very well made another choice. Elias, Jolie—the older woman who'd first answered the door—and I were left in the wake.

Jolie sighed again. "I'm so glad they're gone. Come along. We have work to do."

Jolie's gown swished as she made her way around stacks of things and then past the older woman who'd found a perch on the second step up the left stairway, before disappearing down a hallway.

"I'm Trudie," the older woman said. "I work for Jolie. Have no doubt, she is the force of nature she appears to be."

"I believe it," I said.

"I do too," Elias agreed.

He still made no move to leave me there, and I didn't push him to go. I decided it would still be good to have him with me. It had been so far.

"G'on into the library. I'll gather refreshments and meet you there," Trudie said.

Briefly, I wondered if we should leave a trail of breadcrumbs as Elias and I set off to follow Jolie into the depths of her messy home.

CHAPTER THREE

I have never met a library I didn't love, this one included, even if it was one of the most jam-packed rooms I'd had the pleasure to visit.

Floor-to-ceiling shelves lined the walls, all of them stuffed to overflowing. I thought I saw a piece of furniture peering out, but it was covered by so many items that I couldn't be sure if it was a desk or a table. Behind it on a narrow inset of wall space was a small island of order. A portrait had been hung. Nothing blocked the view of the beautiful and exotic brunette with the pinned-back hair and light-colored tea dress. I wondered if the portrait was Jolie, but it didn't much look like the version of her that I'd just met.

Stacks of books, newspapers, and magazines covered the floors, though there was an obvious walking path, and, like a pot of gold at the end of a rainbow, a green velvet-topped table with four chairs turned out to be our destination. The setup was next to two tall windows that offered an extraordinary view of the side grounds, giving me the view that I'd been hoping for and offering proof that Homer was really good at his job. I couldn't help but wonder why the house itself hadn't been given such attention.

I tried to change my perspective and not think of it as shabby. Surely there was a better description. Maybe well loved, or just cozy, but I couldn't quite get there. There were too many cracks in the walls, and dust covered every exposed surface. Everything seemed to lean, if only slightly. Again, I noticed that I didn't smell any garbage, which made it all bearable.

Jolie stood by the table as we made our way to join her. "Come sit. This is my favorite place in the entire house. Refreshments before business, I always say. I know you're not here for the books," Jolie said to me as we each grabbed a chair. "Thank you for playing along, though. I didn't want . . . anyone else to know what we've found."

I nodded. "I figured."

"Look." Jolie pointed out the window. She squinted at Elias and me.

I took another glance outside. The view reminded me of lovely Scottish landscape painting. Green grass-covered small hills. A walking path that lined the perimeter had been bordered with flowers and healthy shrubbery.

"It's lovely," Elias said.

"It is." Jolie sighed and then signaled for us to sit. "I like to bring my guests here first so they may get a partial answer to the question I know everyone has—how can I possibly live the way I do in this house?"

Neither Elias nor I discouraged her from continuing.

"I can sit here and look out to a beautiful world without all this clutter I've made." She smiled sadly. "I'm aware of my . . . problem. Unfortunately, I haven't been willing to do whatever it is I need to do to make a change. It's just Trudie and me here in the house. My groundskeeper has a wee house out on the property. He's lovely, but he only comes into the house when

Trudie makes him lunch. Anyway, I don't *have* to answer to anyone." Her expression darkened. "Except maybe Bowie."

"Aye?" Elias said.

"I don't mean to plant any ideas, but can't you always get a new attorney?" I asked.

She frowned. "Apparently, I signed something quite a few years back that gives her some sort of power over me if I show any sort of signs of mental failure. I'm one hundred percent 'with it,' but all this mess," she signaled with her arm, "is a mental health issue according to some professionals. Bowie has me where she wants me, but . . . well . . . we'll see."

"Do you think your attorney is out for your best interests?" Elias asked.

Jolie fell into thought, her eyes going down to the worn velvet on the table. "I think she used to be."

Elias and I shared a look.

"Did something happen?" I asked.

"I . . . I'm not sure." She looked toward the doorway and then back at Elias and me. She lowered her voice. "Shortly after we found . . . the thing last week"—she glanced quickly at the doorway again—"I got a visit from Bowie. I hadn't spoken to her in months. She said she needed to have a serious conversation with me. She wanted me to get this mess cleaned up. She said nothing about the item, but I'm suspicious of the timing. I don't want to believe that someone told her, so I'm operating on the hope that she truly doesn't know about it. I guess, again, we will see." She paused, but we could tell she would go on. "But even if it's only about the house, I'm not happy with her sudden interest."

I would have probably agreed with the attorney that the mess did need to be cleaned up, but there was more to be considered here, even if I wasn't yet sure of the extent of it all.

"I'm sorry. Is there anything I or Edwin could do to help?"
I was sure he'd be okay with the offer.

Jolie smiled sadly. "I have friends, Edwin included, who
care for me and for whom I care. I don't go out much and I
don't invite people here—I'm embarrassed by my affliction—
but Trudie has been there through thick and thin. I thank
you for your offer, and I will remember it if I need Edwin's
assistance."

"He will be happy to hear that."

I was suddenly startled by movement in the side yard. "Oh."

"What's he doing out there?" Jolie asked as we all watched
the young man in the bright orange sweater, the one we'd just
seen in the entryway, walking down the path Jolie had just
pointed out.

"Alban Dunning, his name?" Elias asked.

"Aye," Jolie said.

Elias scooted his chair back. "Shall I ask him to leave?"

"No, not yet," Jolie said. "Let's see what he does."

Alban was probably in his thirties. With a head full of dark
curls and that sweater, he would be impossible to miss. With
his hands in his pockets, he strolled along as if he knew what
he was doing. He did not appear to be in a hurry.

"Where does the path go?" I asked.

"I put it in myself. It ends at my property line, but that's
maybe a quarter of a kilometer down and around. However, he
can keep walking unimpeded from there, all the way around
and to a small shopping area with a coffee and pastry shop.
Many people walk the path." Jolie smiled. "Some wave at me
through the windows. I've come to expect seeing some people,
but I've never seen Mr. Dunning until today."

"There were two other vehicles out front. Maybe he rode in
with Gilles and then decided to walk back." I shrugged.

"I don't know."

Just as he disappeared from sight, Trudie came into the room carrying a tray.

Elias stood and hurried to help the older woman with the tray that appeared to weigh more than Trudie herself.

"Ta, lad," Trudie said.

As Elias placed the tray on the table and then did the honors of dispersing mugs and filling them with tea, I watched Trudie. Based upon Jolie's suspicious glance toward the doorway, I'd immediately wondered if maybe she had played a part in Bowie's sudden insistence about cleaning up the house.

Of course, looks could always be deceiving, but it was near impossible for me to believe that this tiny, old woman could be anything other than she appeared to be. She was comfortable enough to take a seat and let Elias continue to disperse the refreshments. I could tell how her and Jolie's existence together in the house was easy and routine.

I also watched Jolie, who did not behave in a way that made me think she was suspicious of Trudie. Maybe her glance toward the door was just a reaction, perhaps something to add drama.

I continued to digest my first impressions—that Jolie was a free spirit and Trudie was a quiet, reserved woman who'd probably been brought up to behave as if she was part of the background, probably told not to speak until spoken to.

Those were just my impressions over tea and cookies, though, and they could have been completely off base.

When the conversation turned to the item I'd come out to see, still no one said aloud what it was—or what it might be. Jolie did not ask Elias to leave; in fact, she seemed to enjoy our company.

The three of us did not mention seeing Alban to Trudie, and we didn't spot him returning during the half hour or so that we sat there.

Elias charmed and regaled us with stories of his adventures driving a taxi—his close calls, his rides with famous people. He'd mostly retired by the time the driving apps had taken over, but there were still a few celebrities who would give him a call for rides when they were in town.

I hadn't expected such a social gathering. Elias's original plan to drop me off and return to pick me up later seemed to have evolved. Jolie and Trudie both appeared pleased to have some company.

Jolie had been born in the West Rosebud House and had lived there all her life. She'd studied business at university, but once she'd finished school, she'd had no interest in working, and she had more than enough money to make such a choice. She'd spent most of her life reading as well as diving into the history of the area. Stephen, her father, had been born in 1920; Vivian, her mother, in 1921. They'd married in 1940, and Jolie was born in 1947. Stephen had made a fortune buying and selling real estate throughout Scotland, mostly in Edinburgh. He'd begun his business with funds from Vivian.

Stephen and Vivian Lannister had built West Rosebud House and lived there all their lives. Vivian didn't see herself as a "collector"—the word Jolie used to describe her hoarding, which was an affliction her mother also battled. Vivian—it was clarified that she was the subject of the portrait on the wall—spent decades without straying much farther than the gardens of the estate, where she appeared to find plenty to absorb her attention.

"My mother was wicked smart," Jolie said. "She knew how

to mix herbs, create medications, tinctures, and creams that performed as promised. She was respected as well as feared some. My father was also feared. He was a landlord, and that wielded a lot of power back then. Too much. It was a different time, though, and I remember him voicing regrets at his less than charitable behavior toward some unfortunate folks." Jolie shrugged. "I've tried to make up for it, though I know he left some bad things in his wake that can never be remedied."

"Maybe your mother helped enough people to make up the difference," I offered.

Jolie smiled. "Aye, she had a wonderful impact." She shook her head. "No need to get melancholy. Trudie had quite a childhood too."

"Oh, I dinnae ken." Trudie shrugged shyly.

"Trudie was kidnapped as a child, raised in Edinburgh, finding out at age twelve that her parents weren't really her parents."

"Oh my goodness," I said, shocked by Jolie's words. "That had to be rough."

"Kidnapped?" Elias said.

"Aye." Trudie nodded. "I dinnae know a thing about it until my birth parents found me. The people who stole me treated me well. I was their daughter, as far as I ken. I still think of them that way."

I didn't know what else to say to that very horrific and odd story other than what I'd already said. Fortunately, it appeared that Trudie was used to awkward reactions regarding her parentage.

Though her eyes brimmed a little with tears, she smiled. "It was all a long time ago. I was loved, by more parents than most people get. That's how I've decided to think about it."

She shrugged. "I started working with Jolie almost thirty years ago."

Jolie put her hand over Trudie's on the table. They were close, and clearly cared deeply for each other.

Jolie turned her attention back to Elias and me. "Well. Is it time to see the item?"

"I would love to," I said.

"Let's go then." Jolie stood, her velvet gown swooshing as she turned away from the table.

Trudie hurried to follow.

As Elias and I stood, he touched my arm.

"Lass, I dinnae ken what you're here to see. It's none of my business. Is it time for me to leave? I can come back later."

"If you don't have anywhere else to be, please stay. Edwin wouldn't mind, and it's all a little," I lowered my voice, "weird here."

"Aye. I have nowhere else to be. I'm relieved to stay."

"Thank you."

"Are you joining us?" Trudie peered back into the room from the doorway.

"Of course," I said.

Elias and I hurried—well, as best we could around the stacks—to join them.

CHAPTER FOUR

We retraced our steps back toward the entryway. I was on sensory overload because there was so darn much to see, but this time through I noticed that the hallway walls were also covered in photos and paintings—these more hidden by the piles of things than the portrait in the library. My eyes could only skim as we moved along, but I guessed I was seeing all manner of nature paintings along with photos of Jolie with her parents, by herself, and with any number of animals. I wished for the chance to really look around. Though it was certainly all a little weird, as I'd said to Elias, it was intriguing too.

Jolie led us toward the tall back windows, veering to the right at the back of the house. Double doors came into view. The expanse of grounds on the other side of the glass was even more stunning than the side gardens—more rolling green hills, lone trees, and flowerbeds were here and there. The scenery just kept getting better and better.

We spotted Homer carrying a heavy-duty landscaping rake as he made his way across the back.

"That's my groundskeeper. He's been a part of Rosebud since Trudie. They arrived close to the same time."

After a shared look with Elias, I said, "We met him out front. He and Elias are old friends."

"Aye?" Jolie said. "Isn't that a small world?"

Homer moved better than I would have predicted based upon my earlier observations, with sure, quick steps.

"Hello, Homer," Jolie called. "I see you know our guests."

"Hallo!" He waved. "'Twas a wonderful surprise." He held up the rake. "I'm on my way to the yellow gardens."

"Very good," Jolie said. "See you later."

After another smile at Elias, Homer turned and made his way up and over a hill, disappearing from sight quickly.

Jolie lifted the skirt of her gown and started walking again. Inside the house, her clothing choices seemed quirky, and out here, as we followed a groomed and cobblestoned path, the purple velvet seemed completely out of place.

The beauty of the grounds was at once serene and stunning, a different view at each turn. Flowers were strategically placed, grass was cut perfectly, intermittent trees seemed to spread their branches to fill just the right amount of airspace.

"I love the yellow gardens. We'll try to have a look before you go," Jolie called over her shoulder. The path was only wide enough to accommodate us walking single file. "I know my house is messy, to say the least, but I'm not crazy. I just like the stuff. Anyway, Homer has kept everything pristine. He's a good man, so you must be one too, Elias."

I smiled at Elias over my shoulder and then turned to face forward again. "Could Alban have come back here?"

"He could have, but Homer would have seen him and kicked him out. Homer created a rock bed to discourage leaving the path. Ankles can be compromised. I suppose Alban is young enough to give it a go, but Homer would have given him the boot."

We moved up a small slope. Once we reached the top, a shed came into view. It wasn't the type you could buy in home improvement stores but appeared to have been constructed by hand and painted to look like a small gingerbread house.

"We put it in here," Jolie said as she stopped and put her hands on her hips in an already familiar pose. She wasn't winded at all. "In fact, Homer is the one who came upon the item. When he brought it to me, I asked him to put it in this shed. I'm certain he knows what I suspect it is, but he's very good at minding his own business. He did as I asked and hasn't brought it up since."

I didn't gasp aloud, but if the item was what Edwin had told me it might be, the outdoor shed wasn't secure enough.

Elias raised his eyebrows at me, and I realized that my expression was distinctly displeased. I sent him a quick smile.

Jolie led us to the shed and opened the door. We made our way inside the sparse space. Shelves lined one wall, but only a few garden implements were scattered over them.

"This shed was intended to be decorative. It's cute, though Homer does keep a few convenient items in here just in case. There's the thing we've come to see." Jolie pointed to a big plastic tub that sat in the middle of the wooden floor. It was covered by a quilted blanket. "That's part of why we thought the shed might work for . . . what we . . . he found."

"Gracious, it's good you decided against bringing it inside the house, considering our surprise visitors this morning," Trudie said. She wasn't winded from the walk either.

"Good point, Trudie. All right then, let's have a look."

The item, a sword, that Jolie was about to uncover might have been something significant to, with a wide lens, Scottish history, and with a more specific focus, to a battle—a very important Scottish battle. Or more than one.

The Battle of Roslin was fought on February 24, 1303. It was a Scottish victory in the First War of Scottish Independence. John Comyn and Sir Simon Fraser ambushed and defeated English troops. It was an important victory for the Scots—one battle in the many they've waged with the English.

The weapons of destruction of the day were mostly swords and knives. Though many had been cast, made of steel, some weren't as effective as others, or so some of the historical records indicated.

But there was one type of sword that still made historians— of all kinds and specialties—swoon. The Crusader sword.

It was the common weapon of the medieval knights used throughout the crusading era, from 1095 to 1291. It was efficient (well, relatively) against the chain mail armor of the time. Eventually, it even took on religious significance.

Created with the mathematical properties of "golden triangles" and "golden rectangles," the sword represented proportions in line with the harmony of nature. People of that day gave it a spiritual value.

The sword could be used with one hand, though later versions did become longer, making it necessary to use both hands to wield.

Jolie had called Edwin the day the sword had been discovered on her property. Though the Battle of Roslin took place in the early 1300s, after the Crusades, Jolie was certain that the discovery was, indeed, a Crusader sword.

Jolie had asked Edwin to come get the sword, take it off her property and do the appropriate thing with it. In fact, there were proper procedures in place in Scotland, but though Edwin wasn't one to profit from historical finds, he was one to make sure that if there was profit to be had, it didn't first go to any government, particularly if something could benefit a person or a group he thought better suited. It was a bit arrogant of him, he knew, but his donations to causes such as hospitals and libraries had done too much good to argue with his system.

Jolie reached for the blanket and lifted.

The item, obviously shaped like a sword, was covered in rust and dirt.

"A Crusader sword?" Elias asked immediately.

"Aye, I think so." Jolie shrugged.

Elias looked at me, his eyes wide.

I nodded uncertainly and then crouched as I peered into the plastic bin. Yes, it was the size and shape of a Crusader. It was approximately thirty inches long and about two inches wide at the hilt.

"What do you think, Delaney?" Jolie asked.

"Well, from first appearances, it appears to be the right size and shape." My eyes went to the pommel. That was probably the part that would tell the whole story.

Unfortunately, it was covered in the same grime and rust as the rest of the sword. However, it did seem to be a well-defined shape.

I looked at the pommel. The first pommels were oval- or cone-shaped. Brazil nut–shaped pommels became popular around the twelfth century, some enamel with family arms. The ones most used by the Crusaders were wheel-shaped.

With the gunk covering it, I couldn't see any sort of enamel, but the shape wasn't much of a mystery—it took the distinct form of a wheel.

"If this sword was used by a Crusader, and if it is a Crusader sword, it *might* have also been used in the Battle of Roslin, though it's something I can't determine immediately. I will say again though, it is the right size and shape."

"How else would it have gotten here if not Roslin?" Trudie asked as she crouched.

I shrugged. "Well, I don't know. Is there any chance the area where it was found has been preserved?"

Jolie cringed. "I don't think so."

Elias made a noise but didn't comment.

"I think we should take a look at the location, maybe ask Homer not to do anything more in that area than he's already done. Cordon it off for now."

"Aye?" Jolie said.

"Yes," I said.

"Would you like me to track him down?" Elias, who'd also crouched, stood.

"Dear man, would you mind?" Jolie asked.

"Not at all."

"Thanks, Elias," I said, hoping the site hadn't been in the yellow garden and was now being dug up even more.

I'd need to examine the sword closely, but the site might tell more of the story, even if I wouldn't be the person to interpret that part. I knew people who could help.

Elias exited the shed and Jolie reached for the quilt. I didn't want to leave the sword there, unceremoniously placed in a plastic bin. There wasn't even a lock on the door. But I didn't know what else to do with it—yet. I wasn't ready to suggest taking it to Edwin, though I might be by the time we left. I would figure it out after we investigated further.

I was now eighty percent certain it was a Crusader sword, but it would take a closer look to tell for sure, probably by someone who had better tools than I did. As my thoughts organized, I realized that this was probably going to be a bigger deal than Edwin and I could handle.

Trudie and I watched as Jolie moved the quilt to cover the bin again.

"I think it would be better to have this under lock and . . ." I began.

I was interrupted by what I could immediately identify as the sound of Elias's yells. I thought he was saying something like, "Help!" but I couldn't be sure. It sounded urgent enough to propel me up and out of the shed.

Once outside, I looked around, spinning in all directions. "Elias, where are you?" I yelled.

"Just over the bigger hill, Delaney—call the police!"

I knew he meant that I shouldn't try to find him first, that I should call the police before I did anything else. But there was something so terrifyingly strained to his voice that I couldn't bear the thought of not getting my eyes on him.

I set off into a run. I stumbled up the hill, taking what felt like a million years to regain my footing. When I finally made it to the top and over, I froze in my tracks.

Three men were there. Elias was holding tight to Homer, but it was the man on the ground who garnered the lion's share of my attention. It was Alban. I'd know that sweater anywhere.

I looked away, because it was all too horrible to continue to see.

"Delaney, call the police," Elias called. Though he sounded exerted, he was much less frantic.

I put my hand up to stop Jolie and Trudie from climbing up behind me. "Stay there." I hoped Elias was okay—he seemed to be—but I couldn't turn around myself. I didn't want to see that ever again.

I reached for my phone and called the police.

CHAPTER FIVE

A weird sort of organized confusion took over, pushing away the horror of the moment, temporarily.

It didn't take long for the police to arrive. One of the female officers took immediate charge and sent Jolie, Trudie, and me into the house, commanding us to stay in the entryway as another officer watched over us.

The woman stayed at the scene outside.

"Dear man," Jolie said to the officer who'd been left to babysit us. "Could we go to the kitchen and get some water?"

"Of course, ma'am," he said. "My name is Crandall."

"Thank you."

Jolie led the way down another packed hallway and into a kitchen. It was just as crammed with things—papers, pots, pans, though still no garbage or old food smells, thankfully.

Officer Crandall looked around the space. I thought he worked to not look like he was slightly appalled by all the stuff. "Would you . . . like to sit down? I can grab the waters."

Jolie made her way to a nook. She lifted a stack of towels off a chair and took a seat. She nodded at the other covered chairs. "Every man and woman for themselves."

Crandall was probably in his early twenties. With short, dark hair and bright blue eyes, he appeared both serious and very young. I watched as he worked to control a smile at Jolie.

However, there was nothing funny about any of this.

We didn't have the entire story yet, but from what I'd seen, Alban Dunning had been killed, and it appeared that maybe the killer had been Homer, the weapon the landscaping rake. Not only that, it seemed that Elias had either stopped Homer or kept him from running away. Of course, I was guessing all of this.

Not knowing the details or the truth was driving me a little crazy, but I was keeping it together for the sakes of Jolie and Trudie. This turn of horror was bound to be a blow, especially when the shock wore off a little, and Trudie's color was already a little odd.

I hoped that Elias was okay too.

While Officer Crandall searched the cabinets and then found some glasses, I texted Inspector Winters as covertly as possible.

He was a friend, and I wanted him here, if there was any way.

I'm at Jolie Lannister's house in Roslin. There's been a tragedy. Police are here. Can you come too? I texted.

He got back to me before Officer Crandall got the waters to the table.

??? Sure. Be there soon.

Crandall cleared off the fourth chair. Before he sat, he asked, "Can I get any of you anything else?"

We all shook our heads.

He looked pointedly at Trudie. "Are you okay, ma'am?"

She nodded.

"I'd like to hear you say it aloud if you don't mind," Crandall said.

Trudie cleared her throat. "I'm fine, young man, just . . . unsure."

"I understand. You don't need to be scared, though. I mean, if you are."

"I was. But I'm fine. I'd like to know what happened."

"Wouldn't we all?" Jolie added before she took a long drink of the water.

"We will," he said. "We'll get every answer. You are safe."

We were all silent a long beat.

"Did you know Alban Dunning before today?" I asked the two women.

"No, and he barely spoke this morning when he was here with the others," Jolie said.

Officer Crandall held up his hand and looked at the three of us. "Has anyone taken your statements?"

"Not yet," Jolie offered.

Officer Crandall rubbed his chin. "Well, let's not talk about what happened until all of your statements are taken."

"Couldn't you do it?" Trudie asked.

"I could, but each statement should be taken separately, and I'd like to keep us all together until I get further word that the grounds have been cleared."

Jolie frowned. I tried to read her mind. Was she wondering about the sword and whether she should say anything about it or not? I would have advised her not to until asked about it, but it certainly wasn't my place to offer advice.

"Homer . . ." I began, but I wasn't sure what else I wanted to say.

Jolie looked at me. "He's like family, Delaney. I . . ." Tears filled her eyes as she looked at Officer Crandall. "I want to know what happened."

The officer leaned toward her. "We'll get all the answers. I promise."

"Hello?" a voice called from the entryway.

I knew that voice. "Kitchen—take the hallway on your left."

Officer Crandall didn't know Inspector Winters was joining us. Crandall sent me a concerned frown and then stood to greet our visitor, first putting himself between us and the doorway.

Inspector Winters shared his identification with Crandall before he looked at me.

"You okay?"

I nodded. "Elias was with me. He's with the other officers out back."

Inspector Winters nodded and then turned around in the hallway, presumably heading outside.

"Friends in high places?" Jolie asked me.

"I guess so. He *is* a friend."

Officer Crandall tried not to look perturbed.

"He won't get in the way," I said to Crandall.

I understood the need to protect turf. Police officers had been dispatched and were investigating, and though I had no reason not to have confidence in them, I was glad to have the inspector interloping.

Crandall forced a smile. "Can I get anyone another water?"

Jolie lifted her glass, saluted me, and then took a big swig. She handed the glass to Crandall. "Thank you, dear boy."

When he turned away, Jolie nodded approvingly at me.

I tried to keep my expression as neutral as possible.

CHAPTER SIX

I got the rest of the story directly from Elias.

About an hour or so after Inspector Winters's arrival, Elias and I were dismissed, well, told we needed to leave but to remain available for any other questions the officers and inspectors might have. I'd been so happy to see Elias walking into the house—unharmed, not arrested. He did have a little blood on him, but none of it was his, and despite all the other horror, I couldn't help but be grateful for that.

More weight lifted off my shoulders once we were both in the taxi, the doors and windows closing us away from the rest of the world. Well, that was my perception, at least.

As Elias steered the taxi up the bumpy drive and out to the road, I saw Inspector Winters talking with other officers behind the house, but he didn't seem to notice us leaving.

"Are you okay?" I asked Elias.

"Fine, lass. Not hurt at all."

"I'm happy to hear that." I swallowed hard. "Did Winters say anything to you?"

"No, lass. He just nodded in my direction. I took it as both a greeting and acknowledgement that he'd get it all sorted."

I took a deep breath and let it out as I inspected Elias, scanning the dried blood on his shirt and arm. "Aggie isn't going to like the blood."

"She'll understand."

"What happened, Elias? And don't tell me they told you not to share the details. If they did, I'd like you to break that promise. Please."

"No one told me to keep quiet, but I'd tell you anyway. I came upon a terrible scene, and I reacted." He paused, seemed to mentally rewind a beat. "I came over the hill and saw the young man we'd seen earlier—that sweater was immediately recognizable—on the ground. The groundskeeper, Homer, was next to him, the bloodied rake in his hand. I rushed to pull Homer away."

"That's not good." In fact, I felt slightly faint thinking about it. I was glad I wasn't the one driving.

"For his part, Homer claimed he hadn't done the deed—both to me and all the police. He said he came upon the man and just reacted as well, picking the rake up off the victim."

"We saw Homer walking with the rake."

"Aye, but he said he had left it there where Alban was found, planning to pick it up after he retrieved some other tools, said it freed up his hands for a few moments."

"What do you think?"

"Lass, I have no idea." He bit his bottom lip. "Obviously there's so much more going on than our few hours there could tell us, but as much as I want to say that I couldnae imagine Homer killing anyone, he's a fiercely loyal man, and I have no doubt that he's loyal to Ms. Lannister. He wouldnae still work for her if he wasnae. If he might kill for someone, it could be her, if I read their relationship correctly. I didnae tell any of that to the police, and I hope Homer is innocent, but that sword. Lass, a Crusader sword?" He whistled. "That would be something, and maybe something worth killing for." He paused. "Still, though, the Homer I know isnae a killer."

"Jolie said that Homer might not have known what it was."

Elias laughed once. "Not a chance, lass. Homer would know there was a possibility the sword was a Crusader, no doubt in my mind. He knows those sorts of things. We are cut from the same cloth, he and I."

"Did you mention the sword to the police? Did anyone say anything about it?"

"No, not while I was there. I didnae tell a soul, I didnae hear Homer say anything, but I wasnae privy to much of what he said to the police. Did you or Jolie or Trudie mention it?"

"Not while I was there. During my statement, I just said we were touring the grounds. Though I didn't hear their statements, I'm pretty sure neither Jolie nor Trudie said anything."

"Aye."

"That was probably the wrong thing for us all to do."

"Aye."

"It just all happened so quickly, and it felt . . . too secretive or something."

"You were there to see the sword. The murder happened while we were there. There's no reason to think the sword and the murder are tied together, but they might be."

"I'll tell Winters the truth."

"He'll be angry for our secrecy."

"Probably, but like you said, maybe Alban's murder has nothing to do with the sword. We are giving it importance because that's why we were there, but according to Jolie, her early visitors didn't mention it. It might have just been a distraction to their investigation." My heart sank as I said the words aloud. I knew we should have told the police about the sword.

"Aye," Elias said doubtfully.

"I know. The police were going to search the grounds. Surely they'll find it, but who knows what they'll do with it. It wasn't the weapon that killed Alban, so at least there's that."

"Aye."

I put my hand on his arm. "Are you really okay, Elias?"

"Och, fine, lass. Just fine."

I pulled my hand back. "Which would be better—should I come with you to explain everything to Aggie or would you rather do it alone?"

Elias laughed. "Alone please. I'll take you to the bookshop."

"Thank you."

It wasn't a long trip back to town and the bookshop, and I probably could have handled it on my own in Tom's car, but I was glad Elias had been with me. If he hadn't . . . well, I didn't know what would have happened. Had him being there stopped more horror?

Was there a killer on the loose on the grounds? In Roslin? Now that I wasn't so stunned, my brain was able to conjure so much more awfulness.

What had Alban been doing on the grounds? Of course, that was a valid question. But there was something else that kept making its way to the forefront of my thoughts.

We'd watched Alban walking along the side gardens. It had seemed odd to both me and Elias, but Jolie had shrugged it off as something that could happen if he wanted to head toward a walking path that would lead him into the village. But, if he'd ridden out there with Bowie or Gilles, why wasn't he with them when they left?

Though Jolie's dismissal had seemed odd at the time, I'd moved on to other things quickly. I'd been there to see the sword. My senses had been on overload anyway. I hadn't thought I needed to be more adamant about how it was strange to see Alban walking through the side garden.

But now, of course, it seemed beyond strange. It seemed like a pretty darn big clue—though what it might lead to, I didn't have the faintest idea.

Elias stopped the taxi in front of the bookshop, and I gave him a hug. He hugged me back and sent me on my way.

"Have Aggie call me if she wants to talk about any of it."

"Will do, lass. Be safe out there."

I waved as he drove away. I faced the shop and steeled myself. Everyone would want to know what had happened at Jolie's—and they'd all be more than surprised to hear the story.

I pulled the door open and was greeted by Rosie's laughter and Hamlet's voice, seemingly sharing a story. I couldn't immediately see anyone, but was overcome with emotion when Hector, our (mostly Rosie's) miniature Yorkie trotted to greet me.

It was always good to see him, but his greetings didn't typically bring me to tears. I picked him up and held him close to my cheek.

"Such a good boy."

"Lass?" Rosie asked as she appeared from the back. She frowned at me. "What's wrong?"

Her tone must have carried to the back because Hamlet's voice stopped, and then he and my friend Joshua, who had become a friend to us all, came around and stopped next to Rosie.

"What's up, Delaney?" Hamlet asked.

They all looked at me with concerned expressions.

"It's good to be here, that's all." I sniffed.

The three of them shared more concerned looks, and Hector whined.

"Oh, no, lass, I don't think that's all. Come back and tell us what's wrong." Rosie took my arm and guided me to the back table as Hamlet and Joshua headed to the "dark side," another building attached to the bookshop that housed office space, the kitchenette, the loo, and the warehouse where Edwin kept many of his treasures—and the room where I spent most of my time. They were off to gather whatever sustenance might be found on the usually poorly stocked shelves in the kitchenette.

I let Rosie guide me and felt even better as Hector got comfortable on my lap. He was good at knowing who needed his attention the most.

"Should I call Tom, or Edwin?" Rosie asked.

"I don't . . . I really am doing better, though it was quite . . . well, it was bad over at Jolie's house. I don't want to bother Tom. I will tell him all about it later, but Edwin might want to know."

"I'll ring him. Take some deep breaths and drink up when the lads bring over the refreshments."

I nodded agreeably as I kept petting Hector's tiny head.

CHAPTER SEVEN

I'd met Joshua when I first moved to Edinburgh. He worked for National Museums Scotland. He and I were museum soulmates. We both loved them, as well as relished walking through them ever so slowly. He currently held three PhDs and was working on a fourth. A year or so ago, I'd thought he was going to be leaving the museum for a position in Inverness, so I'd hosted a good luck dinner for him. Though they'd met before, it was at that party that he and Hamlet struck up new conversations. They were a lot alike. I was thrilled to have been the one to facilitate their friendship, and I hoped it was yet another thing that might keep Joshua from leaving Edinburgh.

Edwin had hurried right over, and I'd reconsidered calling Tom just so I could have all of them around at once, but I didn't. I knew Tom was busy, and I wanted him to be the only audience member when I shared the story with him.

We sat around the table in the back of the greatest bookshop on the planet. Tea and a few saltine crackers had made me feel somewhat better as I told what had happened at Jolie's.

"Lass, I could never have . . ." Edwin said. "Guessed that something like that would occur."

"Oh, of course not."

"She's always been a character. Jolie Lannister." Rosie shook her head.

"You don't like her?" Hamlet asked Rosie.

"I try not to say that about anyone," she said, "but Jolie has always made me . . . tire't. She did used to leave the house, back, oh about forty years ago. She'd come in here, and . . . well, she was always a challenge." Rosie looked at Edwin.

"She was more social back then, though Rosie is correct, she's always been a wee bit odd." Edwin looked around the table. "Did she tell you about her . . . bloodline?"

"Um. No," I said.

Rosie rolled her eyes.

"At one time she claimed she was the rightful heir to the throne."

"What throne?" I asked.

"THE throne." Edwin raised his eyebrows and then lowered them quickly.

"The one . . . Elizabeth . . . ?"

"Aye," Rosie said.

I looked around the table. Hamlet and Joshua seemed as perplexed as I felt. "Was she?"

"Well, I don't think anyone did the DNA research necessary to find out one way or another, but she stuck by her story for a good long time, and there is some available evidence that her mother knew the royals."

"King George VI? Elizabeth's father?" I said.

"Not exactly," Edwin said. "George VI's brother, Edward VIII, was the king who abdicated."

"Right . . . for true love. Wallis . . . something," I said.

"Simpson," Rosie said. "Not one of our favorite people either."

"Aye," Edwin said. "But that was that story that Jolie told. Actually, her mother started the whole thing. Her mother, Vivian, told Jolie that Edward VIII was her biological father. There are pictures on her walls of her mother with him, with them. They were all friends, Vivian's husband as well, at one time."

"Oh my goodness," I said.

Edwin shook his head. "You need to understand that Jolie's parents were just as, if not more, eccentric than she is. Vivian was given to fantastical stories, so when she started telling this one, no one really believed her, but there was a lot of curiosity. Edward and Wallis had no children, which seemed to solidify Vivian and Jolie's belief. Edward was older when he and Vivian . . . well, it was quite the story."

"Not well publicized? This doesn't sound like something I've ever heard before," I said.

Edwin shook his head. "No, it was just something here, for a short time."

"What did they do? I mean, what does one do if they think they have a claim to the crown?" I asked.

"Make a sicht," Rosie said.

"Scene," Hamlet translated the Scots.

"Embarrass themselves," Rosie continued.

Edwin nodded. "I'm afraid much of that is true. It wasn't pretty, and Vivian and Jolie were so vocal—I believe there are newspaper articles from that time—government officials came up and spoke in stern voices to the entire Lannister family."

Rosie tsked. "Even if Edward and Vivian . . . well, illegitimate children of royals arenae considered in the lines of succession. Vivian made a"—Rosie nodded at me—"scene just because she wanted to. That's my interpretation."

"Goodness. What about Mr. Lannister?" I asked. "Did he not think he was Jolie's father?"

"I don't know what he felt about it all, but he kept his chin held high, his comments to himself," Edwin said.

"The Lannisters stayed together?"

"Aye."

"Was it a scandal or a rumor? How did everyone look at it?"

"Nowhere near a scandal," Rosie said.

"It was a . . . curiosity for a wee bit." Edwin frowned. "And then an embarrassment for the family, I'm afraid. I have heard that over the years it was because of that claim that Jolie started staying home more, collecting newspapers, looking for the truth, perhaps."

"The house is full of newspapers and magazines. Stacks and stacks of them."

Edwin continued, "It was sad, has been sad for a long time, but there was nothing any of us could do." Edwin paused and then sighed. "I'm sorry for all that happened. It might be insensitive of me to ask, but did you see the sword?"

"I did. She said that the groundskeeper, Homer, was the one who found it. They had it in a plastic tub in a shed. I don't think any of us mentioned it to the police."

"Aye? Good thinking. Maybe," Edwin said. "Do you think it's real?"

I'd told Elias I was going to let Inspector Winters know about the sword, but I hadn't yet. Now, though, with Edwin's words, I hesitated again.

I said, "From first appearances, yes, it does look like a Crusader sword, but I'd like to take a closer look."

"I'll have it delivered here," Edwin said.

We all looked at him.

He shrugged. "Well, Jolie will want me to continue to research it, no matter what. I'm happy to do so, and it might give her a welcome distraction. It might give us all one. If the police haven't taken it." He paused. "This will also give me another reason to go check on her. She doesn't like being checked upon without some other reason. Now, I can really find out how she's doing. I'll head over there this evening."

Rosie was frowning at him but didn't vocalize her thoughts.

"I've worked with Gilles Haig only a little, but he seemed lovely, honest," I said. "I'm sure Alban must have been too."

"I've known Gilles for years. He is very well respected about town. I can't say I ever met the lad, though."

"How about Bowie Berry? She's Jolie's attorney."

"I don't know her, but I can inquire."

"I wasn't around any of them nearly long enough to know much of anything, but it sure seemed that Bowie had pushed her way into something Jolie didn't want her to be involved in. Jolie was suspicious that it might be something about the sword."

"Aye, I will talk to Jolie about that too."

Rosie's expression softened. Edwin cared about a sword, priceless or not, but this was now about a sense of responsibility he felt for Jolie's well-being.

If he hadn't sent me out to see it, he wouldn't know a thing about what had happened today. But he had sent me, and though he would never blame me for anything, it was enough to make him think he should be more engaged.

I looked around the table. "I'm sorry for my . . . well, my small breakdown. Everything suddenly felt overwhelming."

"Nonsense, lass, that's what we're here for," Rosie said.

"I do feel much better. Thank you."

"All right. I'm off." Edwin stood from the chair, and with his long, sturdy legs, made his way around to the front of the store. From there he said, "I'll ring you all later."

I told the others that I was going to spend some time in the warehouse on the dark side as Hamlet and Joshua turned their attention back to some old documents they were evaluating.

Rosie and Hector would greet customers.

As I stood from the table, my eyes caught Joshua's, and I thought he looked away too quickly. He'd been silent as I'd shared what had happened—too silent, I suddenly decided. He wasn't the silent type, and he was always supportive.

I shook it off. I had things to do, questions that needed answers, and the warehouse was a good place to look for them.

CHAPTER EIGHT

The warehouse was a locked room in the back of the dark side. One of the tasks I'd been hired for was to organize the numerous items inside it, atop shelves that filled two walls. I'd made a good dent, but I still had plenty to do. I loved everything about the warehouse—all the stuff, the light from the windows at the top of the ceilings, even the sounds and smells. I could spend hours in there and not even feel the time passing. I did, often. I had the greatest job on Earth.

Today, behind the locked and large red, ornate door, I first thought about calling Tom, but he really was supposed to be busy. I was fine. I would tell him everything later, when neither of us could be distracted. I turned my focus to work, though maybe because of what had happened, knives were on my mind.

I'd found several bladed weapons in the warehouse. I'd purchased a lockable bin to keep them safe from further exposure, as well as clumsy hands.

The warehouse used to be a secret from the rest of the world, if maybe poorly kept. Now, with its tiny spark of celebrity, it seemed only prudent to secure potential danger.

I had a whole other bin with firearms, though Edwin had been shocked there'd been any in the warehouse. He'd commented that me finding them only solidified his decision to hire me to get things in order.

I gathered keys from my desk and crouched next to the knife bin. I unlocked it and lifted the lid.

Inside were twelve implements, none of them Crusader swords, but some valuable. All of them were at least interesting.

My favorite was a claymore that might have been used at Culloden. The mere mention of Culloden brought forth emotion from Elias, Edwin, Rosie, and Tom's father, Artair. Even Tom to some extent. It was a battle they still felt in their souls; at least that's how I'd witnessed it.

The Battle of Culloden was the final battle that came at the end of the Jacobite rising of 1745. All Scottish battles were bloody, but Culloden was particularly so.

The English won, which is still something that many Scots, particularly the older generation, still haven't been able to forgive. Especially as the English forces had gone to Inverness and slaughtered Scottish civilians. Over time, I'd become imbued with a Scottish patriotism as well, and the thought of Culloden now brought tears to my eyes too.

I blinked them away today as I gathered the claymore and took it to my desk. Crusader swords were similar to claymores, though the Crusader hilts were shorter and for the most part lighter in weight.

For a time, it was thought that the Scottish troops were defeated with muskets and cannon fire, but newer research had determined that those weapons weren't a part of the battle as much as swords and knives were. The Scottish forces weren't defeated by weaponry as much as they were simply outnumbered.

Of all the items in the warehouse, the bladed weapons had been the things Edwin had struggled the most with getting rid of. Not to the extent of Jolie's affliction, but Edwin did like to hold on to things—his collections. Together we'd found other homes for many things, either other collectors or museums. Edwin had sold some items and then donated the money, mostly to children's charities.

But he had not been able to part with the blades—though not because of the violence they'd inflicted, at least not directly.

Edwin's reverence for them was about the lives that were lived before they were taken down by the blades. He would get choked up just pondering it. The steel that had witnessed a final breath, fearful, yet knowing, eyes.

The murder of Alban Dunning was the most important mystery of the day, of course, but Edwin would do what he could to make sure the sword, Crusader or not, was attended to.

A knock sounded on the warehouse's door. I'd come to know my coworkers' knocks, but this one didn't sound familiar.

Visitors were not invited to explore the dark side. I always locked the door. It was kept open and unlocked only when Edwin visited.

I gathered the claymore, set it back in the bin, and locked the top.

"Who is it?" I asked loudly at the door.

"Joshua."

I turned the latches and opened the door. "Hello."

Despite how close we were, he'd never once been inside the warehouse.

He smiled. "Rosie and Hamlet said I could come over. I hope it's okay."

"It's fine. It's great! I can't believe you haven't seen it sooner."

"I just didn't want to overstep, but I'd love to see the place today."

"Come in."

Tall, thin, with dark, wavy hair, and big black-framed glasses, Joshua cut a sharp figure. His bright, intelligent eyes didn't miss a thing. Today, they took in all the items in the room. He was so brilliant that I knew if I later asked him what he'd seen on the back second shelf, he'd be able to remember and name everything.

"Delaney, if I were you, I might never leave this room. Ever. I would die of starvation, but it would be a happy, contented death."

"I know. It's fabulous."

But there was something about his demeanor that made me curious. What was really going on? His normal open friendliness seemed somewhat guarded today.

I made my way back to my desk and leaned on the edge. "Take your time. Look around all you want."

Joshua took a few more minutes to soak in everything before he turned to me, a serious expression on his face. "I need to talk, Delaney."

"I figured."

"Hamlet and Rosie already know why I'm here."

"Goodness. What's going on, Joshua?" My stomach fell. "Are you leaving Edinburgh?"

I'd be happy to have another going-away party for him, but I would prefer not to.

He shook his head. "No. In fact, I've been given even more responsibility at the museum. I will probably be there for a long time."

"That's good news."

He seemed uncomfortable.

"Joshua?"

"Just this morning I met with the new Treasure Trove Unit director."

"That's interesting." But as I said the words, I wondered if it really was, and what that might mean to all of us at The Cracked Spine. "Oh." I looked around. "Hang on."

"Yes, I see what you're thinking, but it's not all that bad . . . I don't think."

It is Scottish law that if one finds something that might be of Scottish historical or archaeological significance, it is to be reported to the authorities. The authorities could mean any museum, but the top rung of "authorities" is the Treasure Trove Unit of the Scottish government, and it was housed in the main museum building in Edinburgh, the place Joshua had worked for years now. I knew that. Edwin knew it too—we all did. Though we'd all discussed the Treasure Trove, we also turned a blind eye toward certain items in The Cracked Spine collection.

"I'm sure Edwin would want to follow the letter of the law." As I said the words, I wondered if they were true.

Joshua raised his eyebrows at me.

"Okay, maybe not all the time," I acquiesced.

Joshua laughed. "Let me ease your concerns some. When I spoke with the new director—his name is Cramer Donnell—he asked me about my friendship with you, with everyone at The Cracked Spine."

"He did?"

"Sure. You and I have only been caught a few times by the museum's night security team, but word gets around. Everyone knows of Edwin, and the warehouse, of course. Anyway, I told Cramer that in the course of our friendship, I hadn't seen one thing that the museum would be interested in or concerned about."

"But, now you've seen the warehouse."

"Not really." Joshua winked. "I know Edwin does good things with his money, his collections. I wanted him, all of you, to know that I'm not interested in causing any problems with any of it."

"Won't that get you in trouble?"

"No one will know. I am comfortable with all of you at The Cracked Spine keeping things close to your vests."

"I sense there is a 'but.'"

"There is, I'm afraid." He frowned. "If the sword is, indeed, a Crusader, I'm afraid I'm going to need to get involved." He paused, then hurried his next words. "In a collaborative way, though."

"That makes sense," I said, wondering how Edwin was truly going to feel about this. Still, a Crusader sword *was* a pretty big deal.

Edwin had been friends with a few Treasure Trove directors over the years. I'd heard some of the stories, not all of them complimentary. I didn't recall him mentioning the name Cramer Donnell.

Edwin would not want anyone to have more decision-making power over the item than he did—especially a sword.

As if reading my mind, Joshua said, "Rosie and Hamlet told me about Edwin's love of all things stabby."

I laughed. "That's one way to put it."

"They also said that Edwin might have thought to get ahold of the director anyway."

"I don't know . . ." In fact, I didn't think he would have considered it at all.

"Me neither, but, well, Delaney, your friendship means the world to me. I'm fond of everyone at The Cracked Spine. I would never do anything to put any of you in jeopardy."

I thought that was a strange turn of phrase, but I didn't want to push our luck and ask if Joshua meant he was just going to look the other way. "Thank you," I said.

He tipped his head gratefully. "Will you call me if Edwin brings the sword in?"

"Yes. Right away."

"Appreciate it." He stood and made his way toward the still-open doorway. He paused. "Hamlet and I are going to dinner. Do you and Tom want to join us?"

"I would love to, but I have too much work. Another time?"

"Definitely."

I closed and locked the door behind him, and thought through our conversation.

As I heard him climb the stairs to make his way back to the light side, my back against the door, my eyes went to the locked bin with the blades. I was glad I'd put the claymore away—not that a claymore was a Crusader, but still.

Life certainly wasn't black and white. I knew that, of course, but even though we all dealt with old, valuable things, I couldn't have predicted this moment, when my loyalties might become questioned or challenged.

No one at The Cracked Spine would want to put Joshua in a tricky situation, but it appeared it might be happening anyway.

CHAPTER NINE

"Cramer Donnell?" Tom asked as he wiped his fingers on his napkin. Our breakfast habit was toast, jam, and coffee. We always tried to make breakfast time together a priority.

"That's the name Joshua gave me."

"I'm not in that world, but I don't remember reading about a new director."

"He asked Joshua about all of us at the bookshop."

Tom frowned, but then forced a smile. "That might mean nothing."

I laughed. "I don't know what it means yet, but it's probably something."

"I think it could be fine, just the new director doing his due diligence."

"Right. Maybe."

"Aye."

"Edwin is picking me up this morning. It was too dark last night to gather the sword by the time Edwin reached Jolie, and she didn't want company. She asked that he and I come out this morning. We aren't going to call the Treasure Trove offices. I'm not going to call Joshua. Shoot, Tom, I haven't even told Inspector Winters yet." I frowned.

Tom met my expression. "Delaney, you know that Edwin would not want you doing something that makes you uncomfortable. Let him know."

"The problem is I think I'm okay with being a little sneaky. For now."

Tom nodded. "Lass, you are incapable of doing the wrong thing. It will be fine."

"We'll see."

"I am wondering if Edwin is doing something that might get the two of you in trouble. I'll have some bail money on me just in case, but . . . I hope it doesn't go that way."

"Inspector Winters will get us out of any jam. I think."

"Aye. Maybe."

Tom had gotten home so late the night before that we hadn't had a chance to talk about everything that had happened. After I told him about the murder, all the other things seemed too unimportant for a late-night conversation. We'd gone over everything else this morning.

I'd checked all the usual news outlets but hadn't heard anything about the murder. Roslin was only a short distance from Edinburgh, but maybe it was far enough not to be a news priority.

"I did text Inspector Winters that I'd like to talk to him this morning but haven't heard from him yet."

"What are you going to tell him?"

"I'm not sure yet."

"Play it by ear?"

"Right." I smiled at the American expression. Since our visit to Kansas and my family, Tom had commented that though he would always be Scottish through and through, he thought he should pick up a phrase or two that might remind me of my own homeland.

It was adorable.

He and his employee Rodger had been working on yet another plumbing problem in the back part of the pub. Between that and a busy football season (soccer, as far as I was concerned, but Tom couldn't force himself to switch to that American vernacular) with the place overflowing with revelers, he'd been abnormally busy. He and Rodger had completed the plumbing now, though, and he was looking forward to a day of just pouring drinks and cheering matches played on the television.

After we cleaned up, I walked him to the front door. He pulled me into a hug and kissed my forehead. "Be safe, love, and let me know if you need the bail money."

"You'll be my first call."

"And if you don't get arrested, do you have time for dinner tonight?"

"Absolutely."

From the doorway of our blue house by the sea, I watched him get into his car, and I waved as he drove away. Most of the time, I rode into Grassmarket with him, and when I didn't it was rare that I stood in the doorway and watched him go, but it felt right today.

Just as Tom's car disappeared from view, Edwin's came into sight. He was on time. As he pulled into the driveway, I signaled that I needed a second. I ran inside, made sure all the appliances were off, grabbed my bag, and hurried back out to the Citroën.

The heater in Edwin's old car had had plenty of time to warm the front seats, and the cold morning, with an assist from the ever-present ocean breeze, made me relish the heat. The warmth along with the cup of coffee Edwin had brought for me took off all the chills.

"Morning, lass," Edwin said as I fastened the seat belt.

"Good morning. How are . . . things?"

"How are you?"

I sighed. "I'm okay, Edwin. I don't think I've quite processed what I saw yesterday."

"It sounds like it was terrible."

"I . . ."

"What?"

"I want to make sure we do the right thing."

Edwin nodded. "We will, lass, but may I add the word 'ultimately'?"

That wasn't quite the way it was supposed to work, but I trusted Edwin implicitly.

"Okay," I said. "Sure."

"I promise."

"Okay," I said a little more confidently. "Thanks, Edwin."

"Thank you. Keep me on the straight and narrow, lass. We'll be fine. I'm looking forward to speaking with Jolie, but I haven't heard any news regarding yesterday's events at Rosebud. Have you?"

"Not a word. I feel like it should be a big story."

"I think it will be, at some point. There are some layers to work through there, and since the Lannisters were once known for stirring things up, I imagine there's some research being done."

I hadn't taken any time to research Jolie and her family the night before. It had been an evening to decompress, and searching for information on the internet didn't usually mix well with relaxation.

"Are we going to get the sword?" I asked.

"That's the plan."

Though I'd worked hard to let go of the stress of yesterday's events, I'd still had a difficult time getting to sleep, because once I'd closed my eyes, thoughts of how I was going to tell Edwin about Joshua's visit started rumbling around in my busy mind. I'd told Rosie and Hamlet that I would have the conversation—that they didn't need to take that task on—but I struggled with the best way to begin with my boss. Now was as good a time as any, I decided.

"Edwin, Joshua visited me in the warehouse yesterday," I said.

"Aye," he said with a tinge of suspicion. "Did he love it?"

"I think he did, but I think he also had an ulterior motive."

"Aye?"

With as little emotion as possible, I told Edwin the details of the visit. I emphasized the fact that Joshua was turning a blind eye to almost everything, except perhaps a Crusader sword.

Edwin listened, keeping his expression neutral. It was the way he often digested new information. He liked to give things time to percolate.

When he finally spoke, he said, "Cramer Donnell is the new man's name?"

"That's the name Joshua gave me. Do you know him?"

"I've never heard of him, and that surprises me. I wonder about his background and how we haven't crossed paths yet. Would you mind researching him for me when you have a moment?"

I grabbed my phone. "I have a moment right now."

Cramer Donnell's picture, as well as the notice from National Museums Scotland regarding him being hired to the position of director, were the first things that came up with the search.

I read the notice aloud: "National Museums Scotland is pleased to announce the acquisition of a new director of the Treasure Trove Unit of the Scottish government. Cramer Donnell comes to Edinburgh from Glasgow, where he spent decades as director of Glasgow House and Abertaf Castle. Mr. Donnell's interest in Scottish history began when he was a wee lad and his family traveled to Culloden on holiday. His experience along with his passion for all Scottish history makes him a perfect fit for the directorship. We are all looking forward to working and exploring many more wonderful finds with Mr. Donnell."

I paused but then continued a moment later, "Seems clear-cut."

"I knew the previous director, a gentleman named Christian Wurther—"

"I've heard that name."

"Aye. Of all the directors I've known over the years, Mr. Wurther was probably the laziest." Edwin tapped the steering wheel with his index finger. "I know you are aware of the fact that I work to ingratiate myself with people in such positions as the Treasure Trove. Museum directors, archaeologists, et cetera. I feel that if we work together, we will all only be of benefit to our beloved country."

"Yes, you've mentioned something like that a time or two."

"Aye, well, some might say—and I'm not admitting to such a thing, mind—but some might say that I am a wee bit too friendly, perhaps too free with buying meals and drinks for people in such positions." He sent me a quick sideways glance before returning his eyes to the road. He lowered his voice. "I've been accused of bribery." He brought his voice back up to its normal volume. "Mr. Wurther was never interested in dinners or evenings at any pub. I thought he was going to be immune to my charms, if you know what I mean."

"I do."

"Anyway, my prediction about him proved incorrect. It was simply that he was lazy. He didn't much care what anyone did just as long as folks left him alone in his office so he might do his own tedious research about . . . well, I'm not sure I ever learned those specifics. Anyway, I think the museum gave him a few chances to reform his ways, but he never did. I'd heard he'd been let go, but Mr. Donnell's hiring is news to me." He sent me a quick smile. "I look forward to meeting him, and perhaps returning to my . . . amusing ways."

"No one is immune to your charms."

Edwin laughed. "Not true, lass, but I'm not out to do harm to the Treasure Trove. It just takes time for some to understand . . . again, my ways."

I nodded. He wasn't wrong, but what neither of us added was that most everyone did buy in, come to trust and believe in Edwin, eventually.

I looked at the picture of Cramer Donnell. A thin man with short, brownish hair, his toothy grin made him seem approachable and friendly. Looks could be deceiving, though.

As we stopped at a traffic signal, I shared the picture with Edwin.

"Very nice. Now I'll see him coming." He winked at me before he took off again.

I saved the picture on my camera and then turned my eyes forward, anxious to see Jolie—and, I admitted to myself, the sword too.

CHAPTER TEN

It had been cloudy the day before, but not as dreary as it was this morning. It was colder now too.

Unquestionably, the weather made the decrepit house seem shabbier. Even the beautiful grounds seemed off-color, maybe sickly. A murder would do that.

Maybe the grounds missed Homer, if he wasn't there. Had he been charged and arrested? Was he behind bars?

I wished Inspector Winters would check in with me.

Edwin lifted the knocker this time, allowing it to fall once.

A moment later, Trudie opened the door. Her small frame, like everything else, seemed even smaller today. Her eyes were rimmed in red.

"Hello," she said as she pulled the door wide. "Oh, I'm so, so happy to see you, Delaney."

"Oh," I said as she stepped out and pulled me into a hug. I hugged back and gave her a moment.

When she finally released me, she stood back and looked at Edwin.

"You're Mr. MacAlister," she said.

"Edwin."

"This is Trudie," I said.

"A pleasure to meet you." Edwin extended his hand and bowed a little.

"I've heard about you for years. I cannae believe we havnae met." She took Edwin's hand in both of hers.

"It is a pleasure," he repeated.

When Trudie released Edwin, she sniffed and wiped her fingers under her eyes. "You've come at the right time. Jolie is . . . not well. She won't let me call the doctor, and I . . . I don't know what to do."

"Take us to her," Edwin said.

Hurriedly, we followed Trudie inside. Nothing had been cleared away, so the paths were still limited to the spaces in between all the stuff. I saw surprise brighten Edwin's eyes, but he was far too polite to offer a comment.

Once again, seeming to defy her age, Trudie took off up the left stairway, her legs moving evenly and easily. I followed behind her and Edwin brought up the back.

The stairs also held piles of things, but there was enough room so they weren't completely precarious—though probably not safe enough to meet any code standards.

"I've already sent Bowie away. She knocked earlier. I thought she was you, so I answered the door. I thought she might mow me over, but she's all bark, no bite," Trudie said over her shoulder.

I could imagine the scene and was glad Trudie hadn't been intimidated. I looked over my shoulder and shared raised eyebrows with Edwin.

Trudie jetted down the hallway off the landing. Surprisingly, there were very few stacks here, but there were a number of shoeboxes. Ornate red, gold, and blue worn carpeting covered the floor, and wood panels lined the bottom half of all the walls. One broken ceramic bust lay on the floor, the head and face too disfigured to know who might have been the subject.

Trudie knocked on the second door to our right, but she didn't wait for an invitation before opening it.

"We've company," she said. "Delaney and Mr. MacAlister are here."

Neither Edwin nor I waited for an invitation either. On the way up the stairs, my imagination had gone into overdrive and Trudie's "not well" turned into "deathly ill."

"Oh," Jolie said weakly.

Or that's who I thought was speaking. The room was shrouded in complete darkness. Once inside the door, Edwin and I stopped next to each other. I assumed he was blinking as I was, trying to see where we were and who was in there with us.

We heard the swish of curtains before we could see that it was Trudie who was opening them. Though there were dark clouds outside, it was now certainly brighter than the closed-off room, and the new light was squint-worthy. The large windows looked out toward the back of the property.

"No! Close those, Trudie," Jolie exclaimed. She pulled a quilt, one patterned very similarly to the hallway carpeting, over her head. "I'm not ready for visitors."

"Och, of course you are. We cannae be impolite to Edwin MacAlister now, can we? And lovely Delaney?" Trudie nodded encouragingly at us.

Edwin took the hint. "Hello, Jolie, it's lovely to see you."

Were it all not so serious, it would have been a silly and laughable thing to say since all we saw of Jolie was the mound her body made in the giant, wooden four-poster bed.

"Always good to see you too, Edwin," Jolie said, still from her hiding place.

I bit the inside of my cheek to quash the awful, awful laugh that threatened to erupt.

"I'm going to gather things from the kitchen," Trudie said to the bed. "Would you like me to bring them up here or would you like to come downstairs?"

We waited a beat and then another.

"Bring them up here," Jolie said, reluctantly.

"Aye. Right away." Trudie nodded at Edwin and me as she left the room.

Even neater than the hallway, Jolie's room was almost pristine. The only thing resembling a stack of anything were a few handkerchiefs on a makeup table.

All the furniture was old, dark wood, carved with curlicues and spires on the ends of all the rounded knobs.

There was no television in the room, but there was an old radio sitting atop a dresser, and a crank turntable for 78 rpm records, though I didn't spot any of those anywhere.

"Jolie?" Edwin took a couple tentative steps toward the bed. "How are you, dear?"

"Oh, well, not great."

"I understand. Let us see you. Let's chat a bit."

Slowly the quilt came off her head and moved down to her chest. She wore a cap and a nightgown that also seemed to match the curtains and the carpeting. Jolie had an affinity for red, gold, and blue patterns.

When her eye landed fully on Edwin, a big smile lit her face. "Oh, Edwin, it is so very good to see you."

"Same, dear." He smiled as he stepped all the way to the bed and reached out his hand.

Jolie took it, and for a moment, they only smiled at each other.

And I realized something. They had been very close at one time—romantically, I was sure. Though I shouldn't have been surprised, I was. Edwin hadn't told me about that part, but as I watched them now, there was no doubt in my mind that they had been a couple.

And it was clear that their feelings for each other, though diluted, were still a part of them. The emotion that filled the room was heady, reminding me of roses and leather-bound books.

I smiled goofily.

"Delaney," Jolie said as she released Edwin's hand and sat up higher in the bed. "How are you, my dear? Yesterday was harrowing. How's your lovely friend, Elias?"

"He's fine." I hoped he was. I hadn't spoken to him again. "I'm fine. I'm so . . . sorry." I stepped closer to the bed. "Have you heard any details? How's Homer?"

Jolie's smile turned into a frown. "I don't know anything except that Homer was taken away by the police, and I'm sure it's all one big mistake. Homer could never kill anyone, unless he was protecting either Trudie or me."

"Maybe that's what was happening," Edwin offered.

"That lad was a threat to us? I simply can't imagine how."

Jolie was fine—at least not physically ill—so I continued. "Can you remember the meeting with him and the others? Maybe there is a clue somewhere in that."

Jolie cocked her head at me. "Are you here to investigate the lad's murder or pick up the sword?"

I looked at Edwin and back at Jolie. He spoke before I could. "Mostly, we're here to make sure you're all right."

Jolie laughed. "No, you're not, Edwin dear. You would have just called again if that were the case. I know you want that sword, and I'm prepared to give it to you, but, Delaney, are you going to solve this mystery?"

"Maybe." I shrugged.

"How very delightful." Jolie's expression brightened. In a flourish, she threw off the quilt. "Let's get to work."

CHAPTER ELEVEN

Jolie sent us downstairs, where we met Trudie in the kitchen and helped her carry things to the green velvet table in the library. She left us there and went to help Jolie "put herself together."

Edwin made no comment on the state of the house but perused the library shelves instead. I took the opportunity to slip out and look at the paintings and pictures on the hallway walls.

Jolie was recognizable, even in the pictures of her as a child. She'd always had a slightly pointy chin and eyes that seemed to be smiling even when the rest of her expression wasn't.

I sussed out her parents—Jolie resembled her fair-haired father much more than her brunette mother, though Jolie was completely gray now. Family pictures showed three people who cared about each other enough to either stand close to one another or wrap their arms around one another. There weren't a lot of big smiles, but there were some. Most expressions seemed content but reserved.

There were many pictures of Jolie aboard different boats. In most of them, she wore fisherman gear with thick overalls and waders. She seemed to be very happy on the water.

I came upon one picture that I couldn't help but snap a copy of with my phone.

Edwin and Jolie were young, both of them stunning in their beautiful clothes as they gazed at each other while the picture caught them in an unguarded moment on a dance floor. My guess had been spot-on. You didn't look at just anyone the way they looked at each other.

Tears came to my eyes as I gazed at the picture. I was grateful I'd come to know my boss at The Cracked Spine, but what I wouldn't have given to know this younger version of him, and Jolie too.

They were both clearly living their best lives. I would ask Edwin for the story behind the picture at some point, but for now I had other things to see.

The most jaw-dropping find was a picture with Jolie, her parents, Wallis Simpson, and the former King Edward VIII. They wore the clothes of the time as Edward held in his arms a toddler version of Jolie. He was all smiles, as was Vivian. Jolie's father didn't appear quite as happy, and Wallis Simpson frowned. I pondered the history and mystery behind the picture.

"Did Edwin tell you?" Jolie asked from the end of the hall-way.

I started. "Oh. I . . . well, he mentioned something."

Jolie smiled. She was now dressed, and her hair was done up in a bun. She wore a regular old sweater and jeans today, and she seemed much more youthful than she had either the day before or the few previous minutes up in her room. "I'll tell you the details at some point." She started walking in my di-rection. "For your information, my mother stood by her story until the day she died. She claimed that Edward was my father. She twisted that into meaning I had a right to the throne."

I nodded. "Has anyone done any DNA testing?"

"No, lass, it wouldn't be worthwhile. I'm not welcome into the royal family. There's no need to make it more uncomfortable for everyone."

I wanted to comment on how much she looked like the man who'd married her mother, but then I realized that he resembled Edward. They were both rather ordinary-looking men with inquisitive eyes and thin lips. I decided to keep that observation to myself.

"Let's talk about our current-day mysteries." She walked past me and into the library.

With one more glance at the picture, as well as the one of Jolie and Edwin, I followed behind.

"Bowie led them all into the house," she went on, once we were all gathered. "In fact, Gilles seemed uncomfortable to be there. Alban, may he rest, appeared to just be tagging along. He didn't speak other than basic greetings. No eye contact," Jolie said. "Seemed shy."

"Gilles was uncomfortable?" I asked.

"Aye. I think so. He frowned a lot, didn't have much to say, though he answered Bowie's questions about how long it might take to clear things out of the house."

"He's an estate man," Edwin said. "Did Bowie want your house cleared out or your items sold?"

"I think she wanted everything sold but told Gilles to get things cleaned up too. Both."

I looked at Edwin and back at Jolie. "Did . . . did anyone ever talk about exploring the grounds?"

"No, why?"

"You suspected they might have heard about the sword. I just wondered . . ."

"I see. No, that didn't come up." Jolie paused. "There was no mention of the sword, but I was—I am—suspicious of the timing."

"Why?" Edwin asked.

Jolie shrugged. "I hadn't talked to Bowie in months. The sword was found the week before. That's all."

"When I got to the door, I heard loud voices."

"It was mostly me." Jolie looked at Edwin. "I was very angry. They came in here, Bowie demanding things from me that I didn't feel she had the right to demand. I raised my voice, and so did Bowie. But maybe she does have the right—those papers I signed."

Edwin nodded. "I can work on that if you'd like."

Jolie smiled at him. "Maybe, Edwin. It's not your job to rescue me. Trudie sent her away today. I'll figure it out . . . but if I don't, then aye, maybe I'll ask for your help."

Edwin nodded again.

"I'd heard of Gilles before yesterday, but he and I had never met. He has a wonderful reputation, I think," Jolie said.

"Aye," Edwin said.

Jolie tapped her finger on her mouth. "I did get a call a week ago from a young man. He said he worked at an estate consignment house. He wondered if I was interested in their services. I asked him why he thought I might be. He hemmed and hawed a moment and didn't give me a straight answer before he hung up. I wonder now if that was Alban. Until this moment I had forgotten about that call."

"You don't think it was Gilles?" I asked.

Jolie shook her head. "No, it was a young lad. Gilles's voice is distinctly older. If I'd thought about it when they were here, I would have asked if it had been him."

"Do you know if Alban rode out here with Gilles—or did he walk? Maybe he really did live close by?"

"I don't know." Jolie reached for her tea.

"Jolie, did your solicitor, Bowie, really not ring you beforehand to schedule the meeting?" Edwin asked.

Jolie glanced at Trudie who shook her head. "She didn't. Trudie takes most of my calls, but I did answer the phone—we still only have a landline—a few months ago when Bowie rang just to ask how I was doing."

"I haven't talked to Bowie in over a year," Trudie added. "The last time we spoke it was about a key to a safety-deposit box that Jolie wanted to open."

"Did she bring the key?" Edwin asked.

Jolie shook her head. "No, but she met me at the bank and gave me the key."

"May I ask what was in the box?" Edwin asked.

"Some of my mother's silverware." Jolie shrugged. "I'd forgotten all about it, but when I remembered, I thought I should retrieve it, or at least see if it was there. It was. All of it. Bowie had the key all along. She could have accessed the box at any time, but she didn't. Until yesterday morning, I trusted her completely."

"The surprise meeting was enough to cause you not to trust her any longer?" Edwin asked.

"Aye. Edwin, it was a true ambush. She showed up here, demanding that I get this place cleaned up, *telling* me that Gilles and Alban were going to inventory the place and take care of selling everything."

"She had no right," Trudie said.

"Well, she might," Jolie said. "I gave her the power to make such decisions for me if it appears I'm not able to do so."

"But you're fine," Edwin said.

Jolie sent him a withering look. "Edwin, look around. It doesn't appear that I'm fine."

"Your acknowledgment of that fact does much to prove you are," he responded.

"Still, though, she can use this all against me."

"She would have a fight on her hands," I said.

Jolie sighed. "One she might win, I suppose. It's that thought that sent me under the covers. I don't want a battle, and I'm not sure I have it in me to win one."

"We would all vouch for you. You wouldn't be alone," Edwin said.

"That's true," Trudie agreed.

Jolie smiled. "Well, thank you all, but . . . well, I am going to stop feeling sorry for myself right this minute. I will come up with a plan that's better than hiding in my bed. Alban's murder is more important, and I assure you that Homer did not kill him."

"Unless he was maybe defending you?" I said.

"Well, even then, he would have done other things first, like maybe yell to warn us off. I don't know, but he's not a killer."

"The police will figure it out," I said.

"I hope so." Jolie sighed. "I would like to know more about Alban, but I'm not willing to leave the house to ask questions." She leaned toward me. "But you are. You will be asking questions?"

I lifted my eyebrows at Edwin. It was pointless to try to fight it. "Yes, I think I will."

"Excellent! You must ring me with anything you discover."

"I will."

"Good." Jolie looked at the watch on her wrist and lifted her eyebrows. "Oh. Shall we gather the sword and get you on your way?"

It was an abrupt move, but maybe she was tiring, or she had something else to do.

"Do you have an appointment?" Edwin asked.

"Oh, never mind about that." Jolie stood. "Let's go get it."

With Jolie in the lead again, we took the same route we had the day before. The clouds had become even more ominous, and, though I was sure it was only my imagination, there was no question that the estate's grounds seemed less perfect than they'd been when Homer was there.

I'd had the thought that if he had been the killer, of course it was better that he wasn't there. I wasn't going to say that aloud because the women seemed certain that Homer wasn't the one who did the deed. Nevertheless, if he was . . .

We were quieter today. I glanced in the direction where I'd seen the horror, but no one made a move to go that way.

It was a relief to find the quilt-covered tub still inside the shed, but I still held my breath as Jolie reached for the blanket and lifted.

It was still there.

"The police didn't search here?" I asked.

Jolie shrugged. "If they did, they didn't say anything."

"Gracious." Edwin's exclamation was quiet and breathy.

"Aye, I agree," Jolie said. "Take it, Edwin. Get it out of here. I can't pinpoint how Bowie might have learned about it or if it was the reason for her showing up yesterday. I have no idea if it had anything to do with Mr. Dunning, but I want it gone. I want it out of my care."

Edwin nodded. "Are you sure?"

"I've never been more certain about anything." She glanced at her watch again.

Edwin and I shared a look, but he didn't ask again about an appointment. It was clear that she wanted us to hurry along.

I caught Trudie's gaze. Her wide eyes made her seem perplexed, but she didn't comment either.

The tub wasn't heavy, but it made more sense for Edwin and me to both carry it, one of us on each end. We made the trek back to the house, walking around the structure instead of through it.

Once in the front, Jolie seemed to be looking for someone heading in our direction from the road. She was still in hurry-up mode, and I was sure Edwin felt like I did—as if we were being pushed to get out of there.

Once in the car, Jolie and Trudie waving at us in our rearview mirror, Edwin said, "I wonder who's on the way."

"Someone she doesn't want us to talk to."

"Aye."

Once off the circular driveway, Edwin steered his Citroën onto the two-lane road that would lead us through the village of Roslin and then to Edinburgh. The roadway wasn't wide, and it was easy to see into the vehicles driving the other way, the ones heading toward the estate.

If I hadn't just looked up who he was, I would not have recognized the man driving the black sedan coming toward us. I might have recognized his passenger.

I twisted my neck as the cars passed each other.

"What is it, lass?" Edwin asked.

"I'm pretty sure that was Cramer Donnell driving that car, and I'm one hundred percent sure that the passenger was Joshua."

Joshua and I had made solid eye contact, his neck twisting just as mine had.

"Oh. Should we go back?"

I thought a long moment. "No, I don't think we should."

"Aye. I like that answer." Edwin looked in his rearview mirror. "Do you think they'll turn around and chase us?"

Again, I thought a moment. "I don't know, but I doubt it. Let's get the sword someplace safe. Quickly."

"Aye, lass, aye."

CHAPTER TWELVE

I stood in front of the bookshop and watched Edwin and the sword drive away. Wherever he was taking it, he wasn't telling. I assumed it was because he wasn't quite sure what to do with it yet. He would tell me when he decided.

I couldn't shake the sense that we'd somehow done something wrong. But we hadn't stolen the sword. Jolie had asked us to take it. The part that blurred the lines was that we now assumed that she had also called Cramer, the Treasure Trove Unit director. We couldn't know what she'd said to him. Edwin and I had debated whether he should call her and ask but decided that maybe it was best not to know.

My conversation with Joshua the previous day had put me in a precarious position, and a part of me resented it. If we hadn't spoken, the Treasure Trove wouldn't have even come to my mind—well, at least not right away.

Edwin and I had also discussed when he might make a call to Cramer, or maybe just Joshua, about the sword being in his possession.

As the Citroën disappeared, I bit my bottom lip. How many rare, precious, and priceless (or pretty close to it) items had

Edwin and I worked with, looked at, given away, sold? Too many to count offhand. There had never been one moment before when I'd second-guessed our activities or motives. I still didn't—we would do right by the sword. But with Joshua's heads-up, and spotting him and Cramer Donnell driving to Jolie's, everything had changed.

Hoping for a little Zen, or just some clarity, I took a deep breath through my nose and let it out through my mouth. It didn't help.

Inside the bookshop, Rosie and Hamlet were both helping multiple customers. I grabbed Hector as he greeted me and carried him along as I tried to assist my coworkers with the rush.

It turned out to be the best thing for my nerves. As I helped a young couple find their mother the perfect Jane Austen, and then fell into a wonderful conversation about Mary Shelley and *Frankenstein* with an older gentleman from Bangkok, my groove came back, my nerves settled down.

"Gracious," Rosie said as the bookshop cleared out again. "We haven't been that busy in a long time."

"I have no idea why." Hamlet shrugged. "It's not a holiday, the weather's not the best."

"Just because."

I looked at my coworkers and wondered if Edwin had told them where we were going on our morning errand. They hadn't inquired as to why I was a little late.

I was afraid to bring it up because I didn't want Hamlet's loyalties to feel torn between us and his friendship with Joshua.

Just as I decided I was overthinking it all and remembered that I didn't keep anything from any of my coworkers, my phone rang.

I'd put Hector down at some point and he was already there,

sitting next to the bag, which I'd also placed on the floor near Rosie's desk, and looking up at me expectantly. He never failed to reinforce that he was the cutest dog on the planet.

I grabbed the phone and looked at the ID. "Aggie? Hello."

"Lass," she said, her voice strained even with only that one word.

"What's wrong?"

"It's Elias. He's been taken away by the police."

"What?"

"Aye, your Inspector Winters came for him."

It didn't make sense that Elias had been arrested, but I didn't want to add more stress to Aggie by questioning her for details. "I'll figure out what's going on."

"Ta, lass. Ta." She sniffed as if she'd been crying.

My heart might have crumbled to pieces if I'd had to just wait for answers. We disconnected the call, and I noticed that Rosie and Hamlet were both watching me.

"Lass?" Rosie said.

"What's up?" Hamlet asked.

"I need to go find Elias. He's with Inspector Winters." I grabbed my bag. "I'm sorry I'm leaving again."

"We'll be fine," Hamlet said.

They would, and even if another rush came in, I had to go. With one more scratch behind Hector's ears, I nodded apologetically at my coworkers before I went back through the door I'd come in not that long ago.

I glanced in the direction of Tom's pub but couldn't spot anyone through the window. I could have passed the pub by walking to Inspector Winters's station, which was located at the bottom of the Royal Mile, but I decided to take the bus, a much faster trip.

Once boarded, I thought about texting Tom with an update, but he would only think he needed to join me at the station. I was torn between wanting him to do so and not wanting to mess up his schedule. I chose to leave him alone, for now.

I disembarked after the short (though it felt like it took forever) ride down the hill. I ran into the station.

A woman officer was behind the desk today. I didn't recognize her but told myself to gather my composure as she sent me critical eyes over the top of the reading glasses perched on her nose.

"Hi, I'm here to see Inspector Winters." I smiled, but hopefully not too maniacally.

"Are you now?" She leaned forward on the desk. "Why would that be?"

I was somewhat taken aback by her chilly attitude, but I forged on. "Well, I . . . I guess I need to talk to him about Alban Dunning."

Her eyebrows lifted and she straightened up. "Aye? Well, give me a moment. Name?"

"Delaney Nichols."

She frowned. "Aye. I thought as much. Red hair, American accent. I've been warned about you."

"Oh. I'm . . . sorry."

Finally, the officer smiled genuinely. "It's nothing. Only good things. I just wanted to make you work for it a little."

"Oh." I paused. "Only good things?"

She laughed. "Aye."

"That's good to hear."

The officer cleared her throat. "Are you really here about the murder of Alban Dunning?"

"Kind of." I figured we'd lose our small bond if I lied to her.

"I heard Inspector Winters brought in a friend for questioning, and I'd like to ask him about it."

She cocked her head and squinted her eyes at me for a moment. "I don't know how you did it, but Winters made it clear to all of us that we're to gather him if you ever stop by."

"Really?"

"Aye." She shook her head as she scooted off the stool and headed toward the hallway that would lead to Inspector Winters's shared office. "I'll be right back."

"Thank you."

Again, time seemed to slow down. Was Elias okay? Was he truly being questioned for murder? I couldn't make sense of that, but maybe anything was possible at this point. Aggie wasn't one to panic needlessly. In fact, she was probably less emotional than Elias. The panic I heard in her voice had propelled me here without much thought whatsoever.

Now, as I had a moment to let everything catch up, I suddenly felt a wave of stupid, as if I was behaving entitled. Nevertheless, I wasn't willing to leave until I heard that Elias was okay.

A few minutes later, Inspector Winters appeared, though the other officer wasn't with him.

"Delaney, what's going on?" he asked as he held a cup of coffee.

"I . . . Aggie called me. Is Elias in trouble?"

"No."

"Okay. Is he here?"

"Aye, lass, but he's fine." He frowned at me. "You want to see him?"

"I do. If possible."

"All right. Just down that way, to the interview room—the one you've been in a time or two."

"Thanks."

I hurried toward the room, meeting Inspector Winters as he came around from the other direction. He opened the door and let me go in first.

It wasn't just Elias inside, but Homer too.

"Delaney?" Elias asked, but he nodded a moment later. "Did Aggie ring you?"

"She did."

"I'm sorry," Elias said.

"No need. Is everyone okay?"

Elias and Homer shared a look before Elias said, "Aye. We're fine."

The tone told me that things could probably be better, though.

"Have a seat, Delaney," Inspector Winters said. "Coffee?"

"No thanks." I sat in the closest chair.

Inspector Winters set his coffee on the table and took a chair next to me. For a long moment, we all looked at each other.

Homer spoke first. "I met you yesterday, aye?"

"Yes. Hello, Homer. Are you okay?"

He nodded and leaned his elbows forward on the table. "I wanted Elias here with me."

"Oh. Why?"

"I cannae afford a solicitor." He shrugged.

"Jolie can," I said immediately. If he wasn't willing to ask her for help, I was. She cared deeply for Homer. I was sure she would want to help him.

Homer shook his head. "No, lass, I dinnae think so."

"She's run out of money?" I asked bluntly.

"No, I willnae ask her."

"Why not?"

"It's not her responsibility."

I would have begged to differ, but the look in Elias's eyes told me it wouldn't be a welcome opinion.

Homer continued, "I just wanted a friend here with me. Inspector Winters was good enough to round up Elias."

It was a weird set of circumstances, but since Elias had witnessed something—after the murder itself, I thought—maybe this was Inspector Winters's way of getting both of their viewpoints or trying to catch one of them in a lie.

I wondered if I should call Edwin and have him send an attorney over. But it was Inspector Winters, after all, and I trusted him.

"I think he should have an attorney too," Inspector Winters said. "However, with the two of you here for him, I feel better."

"Has he—" I looked at Homer. "Have you been arrested?"

"No, he hasn't," Inspector Winters said, "though he's not off the hook yet. We are investigating, but there were enough questions at the scene to set him free this morning. For now."

Relief spread through me. I nodded. "Okay, okay. So, what happened, Homer?"

Homer looked at me and then at Winters. I wondered if he'd said much of anything yet, or if I'd arrived at the beginning of the interview. I didn't ask.

"I'd set down the rake, thinking I would need it more later at an area in the other direction, and was walking toward the yellow gardens—it's a plot covered in yellow flowers in the spring. Now, it's not as colorful, but I like to add bulbs or move some around this time of year. I heard yelling—just one voice, male. At this point, I would assume it was Alban—"

"What words did you hear?" Inspector Winters asked.

Homer's eyebrows came together over his closed eyes. "I

think I heard, 'stop!' and 'you don't have to do this' and other things I couldn't make out. It sounded bad, though. You know how it goes—just by the sound of something, you ken something isnae right?"

"Sure," Inspector Winters said. "Then what?"

"I'm afraid I hesitated, but only for a few seconds. I was scarit, but not for myself. I took a moment to think about where Jolie and everyone else might be. It seemed like the yelling was coming from the direction of the shed."

"The shed? The one that looks like a gingerbread house?" the inspector asked.

"Aye. I ken that Jolie liked to take her walkabouts out that way, so I thought that's where they were all going."

"I can confirm," I interjected. "That's where we went."

"Why?" Inspector Winters asked.

Homer shrugged, and I suddenly felt horrible for him. He was keeping a secret when now wasn't the time to keep them, and he was as ashamed as I was about keeping it.

I leaned toward him on the table. "Homer, it's okay. I'm going to tell Inspector Winters what was going on. It might be important."

"You are?" Tears filled his eyes.

I felt even worse for him. I'd been dancing around the truth myself for two days, and I hated that feeling. What in the world was wrong with me, us? To hell with that stupid sword.

"Inspector Winters, I was out there to look at an item that was found on Jolie's property. Elias had driven me, so he came inside with me."

"What item?"

The relief I felt as I told the story was mirrored in Elias's and Homer's relaxing shoulders. We'd all been lying, again, about a stupid . . . thing! We'd all felt the stress, and no one wanted to be the one to spill the beans, even if it seemed no one—Jolie included—had instructed anyone to keep the secret from the police. We'd all just somehow assumed. There was no longer a choice in the matter, though.

"This is good, Delaney. Thank you," Inspector Winters said.

I smiled weakly. I needed to get ahold of Edwin and Jolie to let them know what I'd told the police.

"Inspector," Homer said, "I cannae imagine the sword had anything to do with Mr. Dunning's murder. It was a well-kept secret until Jolie shared it with Edwin, Ms. Delaney, and Elias." He nodded toward us. "Jolie asked Trudie and me to keep it a secret before the murder occurred, so I guess we all did afterwards too."

"Tell me the circumstances of you finding it," Inspector Winters said.

Homer folded his hands together on the table. "It was just last week. I was working the grounds—"

"Where?" Winters asked.

"In an area we call Bountiful. It's away from the house directly off the public walking path and near a bridge."

"It's a public path?"

"No, but Jolie allows people to use it. Word has gotten around. I found the sword over a small hill from the path."

"Jolie is okay with strangers taking the path?"

"Aye. She welcomes them there but doesn't like them walking deeper onto the grounds. The bridge isnae easily noticed as you walk along the path."

"Okay. Go on."

Homer shrugged. "I was weeding, digging up some things, moving them here and there, and my spade hit a sharp item and made a dull clink-thud noise. Carefully, using only my hands now, I dug it up and out of there. Of course, I realized immediately that it was a sword, so I was careful." He looked sheepishly at Elias before he continued. "I ken what it might be immediately."

"Aye," Elias said. "I figured."

"I gathered it and hurried it back to the house."

"Did anyone walk by on the path as you were digging it up?" Winters asked.

"No. I looked around, made sure."

"Could someone have been hidden from sight and observing?"

"Aye, there are plenty of things to hide around, but I looked. I didnae see a soul."

"Did Alban live in Roslin?" I asked Inspector Winters.

"No. He lived in Edinburgh."

I knew that both Elias and I had told the police that we'd seen Alban walking down the path before we'd set out on our own "explorations."

I swallowed hard. I didn't want to point the finger of suspicion at anyone, but I continued, "I wondered if maybe he and Gilles had had some sort of argument and Alban just said he'd walk himself back to . . . somewhere? It doesn't seem reasonable that he'd walk to Edinburgh, but maybe somewhere in Roslin, where he could get an Uber or something?"

"Aye. We talked to Gilles," Winters said.

"I don't suppose you want to tell us what he said."

"I do not, but we are exploring possible Roslin connections."

That seemed reasonable.

Inspector Winters looked at Homer again. "After you pulled the sword from the ground, what did you do?"

"I hurried it to the house and showed it to Jolie and Trudie. They didnae understand what it might be. When I told them, they asked me to put it out in the shed. Jolie said she knew some people and would make some calls."

"She asked you to put it in the shed? That seems unsafe, unsecure," Winters said.

"I thought so too," Homer said quickly. "I asked her if she was sure. She said she was."

I'd considered the same thing—why had such a potentially valuable item been kept in a shed out in the middle of an otherwise vacant expanse of Jolie's property?

I didn't think Homer was lying. What would Jolie say when she was asked about her idea for a storage location?

I cringed inwardly. She was not going to be happy with me.

The relief I felt over the truth being out there far outweighed my concern, though. It would hers too. I still didn't see a tie to Alban's murder, but Inspector Winters was asking enough questions that he seemed to suspect a possible tie.

Inspector Winters nodded. "Then what?"

"Then I just got back to my job. I checked on the sword a few times a day, but Jolie didn't give me any further instructions."

"Okay. When you heard the male voice, were there any words about swords or weapons?"

"No."

Inspector Winters fell into thought. The rest of us waited silently. He looked up a moment later. "We didn't have much of anything to help us find Mr. Dunning's murderer. I can only hope this gives us a lead. I wish you all would have told us sooner."

The three of us shrank a little in our chairs.

"Sorry," I said.

"I didnae have anything to do with the lad's murder," Homer said. "I'm sorry too."

Inspector Winters looked at Elias.

"I'm sorry too, Inspector."

"Right."

"Is there any evidence at all?" I asked.

"A wee bit, but not much. No, I'm not going to tell you what it is. You need to stay close by, Homer. Don't leave Roslin or Edinburgh."

"I have nowhere else to go."

"I'll run you home," Inspector Winters said.

"I can, Inspector," Elias said.

"That's up to Homer."

Homer looked at Elias. "That would be lovely. Ta, friend."

From Aggie's call, I'd thought Elias had been escorted by Inspector Winters, but he'd followed behind him in the taxi. If I'd noticed it parked out front, I might have relaxed sooner. I should have taken the time to ask Aggie a few more questions.

As we left, I felt appropriately chastened. In fact, Inspector Winters could have arrested us all for interfering in a murder investigation. I was glad he just let us go, even if I did feel his deep disappointment.

I'd been the one to text him to come out to the scene and had kept the information about the sword from him. I would look for a moment I could redeem myself, but at least he now had the information.

I rode along with Homer and Elias, both hoping to talk to Homer some more as well as maybe give Jolie my confession in person. I considered texting Edwin, but decided I needed to tell him in person too.

However, the conversations inside the taxi on the short drive to Roslin were about the men's younger days when they worked together on the docks.

They both spoke with so much Scots that I had a hard time following what they said. I'd prided myself on my acclimation to my new country, how I now rarely needed Hamlet to translate something Rosie said to me. The ride to Roslin told me I still had work to do.

As we pulled into the circular driveway, Homer thanked us both. We got out of the taxi and made our way to the front door. It was locked.

Homer looked at this watch. "If Jolie's keeping her schedule, she and Trudie are out for a walkabout. They travel about five kilometers, if you want to track them down or maybe wait for them."

"No, we'll head back." I was sure Aggie was anxious to get her eyes on Elias again. Besides, if I had a preference, it would be to talk to Edwin before Jolie. I also thought Homer might share with her what I'd confessed and thought it would be better coming from him anyway.

"Aye. Ta again, friends," Homer said before he and Elias shared a hug and he took off down the path, presumably to get back to work. Homer wasn't the type of man who took many days off.

"Can we drive you anywhere else?" Elias called.

"No, I've got things to do."

"Come for dinner soon."

"Will do." Homer waved over his shoulder.

I wished for the chance to see Homer's home, but now wasn't the day.

Back in the cab, Elias first called Aggie to reassure her that he was fine, that the police never even considered him a suspect. He handed me the phone, and I reassured her that Elias was telling her the truth.

Elias put the phone back to his ear. "Delaney and I are running an errand. I'll be home soon, love."

They disconnected the call.

"We're running an errand?" I asked.

"Aye. We're going to talk to Gilles Haig, or at least we're going to try."

"We are? I like that plan, but . . . why right now?"

"I want to know more about why they were out there yesterday."

"Okay? This isn't like you."

"Well, I'm curious."

"Me too. I guess. I . . . let's do it."

I couldn't remember one time when Elias had instigated an inquiring visit to someone. My coworkers had told me that my curiosity had worn off on them a little. Maybe the same had happened to Elias and Aggie, but that didn't seem quite right. There was something else going on here, but the stubborn set of Elias's jaw told me he wasn't going to share his motivation. I was okay with that and sure I'd figure it out eventually anyway.

CHAPTER THIRTEEN

Though Edwin had named the once secret space in the bookshop building a *warehouse,* the more appropriate and official definition would probably be "back room." But Gilles Haig ran an actual auction warehouse. He'd had the business for over twenty years, and as I'd given it even more thought, from what I'd heard, he was respected by everyone.

The way it worked: once a week, cars, trucks, all kinds of vehicles would line up along the street next to the big steel-walled building. They would turn down an alleyway—a *close* in Scotland, though this space was more like an American alley than any closes I'd explored. The vehicles would be unloaded one at a time. Quickly, Gilles and his staff would inventory the items and write the customer a receipt. Then, a week or two later, an auction would be held in the warehouse. Gilles made twenty-five percent, the customers seventy-five of whatever sold.

I'd never been to his place, though I'd heard about the auctions and Gilles's auctioneering skills. I'd wanted to visit, and now I wished I had before today.

Right inside the front doors was a big space filled with tables

that held many different items. It was impossible to digest all
the things we saw, but my eyes skimmed over a Dolly Parton
album cover as well as a doll that I thought I used to have—one
that came with a makeup palette. Furniture, even appliances,
all sorts of things.

"Can I help you?" A voice called from the back.

My eyes zeroed in on a woman wearing a brown canvas
work apron, a big bun of gray hair topping off her round figure.

"We were hoping to talk to Mr. Haig," I called.

"About what?"

I hadn't thought things through that far.

"My wife is his cousin," Elias called. "Aggie McKenna."

My gaze snapped back to Elias. Now I understood his initi-
ating this meeting. He gave me a tiny shrug. I was glad for the
connection. Elias was pleased with the good surprise.

"Aye? Well I don't know one thing about Gilles's family, but
if that's the case, I'm sure he'll see you. His is the office at the
end." She pointed toward one of the closed doors along a side
wall, the door with a carved wood office sign above it.

"Thank you," Elias said.

"You didn't tell me," I said quietly as we made our way.

"I wasnae sure if we'd need to use it or not. They are cousins, aye, but they havnae seen each other for a decade or so.
We'll see if it does us any good."

"Oh. They had a falling out?"

"Oh, no, just busy with their lives."

"I know how that goes."

Once outside the door, I knocked.

"Who's there?" came from inside.

"Delaney Nichols. We met yesterday. Elias McKenna is
here with me."

A few moments later, the door opened. We were greeted by the same man I'd met yesterday, but he looked remarkably different, older and more tired, with red-rimmed eyes.

"Gilles, I'm Aggie's husband. We met a long time ago," Elias said.

"I thought I recognized you yesterday, but I meet so many people." He paused. "Come in. Have a seat."

Elias and I sat on an old couch that had been placed against a wall and Gilles sat in his desk chair. The desk was against the wall, so the seating area filled the middle of the space.

"What can I do for you?" Gilles asked.

"We're sorry for your loss," Elias said.

"Aye." Gilles nodded. "I'm having a hard time processing it all. I didn't want to come to work, but I didn't know what else to do. I'm not focusing well."

"It's a terrible shock," I said.

"Aye. He was a good lad."

"As bad as the timing is, we were hoping to ask you some questions about Alban," I said.

"You? Why?"

Elias jumped in. "Homer was released but he's not off the hook yet. The police are investigating. Homer's an old friend of mine. I guess I'm trying to help him."

Gilles frowned at Elias. "Really? Goodness, it feels like a small world with you here."

Elias nodded.

As Gilles fell into thought again, I took a quick look around the office. It was as if we stepped back in time. It must not have been remodeled since the early 1900s.

"Your office is beautiful," I interjected.

The desk and shelves were all made of cherrywood, fashioned in Art Deco style. I would normally find such designs feminine, but this office was distinctly masculine with a James Bond air about it—sleek and old-fashioned at the same time.

"The warehouse used to be an old railroad building. This room was the manager's office. He was apparently a stickler for neatness and keeping things pristine. When the rails all moved, this building was shut down until I bought it twenty years ago to start the auction house. I came in here, dusted everything, and then kept it as it was." He looked at Elias. "How's sweet Aggie? I haven't seen her for so many years."

"She's well. Healthy."

"Does she still make that shortbread?"

"Aye, the best ever."

"I can vouch for that," I added.

"Give her my best, and tell her that our cousin in Germany, Morton, was released from prison recently."

"Aye? I've not heard of him."

"He's quite a character. Ask Aggie."

"I surely will. She sends her best."

"The police let the groundskeeper go?"

Elias and I nodded.

"I thought they had him red-handed." Gilles cringed. "That was a poor choice of words. I thought they caught him in the act." His sad eyes scanned us. "I heard that one of you found the groundskeeper with Alban's body."

"I came upon the scene, but Homer was removing the rake off . . . Alban. Homer wasnae the one to . . ."

"I see. So, the police don't know what happened to Alban?"

"They say they have a clue, but they're not sharing it, of course," I said.

"I wish I knew what that was. Maybe I could help," Gilles said.

"Where was Alban from?" Elias asked as he sat forward on the couch.

"He grew up right here in Edinburgh, a good lad, quiet life, kept to himself. He dated a wee bit, but he was . . . well, he was just one of those people who seemed to like being alone. He was drawn to the job here because he did it mostly on his own. When people drop off their items, we do a quick inventory, but we do a thorough one before auction. Alban always took one side of the warehouse and my other employee, Helen, the other. She'll be doing the whole thing now, until I get someone hired. He loved the tediousness of it, the research involved if he found something that needed an extra look. We're an honest group. If we find something more valuable than a customer might have thought, we let them know as quickly as possible.

"Alban was good too—fast and accurate. Helen isn't all that social either. They worked well together." Gilles smiled sadly.

My throat tightened and I blinked back some tears. "Did you know anything about his life outside of work, his friends, if he had any enemies?"

"I'm not aware of any friends, nor could I imagine he had any enemies. He always kept so much to himself." Gilles rubbed his chin. "He ate the same thing for breakfast and for lunch every day. An egg sandwich for breakfast and a tuna sandwich for lunch. He walked to work—lived only a few blocks to the south, in a flat above Joby's Coffee Shop—and walked home, stopping by the small restaurant—Bonnie's—down that way every night for dinner. He was a creature of habit and didn't like it when his routine got disrupted. It would put him out of sorts. It happened yesterday when I brought him with me out to Ms. Lannister's. He didn't like it, but he worked hard to hide that fact because sometimes in-home visits are a part of the job."

"When did you know about the visit?"

"Ms. Berry showed up yesterday morning earlier and demanded that we go with her."

"Demanded?" Elais asked.

Gilles nodded.

"Pardon me for asking this," I began. "But you must have felt obligated to go?"

"Not obligated, but I was curious. I'd heard of the Lannisters. It seemed prudent to go, but . . . well, Ms. Berry didn't tell us we would be arriving unexpectedly. It bothered us both." He paused. "As I got in my car, Alban said something to Ms. Berry. I didn't hear the words, but he was bothered, enough that he requested that I let him walk back on his own."

"That's a long trip," Elias said.

"I thought he'd catch a taxi or an Uber in Roslin."

"Did Ms. Berry mention any specific items she wanted to look at?" I asked.

"No, just . . . everything."

I was sure he was being honest. If Bowie Berry knew about the sword, I didn't think she'd told Gilles about it.

"Gilles, was it out of character for Alban to be upset enough to want to walk on his own?" I sat forward on the couch too.

"I'd never seen him upset like that, but I knew he didn't like to have his schedule interrupted. That on top of us being a part of . . . what was the word Ms. Lannister used? An *ambush*? I guessed he was upset about being part of something that wasn't on the up and up. I was too, but Alban and I didn't get upset in the same ways. Alban didn't like any sort of confrontation."

"What about his family?" Elias asked.

"I don't know anything about them. Helen told me she learned his childhood was rough, as if maybe his house was full of anger and violence. He never seemed to want to share those things with me, and I never pushed him on it. Helen probably had more personal conversations with him than I ever did, and even then, I can't imagine they were too deep. I think . . . well, I think he just wanted to live without disruption. He liked predictability—no, 'liked' isn't the correct word. He *needed* it to be able to function at his best."

He held up a hand as if he wanted us to give him a moment. We waited silently.

Gilles continued, "On the way to the Lannister house, he was quiet but okay. I told him I was intrigued by the idea of meeting Jolie Lannister. He had no comment, but that wasn't unusual. I concluded that he became most upset when we got there and we hadn't been expected."

"The scandal?" I said. "Jolie's . . . parentage?"

"Aye. I'm old enough to remember it. I think Alban knew some of it too."

"So, he was embarrassed by what happened, how Ms. Lannister was surprised?" Elias asked.

Gilles smiled sadly again. "Maybe. He told me he needed to walk, so I let him. He was a grown man." Gilles stood and went to the door. "I haven't asked . . ." He opened the door and called, "Helen, could you come in here a moment?"

We heard a distant "aye." She said it again when she stood in the doorway.

"This is Elias and Delaney. This is Helen." Gilles stood back from the doorway. "Helen, did Alban ever mention anything to you about Roslin?"

"The village where he was . . . ?"

"Aye."

She shook her head. "No, never."

"He never mentioned walking around out there or knowing the area?"

"No, Gilles. Never. He came to work and went home every day as far as I know."

"What about on his days off?" I asked. "Did he mention what he did on those days?"

"Aye, went to the library. He checked out books every week," Helen said.

"I didnae know about that," Gilles said, sadly.

"He didnae talk about it much, but, aye, he loved to read."

"I never once saw him with a book," Gilles said.

"No, he would never bring one to work. Work was about work, but sometimes we would talk about the things he'd read. He was much more willing to discuss things he'd read than about his own life."

Gilles shook his head but didn't say again that he hadn't known that part of his employee's life. "Thank you, Helen. If you think of anything we should tell the police, let me know."

"I thought they caught the killer."

"No, the man they took away wasn't the killer," Gilles said.

"Oh." Helen frowned. "Poor Alban."

"Aye."

The sound of a door slamming startled us all. I jumped in my skin.

"Hello?" a woman's voice called.

Helen stepped back from the doorway and repeated what she'd said to Elias and me when we'd come in: "Can I help you?"

"I'm looking for Gilles Haig."

Heels clacked on the cement floor, heading in our direction.

Helen looked at Gilles as if to ask what to do.

Gilles nodded and she stepped back and made her way back into the warehouse.

Bowie Berry appeared and filled the doorway with an attitude that couldn't be denied.

"Oh," she said as she took in the rest of us in the room. She put her hands on her hips and said, "Well, two birds, one stone and all of that. Hello, everyone."

Gilles said, "Hello, Ms. Berry."

"There's something you can do for me, Mr. Haig." She looked at me. "You too, Ms. Nichols."

Usually, I would want to talk to Bowie Berry, but I didn't like the tone she'd brought to this get-together. There was nothing I wanted more in that moment than to run out of there, but from her attitude and her stance filling the doorway, I was pretty sure she wouldn't hesitate to tackle me if I tried. I was curious about her motives, but I wasn't ready for a confrontation either.

"I'd love to stay and chat, but I've got a pickup that I cannae be late for." Elias stood. He picked up on my sense of being trapped. "Delaney, we have to go."

"Right." I stood too.

"Wait." Bowie put her hand up.

Elias grumbled.

"No, I won't keep you," she said to him. "But I do want to speak with you both. Look, I promise I only have Jolie's best interests in mind. Maybe I could ring you, meet you for coffee or lunch? My treat."

"Do you have a card?" I asked.

"Aye." Bowie opened the salmon-colored leather clutch that matched the color of her dress. She dug around a moment. "Dammit." She closed the purse after she grabbed her mobile. "Of course, when I need one the most, I don't have one. What's your number?"

Though I really didn't want to, I gave her my number. After she typed it in, my phone buzzed in my pocket before she disconnected the call.

"There. Now we can reach each other. Please, Ms. Nichols, again, I only have Ms. Lannister's best interests in mind." She nodded toward Gilles. "Wouldn't you agree, Mr. Haig?"

"I . . ."

Bowie frowned. "Clearly I need to convince you, too."

I piped up. "What if she doesn't want to sell her estate?"

Bowie sighed. "You don't have the history. You don't know about the meeting she and I had ten years ago when she told me she was worried about her mental health issues, worried that she would become more and more like her mother and that wasn't a good thing." She cleared her throat. "I won't say more about that, but know that"—she cocked her head at me—"Ms. Nichols, did you know Jolie before yesterday?"

I didn't answer. I didn't like the way she asked the questions. Neither did Elias, based on the grumble he let out, under his breath. Maybe I just didn't want to hear her version of the truth—at least yet.

"We need to go," Elias said.

Another long beat later, and probably because of his glare, Bowie moved out of the way.

I turned to Gilles. "I'm sorry for your loss. If there's anything I can do, please don't hesitate to call me."

"Ta, lass. I appreciate your visit this morning. Alban will be missed."

"Yes, he will."

With a controlled scurry, Elias and I left the office and then the warehouse.

CHAPTER FOURTEEN

Once in the taxi, Elias said, "It felt like time to go."

"I agree. I'm curious . . . I don't want to do anything to harm Jolie Lannister, but I'm not prepared to get between her and her attorney. I don't know any of them that well. Edwin might, but I don't." I paused. "Though I wouldn't mind eavesdropping."

Elias looked at me.

"Just saying, but no, I don't want to go back." I bucked the seat belt. "I have another idea if you're not busy, though . . ."

"Not at all. What should we investigate?"

"Want to drive by Alban's flat?"

"Aye. Above a coffee shop, just down the way?"

"That's what I remember."

"We'll be there quickly."

Joby's Coffee Shop was more than just coffee. It was also a candy shop—hard candies of all varieties. I'd visited it once before with Tom, but I hadn't remembered when Gilles mentioned the location.

I did now, and my mouth watered with the memory of the orange cream drops, but we didn't stop by the shop, sadly.

Lots of flats were located above main level businesses in Edinburgh. I'd visited a range of sizes and décor. I loved them all. Though I'd been lucky to live in a small house behind Elias and Aggie's place and then move into the blue house by the sea, I'd imagined myself in many of the flats I'd visited. For the most part, they were cozy and comfortable and quaint.

It seemed both a good and bad idea to live above a sweets shop.

There was no obvious police presence in the area, and Elias found a parking spot right in front of the building. We took that as encouragement to explore further.

We climbed the stairway next to the sweets shop and were greeted with two doors on a landing. Back farther, there was another stairway leading upward. The building had multiple levels with flats.

"I didn't see a residence directory near the doorway," I said.

"No, the front door is left unlocked. No need to buzz anyone to be let in."

"We should have asked Gilles for a flat number."

"Aye."

As we stood there, one of the doors opened and a young woman exited. She was probably in her thirties (like I thought Alban had been, though I had yet to confirm), and carried a few crocheted shopping bags.

"Uh. Hello," she said with an obvious American accent.

"Hi." I smiled, though it felt way too weird to just ask for the location of a murdered man's flat.

"Can I help you?"

"I . . . we're . . ."

The woman glanced toward the stairway. Like Bowie was in our way, we were in hers, and we were starting to bother her.

"I used to work with Alban Dunning. He had some of my books. The police told me to meet them here to gather them." Goodness, that was one quick lie. I should have been ashamed of myself, but I wasn't—if only because the woman didn't seem concerned now.

She relaxed and said, "I didn't know him at all, but such sad news. His flat was up on the next level—unit four—maybe the police are up there waiting for you."

"Of course! We should have thought to look. Thank you."

"You're welcome." She smiled quickly.

We stepped toward the other flight of stairs, getting out of her way easily. She trotted down and out the front door.

I looked at Elias. "That was a terrible lie."

He shrugged. "No harm done."

We walked up to the next floor, where units three and four were located.

There was nothing interesting about the door to Alban's flat—no decorations, no nameplate, nothing.

"Well, this is sad," I said as we stared at the door. "Just seeing his door, knowing he'll never . . ."

"Aye, but is it unlocked?" Elias grabbed the driving gloves he always carried in his back pocket and put them on.

I didn't stop him as he reached for the knob. It was most definitely locked.

"Want me to jimmy it?" Elias asked. "It would be easy."

"No. I mean, yes, I would love to see inside this apartment, but, no, let's not break the law. I'm having a hard enough time dealing with all the lies of the past couple of days. I can't take that sort of illegal activity."

Elias shrugged. "Aye, then. Shall we speak to the candy shop owner? Maybe he's the landlord too."

"That's a great idea! Let's go."

We made our way down the stairs not seeing anyone else until we went through the shop's side door.

"Can I help you?" a kid asked from behind the counter.

I didn't remember who had helped Tom and me before, but I didn't think it was a teenager.

"Well, we are wondering if the landlord of the flats above is here, but, also, I would love some candy," I said.

"Aye, the owner of the building is in the back. Shall I grab him, or do you want to place the candy order first?"

"Go get him, lad. We'll think about our order while you're gone," Elias said.

"You bet." He disappeared behind a curtain-covered doorway.

"We can buy it by the pound. I think we should get one of every flavor?"

"Not two?" Elias asked.

"Good point. Yes, two."

An older man appeared from behind the curtain. He seemed familiar.

"I'm Luke," he said. "Can I help you?"

Elias signaled to the kid. The two of them conversed quietly at the far end of the counter as Luke and I moved toward the cash register.

I introduced myself and told him I'd just met Alban earlier the day he was murdered.

"I'm doing some work for the woman who owns the place where Alban was killed," I said.

"The Rosebud House? The Lannister place?"

"Yes."

"And you want to know what about Alban? Why? What was his connection to Rosebud?"

"I don't know." I sighed. "The man who was originally arrested for the crime was released, and I don't know if the police have any suspects. Because of the work I do at the bookshop, my boss's friendship with Jolie Lannister, I wonder if you knew him at all." It was mostly honest, and that felt good.

Luke seemed to accept my motivations. "Alban was a good lad. Quiet. Paid his rent on time. Honestly, I thought his somewhat hermitic ways were a wee bit odd, but what business of that was mine? I've never seen him with anyone and can't imagine he had any enemies."

He paused and studied me a moment—I tried to look trustworthy, but I wasn't sure I could pull off sincerity today.

"One of his neighbors heard Alban's door slam a few days back. The neighbor looked out to see a woman hurrying down the stairs, but he wasn't sure if she came from Alban's place. He told me he asked Alban about it, and all he managed to do was to embarrass him. He felt so bad about asking him that he came and told me he might have bothered Alban and he was sorry for it."

I nodded. "The neighbor across the hall?"

"Aye, but . . . I don't think you should bother him."

"Okay. We won't. Did he say what the woman looked like?"

Luke shook his head. "He only saw her from behind for a second or two and didn't notice much."

"Did you ask Alban about it?"

"Of course not. None of my business who he has over. The

neighbor just wanted to make sure he was okay, but even he felt too nosey. Alban wouldn't admit to the slamming door being his, the woman coming from his place."

I wouldn't knock on the neighbor's door and ask for more details, but I sure wanted to.

"Thank you, Luke. Have you talked to the police?"

"No. Not really. They stopped by to tell me what happened, but they didn't ask questions. They said they'd be back, but I haven't seen them. Maybe I should let them know about the door—even if it might not mean anything at all."

I jotted Inspector Winters's number on a piece of scratch paper and encouraged Luke to call.

"It couldn't hurt," I said.

"Aye." Reluctantly, he took the paper and put it in his pocket. No one liked to get involved.

Elias, now loaded up with a bag of candy, met me at my end of the counter, and paid the kid.

"Ready, lass?"

I nodded and we thanked Luke and the employee for their time before we hurried back to the taxi.

"Did you learn anything?" Elias asked me.

"Maybe. I'm not sure, but the police might want to know about it."

I told Elias what Luke had said.

"Might not be anything," he said.

"Or it might be." I sighed. "Goodness, you need to get back to Aggie. I'm sorry I've kept you all day."

"Not to worry. She texted me, invited you over for dinner. Tom too."

"That sounds amazing. One second." Tom had already mentioned having dinner together. He enjoyed Aggie and Elias just as much as I did. I texted him with the invitation and was greeted quickly with: Sounds delicious. Meet you there?

"We're on," I said to Elias.

"Wummersome!"

He was correct—it was sure to be a *wonderful* evening.

CHAPTER FIFTEEN

"You've been busy." Tom smiled and reached for another helping.

We sat around Elias and Aggie's kitchen table, enjoying one of Aggie's specialties—chicken parmesan. Between the two of us, Elias and I shared our day's activities.

"Did you let Inspector Winters know what Luke said?" Aggie asked.

"I sent him a text but didn't hear back. It got late." I nodded toward the darkened window. "I had a surge of panic when I remembered I'd ignored the bookshop most of the day, but when I talked to Rosie, she said all had been well, and she'd see me tomorrow."

As it was, I felt discombobulated, like I was forgetting something I was supposed to do. I kept going over the tasks I was going to attend to at work and reassured myself, again and again, that all was well, I hadn't missed a deadline.

"Aggie, your cousin, Morton? Gilles said he was out of prison in Germany," I said.

"Aye. I hope that's good news. I hope he's reformed his ways."

"What did he do?"

"Stole from a jewelry store." She shook her head. "That's what he was imprisoned for. I'm sure he's stolen much over his life and gotten away with some of it, but not all. He's served time before."

"I'm sorry."

"Believe it or not, from all I know he isnae a violent man, just a very cagey thief. He's been in Germany a long time. We havnae spoken since we were bairns."

I didn't think Aggie and Gilles's wayward cousin had anything to do with Alban Dunning's murder, but it seemed important to rule him out of any possible suspicion.

"Were you and Gilles ever close?" I asked.

"No, not really, we're some number of cousins somehow removed. My mother and his father were . . . I believe . . . second cousins, so we would see each other at larger family events, but when we visited family on holiday, my parents would mostly go to my grandmother's place in the country. Gilles wasn't usually there for those—she wasnae his grandmother. He was a lovely lad when I was around him, though. Quiet, but funny too." Aggie smiled.

I couldn't imagine him being funny, but the current circumstances were far from comical.

Aggie continued, "I saw him at the auction house about ten years ago. I was helping a friend drop off some things and there he was. We spoke briefly, told each other we would stay in touch, and, like happens far too often, we never did."

"I'll take you over one day. I think he'd like to see a friendly face," Elias said.

"Ta. I would like to do that." Her face got serious. "Now, why would Inspector Winters come over here this morning and insist that Elias go with him? Couldn't he have just asked politely? Or called? I wouldnae have been so worried about him. I'm sorry I disrupted your day, Delaney."

I smiled. "Well, I had a wonderful day, so don't think twice about it. Elias and I make a good team."

"Aye, we do. The Delaney and Elias Investigative Agency."

I loved my job at The Cracked Spine more than anyone should ever be allowed to love a job, but for a brief instant the idea of a detective agency with Elias took shape in my mind, and I didn't hate it.

However, I didn't think anything, even working with Elias investigating crimes, could wrangle me away from the bookshop.

"Let's keep that in our back pockets, just in case," I said.

Elias laughed. So did Aggie, but I didn't think she found it quite so humorous.

"The description of Alban Dunning that Gilles gave you reminds me a little of Gilles when he was a teenager. He might have been funny, but he was also somewhat of a loner," Aggie added.

"We didn't ask a thing about him and his life," I said.

"I wonder if the police suspect him at all," Elias said.

"Surely not," Aggie said. "No, Gilles couldnae harm a fly. At least the Gilles I used to know."

"I don't think he's been brought in for questioning," I said.

We were silent a moment as we pondered the possibility. I decided that Elias and I should probably keep our day jobs and not start up a detective agency—we should have at least given more thought to Gilles as a suspect. He was, after all, one of the last people to see Alban Dunning alive. He was such a nice man, though. But wasn't charm a trait of many serial killers? A chill ran up my spine, but I shook it away.

Tom told us about the out-of-control hen party—*bachelorette* in my American vernacular—that stopped by the pub today. The bride-to-be and the maid of honor got in a fist fight and Tom and Rodger had to separate them until the police got there.

"Is the wedding still on?" Aggie asked.

"I'm assuming not," Tom said. "The fight was about some time the groom and maid of honor spent together on a London trip."

"Not wise," Elias said.

"No." Tom shrugged. "Better to know now, though, I suppose."

When I'd met my husband, I'd been told stories of his seeming fear of commitment. They weren't pretty stories, and, in fact, he'd apologized to a few of his previous girlfriends since he and I had been together. The thought of that made me realize there might be someone—one of his exes—I should talk to. I filed away the idea for later.

We enjoyed dessert and more conversation before Tom and I left to go home. It had been a perfect evening.

The next morning, however, was much less peaceful.

CHAPTER SIXTEEN

"Lass, wake up." Tom was gently shaking my shoulder. "Your mobile."

I sat up as a zip of anxiety shot through me. It was early—something was going on. I fumbled for my phone. Edwin was calling.

"Hello, Edwin?"

"Lass, good morning. Have you seen the newscast?" His voice was more strained than I'd ever heard before. Edwin rarely allowed stress to show.

"No. What's going on?"

"Turn on the telly. They're about to cycle back to the top story."

I threw off the covers and leapt out of bed. With Tom at my heels, we hurried into the front room and I flipped on the television. It was early—not even 8 a.m.—but Edwin was an early riser. He read several newspapers and always caught the morning news before the rest of us had brewed our coffee.

The camera zoomed in for a close-up of one of the newswomen I'd found familiar and mostly trustworthy.

"Our top story takes us back in time in more ways than one.

Ms. Jolie Lannister was once a local celebrity of sorts because of her mother's claims that Jolie had to the British throne. Now she's in the news again. It seems that a local lad was murdered on her property two days ago, and now a priceless item stolen. We are gathering information about the murder, but the police have told us that they aren't sharing details until they're sure all the victim's family members have been properly notified. However, the new director of the Treasure Trove Unit at the National Museum, Cramer Donnell, approached us with the story of the theft. Our own Micah McCrory interviewed Mr. Donnell yesterday:

REPORTER: Mr. Donnell, you are claiming that someone stole a sword from Ms. Lannister?

CRAMER: Aye. I was to go out to her home earlier today and gather it from her. But she said it was gone, taken.

REPORTER: Stolen?

CRAMER: She said "taken." And I'm sure I know who stole it.

REPORTER: Who?

CRAMER: Edwin MacAlister of The Cracked Spine bookshop in Edinburgh.

REPORTER: Have you called the police?

CRAMER: I have, but they are more concerned—as they should be—with investigating the murder that took place on Ms. Lannister's property.

REPORTER (as he looks at a note): The name of the victim has not been released. Do you know who it was?

CRAMER: I'm not at liberty to share that.

REPORTER: Perhaps the two incidents are tied together?

CRAMER: That's why I'm speaking with you. (Cramer looks into the camera.) To the police officers who seem to

be slacking on the job, please investigate this issue as
quickly as possible. That sword is priceless.

I flipped off the television. My stomach was turning as I still
held the phone to my ear. I remembered what I'd been meaning to do the day before—call Edwin and tell him what I'd told
Winters.

"Oh, Edwin, I forgot to tell you I told Inspector Winters
about the sword—but that still doesn't feel like what's happening here."

"Oh. Well, then the police do know. That's very good news,
Delaney. I think I see what happened. Mr. Donnell called the
reporters and they decided to turn it into something. If they
had done their follow-up better and contacted the police about
the allegations first, maybe this wouldn't have even occurred.
No matter that they've got it wrong, it's out there now. All
right. I'll pick you up and we'll go talk to Inspector Winters or
whatever other police we need to speak to together."

"I wanted to tell you in person. Oh, Edwin, I should have
at least called you, but it got late . . ." I did a literal smack of
my head.

Of all the things I didn't expect to hear, Edwin's chuckle
was toward the top of the list. "Oh, lass, not to worry. We'll get
it ironed out, and like I said, this is actually very good news."

I was momentarily speechless.

"Lass?" he said a moment later.

"I'm . . . here. I'm just. Oh, what a mess."

"It will be fine. I'll be by to gather you in half an hour."

"I'll be ready."

I disconnected the call and looked at Tom and said, "Oh
no, I've . . . oh, no."

He guided me to the couch. "Tell me what happened."

Though Elias and I had shared our whole day's activities the night before at dinner, I hadn't remembered the part where I hadn't yet *told* Edwin about my time with Inspector Winters and the meeting with him, Homer, and Elias.

"Lass, it's fine. Edwin didn't steal anything. It will get sorted. He's right—you telling Inspector Winters is a good thing."

"I think Edwin laughed a little. I don't think it's funny at all. Now he's on the news, being portrayed in a bad light."

Tom shrugged. "Edwin likes a good adventure. Isn't there a saying—there's no such thing as bad publicity?"

"Sure, but . . . a thief, maybe tied to a murder? Not good."

He pulled me into his arms and told me again that it would all be okay. I wouldn't have minded staying that way all day, but I had to get ready for Edwin's arrival.

Reluctantly, I let go and hurried to get dressed. I watched for Edwin's car out the front window, anxious to get our morning going. He was there only minutes after I was ready. Tom bid me goodbye; he was the one to wave from the doorway today.

"Good morning." Edwin handed me another cup of coffee as I got into the car. The sun was finally coming up, but it was cold outside.

"Oh, Edwin," I said.

"Lass, let me tell you what's really happened here."

"I'm listening." I held the coffee to warm my hands.

"You've managed to get Cramer Donnell to display his real colors long before I would have discovered them for myself. Not only that but I'm sure the police will be none too happy about his criticism of them. You've probably given us a surprising sort of advantage."

"I envy your positive outlook."

Edwin laughed. "It doesn't pay to be anything but positive, lass. Things will always work out."

"I hope so."

Edwin steered the car to Inspector Winters's police station. Traffic was just beginning to build, and I was able to text Winters that we would be meeting him at his office, as well as fill Edwin in on Elias's and my other activities the day before. Inspector Winters replied with: this early?

I sent a yes and hoped he'd be there.

The woman I'd greeted the day before was behind the front counter again, and she didn't waste a moment with any sort of rolling of her eyes. She seemed to expect our arrival.

"He'll be right in. He told me to ask you to go to the room you've become accustomed to."

"Thank you," I said.

"Thank you," Edwin said. "And thank you for your duty to our fine city. We appreciate all you do."

On a less naturally charming person, Edwin's words might have seemed fake or forced, but he was so naturally kind and generous that the police officer only smiled at him. "You're welcome." Then she looked at me and lost the smile.

Edwin and I found our way to the familiar interview room and took seats. We didn't have long to wait before Inspector Winters joined us.

"I know what's in the news," he said immediately. "Has anyone from the police contacted you, Edwin?"

"Not that I'm aware of, but if they stopped by to arrest me this morning, I haven't been home for a while."

"Right. Do you have the sword?"

"I do. It's locked in a safe in my house. Do you want me to retrieve it?"

"No. Not yet, at least." Inspector Winters shook his head. "Who is Cramer Donnell? What do you know about him? This is the first I've heard of him."

"He's from Glasgow," I said. "We know a little about him."

"He's the one I want to question. Well, along with everyone else. I'll need to confirm with Ms. Lannister that she gave you the sword with her blessing."

"I'm happy to wait right here while you do so. I won't run away from arrest." Edwin folded his hands on the table.

"Right. I'll be back in a bit. I'll have coffee brought in. Hungry?"

Edwin and I shook our heads.

"I'll have something delivered anyway. You might be here awhile."

Once he left the room, I looked at my boss and said, "Oh boy."

Edwin chuckled again.

Ultimately, neither of us were arrested. Jolie did, indeed, confirm to Inspector Winters that she'd given the sword to Edwin. She said she'd told Cramer that the sword was gone, but she wasn't going to tell him who took it. He kept asking her if it was stolen. She got tired of his harassment and, apparently, just closed the door on him.

I could picture the entire scene.

No one could track down a record of Cramer Donnell's alleged call to the police. His now seemingly false statements weren't well received, and Inspector Winters told us that Donnell was going to have to somehow prove that he did make the call. The director might end up in some legal trouble. The reporters were just "doing their jobs," apparently.

"However," Inspector Winter said. "Cramer Donnell also has something we all need."

"That is?" Edwin asked.

"He has—well, the museum has—the proper equipment to understand if what you have is truly a Crusader sword."

"I see." Edwin nodded. "You'd like for me to turn it over to him then?"

Inspector Winters sighed. "I've called the museum. I will work to make a deal with officials, going around Cramer. I will speak with the museum director, who knows a friend of Delaney's—Joshua."

"Yes, Joshua's a good friend."

"Right. Well, the sword is going to remain in Jolie Lannister's ownership, even if you do possess it. That's only fair for now. If she wants to truly give it to you again, Edwin, we're going to make it an official transaction. And, there are Treasure Trove Unit laws that must be abided by. Ultimately, they are to have the say regarding such a treasure, after all. However, I'm not going to let them have it—yet. I can slow down paperwork enough to keep it in Ms. Lannister's possession. For a short time. The deal I will make is that the sword will be brought to the museum, but Delaney will be the one to study and research it."

"Me?"

"Aye," he said. "If you're not qualified, you're not allowed to tell me that right now. Pretend you are and do whatever you need to do to get prepared."

"Okay. I will." I wasn't prepared, but I wasn't too far off. Though I didn't want to work with Cramer, I would love to work with Joshua, so I silently hoped that's the way it would all play out.

Inspector Winters turned to Edwin. "I've issued a press release regarding the whole thing. It's vague, but it does say that you didn't steal anything. Who knows what the media will do with it? They tend to like juicier scandals, but according to the police, at least, you are not in trouble. For now. Who knows what the day will bring."

"Thank you. I've been involved with scandals before, and they usually pass very quickly. I'll be fine. Shall I retrieve the sword now?"

"Soon. You and I will do that and deliver it to the museum when I get the details ironed out. Delaney, go to work. I'll let you know when you can make an appearance at the museum. I'm stepping outside of bounds a little bit here, but neither of you is at fault. Delaney told me about the sword yesterday, so I can't be angry about you keeping it a secret. However, I'm not happy with Cramer Donnell and I need to talk to him myself. As well as try to find Mr. Dunning's killer. The reason I've put myself in the middle of all of this is because I'm wondering if everything might be tied together. Is there anything either of you could add that might help me know more?"

"I wondered the same thing," Edwin said.

I told him about Elias and my visit with Gilles and Luke at the candy shop.

Inspector Winters shook his head. "I appreciate the information, lass, but why are you in the middle of this so much?"

"Homer and Elias are friends."

"I don't suspect Homer," he said.

"Do any other officers?"

"Well, I don't know. I don't think so."

"I don't want him to be in trouble. If no other suspects are found, Homer might be on the list again."

Inspector Winters's eyebrows furrowed. "Okay, well, be careful and call me with anything else you find out."

"I will."

"Let's go, Edwin. Let's leave your car here. We'll drop Delaney off at the bookshop."

CHAPTER SEVENTEEN

I filled Rosie and Hamlet in on the morning's goings-on, and assured them that Edwin hadn't stolen anything.

Hector whined with his greeting. This was rare, unless something distressed him. As I held him and talked to my co-workers, he was squiggly enough that I knew something wasn't quite right.

I gave him a long look and then lifted my eyebrows at Rosie and Hamlet. "What's gone on here this morning? Something has upset him."

"Aye," Rosie said with a strained tone.

"What?" I asked again.

"It was me," Hamlet said. "I was upset this morning and I vented to Rosie."

"What were you so upset about?"

Hamlet sighed. "I'll always be more loyal to Edwin, you all, and the bookshop than I will be to anyone or anything else."

"Sure," I said.

Hamlet seemed to search for a way to tell me something he didn't want to share.

"Rosie?" I turned to her.

"Joshua rang him last night, told him that Cramer Donnell was going to accuse Edwin of stealing the sword and the accusation might be appropriate."

"Oh." I moved Hector to my other arm.

"I didn't think it was . . . I didn't think he was going to call the media," Hamlet said. "I decided not to rush to tell Edwin. I should have rung him right away, warned him. Now, I'm afraid he'll think I chose Joshua and Donnell's side."

"Hamlet, he would never think that. None of us would," I said.

"That's what I told him," Rosie added.

"I did something similar," I said.

"No, you didn't, but thank you for trying to make me feel better."

"I did!" I told him the part about telling Inspector Winters about the sword but then completely forgetting to tell Edwin about that conversation.

Rosie laughed. "Gracious."

"Right?" I looked at Hamlet. "It might appear that we are attempting a coup, but it's not something either of us would ever consider."

"That's true—never." Hamlet took a deep breath.

"You've kept him on his toes," Rosie said as she took a more relaxed Hector from my arms. "It's good for him." Rosie looked back and forth at Hamlet and me. "Edwin MacAlister is happier than I've ever known him to be. He still has his bookshop, but he doesnae have to do the day-to-day things he used to have to do. He has people he trusts implicitly, and he loves both of you like you were his own children. He kens you would never hurt him purposefully, and he's been around long enough to ken that we all make mistakes. Everything will be sorted, and, hopefully, Mr. Dunning's killer will be found, sooner than later. I want the both of you to get on with it and let go of your concerns. We've got plenty to do. Get along and let's get to work."

Rosie turned and went to find something to busy herself. It was her way of saying the conversation was over.

"Thanks, Delaney," Hamlet said.

"We're all good," I said.

We fist-bumped. Hamlet made his way back to his table, and I made my way over to the dark side.

Once I locked the warehouse door behind me, I grabbed my laptop out of my desk drawer and got to work researching Jolie Lannister—it was something I'd been wanting to do for three days, but there had been too many interruptions.

There were so many Jolie Lannister links with so much different information, it was both like finding a gold mine and sensing you might be missing a diamond in the rough.

Jolie Lannister and her parents (her mother more than her father) were, at the least, intriguing characters, and at the worst, strange and delusional.

I opened a spreadsheet program to attempt to put the variety of things in some sort of timeline order.

Stephen and Vivian Lannister were in their early twenties when they married—their wedding a big enough deal for the newspaper to post a picture of the bride and groom and a six-column-inch marriage notice. The archived copy was now easily accessible through the newspaper's website.

Stephen had a comfortable amount of money from his family's shipping business, as well as a healthy income from Vivian's family. His ambition was big enough that when he set out to forge his own fortune building a real estate empire, nothing could stop him.

There were many articles about and pictures of the two of them. As a young married couple, they were the life of the party, beautiful and seemingly always happy.

It appeared that there were two turning points that threatened their popularity and contentedness.

Sometime in 1946, the abdicated king and Wallis Simpson came into the Lannisters' lives—in France. I couldn't find any information regarding what exactly brought them together, but there was speculation that Edward or Wallis or both became ill, and Vivian had something that helped them feel better. She and Stephen were there on holiday, in a place her parents had owned. They all either became fast friends or friendly acquaintances. The Lannisters were pictured with Edward and Wallis at a park in Paris as well as in front of the Eiffel Tower, though other than their names and the locations, there were no other editorial comments included.

Jolie was born in 1947 in Scotland, but I found plenty of pictures of the four adults with the infant, including the one I'd spotted on Jolie's wall. I inspected them all for clues that might be found in Edward's smile or stance that hinted Edward was Jolie's biological father, but none of the adults seemed to be signaling there was something going on that shouldn't have been.

It appeared that all the pictures with Edward and Wallis had been snapped in France, which made me curious. A diverted semi-deep dive told me that after Edward abdicated the throne in December 1936, and after some time in Paris, Spain, and Portugal, he was "exiled" to the Bahamas until after World War II. Then, he and Wallis moved to Paris as well as spent some time in New York City.

I couldn't find pictures of the whole group with Jolie any older than about two years old. There was no information regarding any sort of falling out between them. It wasn't until Jolie was a teenager that Vivian began telling the story of her daughter's parentage.

Along the way, though, in the early 1950s, stories about Vivian began to spread. Jolie had mentioned that her mother was good with herbs and those sorts of things, but she didn't mention the accusations of "witchcraft" that had been leveled at Vivian. Edwin hadn't mentioned them either.

When Vivian allegedly helped a family heal from what was probably influenza, some folks thought her methods were questionable—they were frightened by them and their efficacy. It wasn't completely unheard of to recover from the virus, but Vivian's involvement was a distinct curiosity.

Vivian hadn't searched for credit or accolades regarding her tinctures, but journalists from the day reported that the famous and sometimes cruel landlord Stephen Lannister's wife, Vivian, cured them—magically, they were sure.

The reports, probably because there were plenty of people who'd had bad dealings with Stephen, were inflammatory. From this vantage point, I could see the ridiculousness, but back in the days of yellow journalism, Vivian's story was the sort of thing that sold newspapers.

Before long, the Lannisters stopped going to parties, stopped doing much of anything publicly, so much so that Vivian became a bona fide recluse, still offering her services to those who needed her medicines but only distributing them from her own home.

I speculated that Vivian began telling her story of Jolie's parentage with the goal of moving the journalists away from the inflammatory (and, frankly, cruel) accusations they were publishing. That was just a guess, though, but no matter, it didn't work. They only dug in their heels and called Jolie "crazy" and "hysterical" and "delusional" as well as some sort of wicked witch. It was ugly.

I didn't immediately find proof that any member of the royal family publicly admonished the Lannisters.

Wallis Simpson wasn't well liked, and time had only put her in a more unflattering light. I cringed when I read about her involvement with the Nazi Party.

Vivian's stories and claims fizzled quickly after she stopped talking to the journalists, but thirty-five years later, after her parents were both gone, Jolie herself added fuel to the mostly dead embers of her family's scandals.

By that time, there was a large enough population who wasn't fond of the royals, and was intrigued by Jolie herself, to breathe some temporary life to the old scandals.

Jolie, dressed in a velvet gown, though not the purple one I'd met her in, called a press conference at her home and reannounced her mother's claim of her parentage, and that if fair was truly fair, Jolie would be queen, not Elizabeth.

However, despite the royal critics, neither Jolie's story nor the way she delivered it went over well. Jolie knew that illegitimate children weren't considered in the line of succession, but just like her mother, she made the claim. And there was that strangeness about her mother. It was all dug up and rehashed.

Rosebud had begun its obvious decline, and those who'd been inside it were sharing details about the growing mess. Jolie and her reputation were raked over the coals, which only caused her to hide away even more stubbornly. I found no support for her claims. I kept trying to put a time frame on her days with Edwin, but I could only guess that, based upon what I thought their ages were in the picture I'd seen, Jolie's fall from grace happened after their relationship was over. I would ask Edwin at some point.

Long into my search, I did find an article about "officials" visiting Jolie right before she seemed to be silenced, though details of that visit or meeting weren't readily available, even though speculation was, no doubt, that they'd told her to stop talking about all of it.

DNA tests weren't a thing back then, but the result of me reading all these articles was overwhelming sadness for everyone involved. A lock of Edward's hair so that real tests might be done to either confirm Jolie's story or allow her to finally put it to rest would have solved the mystery. Well, answered the questions, not give her the throne.

I also understood that royal lines weren't always as clearcut as they should be or were presented to be, so attempting to confirm such things were shied away from no matter what. Sometimes people didn't want to know answers.

After a couple hours, I sat back from the screen and rubbed my eyes.

I'd learned a lot, but it was mostly the stuff of gossip, fodder for whispers and *tsk*s, and I wasn't a fan of such things.

Another idea sparked in my mind, so I sat forward again and typed into the search bar—"Jolie Lannister and Alban Dunning."

Nothing came up.

I tried again, this time including "King Edward VIII."

A list populated, though it wasn't nearly as long as my initial search.

"Huh," I said as I clicked on the first link that claimed a connection.

I read through, thinking I'd found a mere coincidence, but the idea solidified as I came to the last paragraph of a story about private secretaries to royals and their job descriptions. For each secretary mentioned, the article's writer had reached out to any potential living descendants for familial impressions or any stories that might have been passed down.

It appeared that one of Edward's secretaries was named Oliver Dunning, and Oliver's grandson, a man named Alban Dunning, who lived and worked in Edinburgh at an auction house, was the source the writer had reached out to and spoken with.

"Oh," I said aloud. This now felt like something important.

I grabbed my phone with one hand and scrolled up to the top of the article on my laptop with the other hand. I spotted the byline and a zip of glee moved through me. Another coincidence maybe, but I'd been thinking about her just the day before—one of Tom's old girlfriends, and someone who'd become a friend to me. I'd thought about calling her then, and now I felt like the universe was instructing me to do so.

I pressed Bridget McBride's contact, her number saved on my phone.

"What, Delaney?" she answered abruptly.

Okay, so maybe we didn't get along great all the time, yet. I was going to win her over eventually.

"Bridget—hi. How are you?"

"What's up?"

"Do you have time for a coffee, or a drink, or something?"

"You need something from me."

I figured there was no real reason to lie. "Well, yes, but I'd still like to see you."

Bridget laughed. "Sure. Whatever." She sighed. "Okay, when do you want to meet?"

I looked at the article on my laptop screen. "As soon as possible?"

Bridget sighed. "See you at the pub in half an hour."

She disconnected the call. I looked at my phone to confirm—yes, the call had ended. I knew which pub she was talking about, of course, and though she'd sound irritated to hear from me, just the fact that she wanted to meet at Tom's pub felt like a positive sign.

To the silent phone, I said, "See you there."

CHAPTER EIGHTEEN

"This is a surprise!" Tom said as I walked into the pub.

"Hello, missus." I saw Rodger, Tom's employee.

"Delaney!" another voice said.

Because he was sitting at a spot that was half dark and half well lit, I didn't recognize Artair, Tom's father, until I heard his voice.

"Hello, everybody!" I hugged my father-in-law. The bar was otherwise empty. "The surprises will keep coming. Bridget is on her way."

"Ah, I see," Tom said.

"This is where she wanted to meet."

"Oh dear, well, I cannae decide if I need to hurry away or stick around to see what she does," Artair said.

"Oh, please don't let her run you off," I said.

Artair laughed. "Never. Though I doubt she'll be pleased to see me."

"Or me," Rodger added.

"I'm probably on that list," Tom said.

"She knew what she was getting into. I let her choose the place," I said as I sidled up to a stool. I looked at Artair, whom

I hadn't seen in a couple weeks. "How are you? I hear you've been working on a project."

"I have."

Artair was a librarian at the University of Edinburgh Library, and he seemed to always have one project or another.

"Is it a secret?" I smiled.

"No, but it's a wee bit . . . delicate."

"What's that mean?"

"I am putting together a display of Scottish political parties throughout the years."

"How is that delicate?"

"There are those who would like me to twist some of the definitions the parties gave themselves to work with our current political opinions."

"That's silly. I would think everyone would just want the facts."

"Well, lass, if I've learned anything at all, it's that one person's facts are another's conspiracies."

"That's tough."

Artair smiled. "I'll get through it. They won't intimidate this old man."

"Good for you." A thought occurred to me. "Has the queen's death meant anything to your project?"

"Aye," he said sadly. "I'm not sure I can pinpoint the ways it will be transformed except that I'm looking at everything I do with a new sort of light and shadow. The facts won't change, but my thoughts about them will, of course."

I looked at him, the glisten of tears in his eyes. "You are amazing."

"Och, lass, you have to say that."

"I do not, but I believe it completely."

"Ta."

We all turned as the front door opened. Bridget stood in the doorway a long moment and took in the scene. A smile broke out on her face, and she made her way toward us.

"Artair, is that you?"

"Aye, lass." Artair stood from the stool again as Bridget pulled him into a hug.

Bridget released the hug and held him by his arms. "It is so good to see you."

"Same, my dear."

"Are you well?"

"Right as rain. You?"

"Never better." She let go of his arms and though her smile wasn't as wide now, she did nod in a friendly fashion. "Rodger. Tom."

"Hello, Bridget," they both said.

When her eyes landed on me, the smile disappeared quickly. "Delaney."

I swallowed hard, wondering what I'd done wrong. "Thanks for meeting me, Bridget."

"Aye." She crossed her arms in front of herself. "You know, you can call me for a drink or a coffee or whatever without needing something from me. I thought we were becoming friends. I haven't heard from you in months."

I wanted to protest and argue that I hadn't heard from her either, but that wouldn't be true. In fact, she'd tried to reach me last month, but I'd gotten busy and hadn't returned the call.

"I'm sorry," I said. "No, really, I am sorry. I should have returned your call. I have no excuse for myself."

Bridget gave me the evil eye for another long beat, but then her expression softened. She was a beautiful woman, with long, blond, curly hair, a big smile, and striking blue eyes. "Okay, I've tortured you enough so you might rethink ignoring me next time." She smiled big now. "It's great to see you anyway." She pulled me into a hug.

Over her shoulder, I lifted my eyebrows at the men who appeared to be a mix of surprised and suspicious at her friendliness.

"Thank you, Bridget," I said.

"What can I get the two of you?" Tom asked.

"Gin and tonic for me," Bridget said.

"I'll have the same," I said. I despised gin, but I figured I'd ride the wave of Bridget and me getting along for now.

Tom lifted his eyebrows at me. "Right. Have a seat. I'll bring out the drinks."

We sat at a high table close to the front window, though there wasn't a lot of space in the pub. Known as the smallest pub in Scotland, it was surprising how many football (aka soccer) fanatics could fit and drink inside.

"What's going on?" Bridget asked after we were comfortable. She was now her normal curious self. "I heard about Edwin's thieving ways." She smiled and waggled her pretty eyebrows a couple times.

"That's supposed to have been cleared up. He didn't steal anything."

"Aye. I heard. The truth can be so disappointing."

Tom approached with our drinks, placing one in front of each of us. We both thanked him and then took sips.

I was thrilled to find that Tom had poured me a Sprite but added a lime to make it look like Bridget's drink.

"Well," I continued, "he didn't steal anything. The report was premature."

"Uh-huh. Or the new Treasure Trove director is a . . . shall we say, piece of work?"

"I don't know about that." I had an inkling, but I didn't need Bridget to glom on to any of that since it appeared I would be working near him in the museum. "What I'm curious about is an article you wrote three years ago."

"Okay. Well, that was hundreds of articles ago, but ask and let's see what I remember."

I'd printed it out earlier and grabbed it from my bag. "This one."

She took another sip of her drink as she looked over the article. "Aye, the piece about the secretaries for the royals." She looked up at me. "What about it?"

"One of your sources was Alban Dunning, the grandson of Oliver Dunning. Look in the last paragraph."

Her eyes moved to the bottom of the page. "Right. I spoke with him on the . . . oh, Delaney," she looked at me again and then back at the paper, "Alban Dunning is the name of the man who was killed three days ago on the Lannister property. We just got official word an hour or so ago."

I nodded. "I'm sure it's the same man."

"Well, the name's not all that common."

"And the Alban who was killed worked at an auction house."

"That's right." She shook her head. "What's going on? What do you know?"

"I know a lot, Bridget, but I need to ask you to keep it off the record for now."

"Are you in the middle of this murder too?"

"I'm in the middle of something." I paused. "So, off the record? I'll tell you everything if we can do it that way."

Bridget frowned and studied her drink a long time before she answered. "All right. Sure. Tell me everything, and then when the time is right, I get the story, aye?"

"Of course. I wouldn't have it any other way."

CHAPTER NINETEEN

After I told Bridget everything—well, at least enough for her to eventually spin into a story—I got to my own nitty-gritty. I wanted her to tell me what she remembered about her conversation or conversations with Alban Dunning.

"He was quiet," she began. "I told him I'd come across a tiny tidbit of information that shined a light on his grandfather and how delightful he'd been, how loyal to Edward. Alban told me he had only a few memories of his grandfather, and they were fond. I was trying to confirm that Mr. Dunning had indeed been one of Edward's secretaries or served in some other capacity. It wasn't all that clear. In fact, Alban only sort of confirmed the secretary part. He said he *thought* his grandfather had worked with Edward. I gleaned from my research that the elder Mr. Dunning was a jokester, with a loud laugh. Alban liked hearing that, and he really liked hearing that his grandfather was well respected." She paused. "He said something that I didn't grasp, though later I wished I'd followed up. It was something about his own father, Mr. Dunning's son, not being a good man at all."

"I heard something like that from Gilles Haig. He told me that Alban's childhood wasn't a happy one."

"Well, I don't know what that means, but it's hard to believe that his rough childhood had anything to do with his murder."

"Bridget, do you know about Jolie Lannister?"

"Sure, the old woman . . ." Her eyes got wide, and she sat up in her chair. "Oh no, I have been so busy, I didn't put any of these pieces together. Jolie and her mother once claimed that Edward was Jolie's biological father. I didn't even think about it." She frowned. "I would have eventually, but I hadn't yet. Delaney, do you think it's all tied together?"

"Well, I don't quite know what *it* all is yet, but something is tied somewhere."

"Could Jolie Lannister have killed Alban Dunning?"

"No, she was with me, showing me the sword."

I'd been surprised that Bridget hadn't been more intrigued by the sword, but she'd almost shrugged the item off, being far more interested in everyone's—mostly Cramer Donnell's—behavior.

"And her groundskeeper, could he have done the deed?"

"I guess that depends on what you mean. Was he capable, was he in the right spot? Yes, but he was released," I said.

"That doesn't mean he isn't guilty."

"He's an old friend of my friend Elias's. Elias says he couldn't imagine Homer ever killing anyone."

She made a sound with her mouth. "Anyone can be pushed to kill, Delaney. Surely you know that by now."

I did know that. I'd seen it. I'd contemplated if I could ever kill and decided that if one of my loved ones was threatened, I absolutely could. Well, in theory.

"Homer is like family to Jolie, right?" Bridget said.

"Bridget, he was cleared by the police," I repeated.

"No, that's not what you said. You said he was released for now."

"Right. I hope you don't cause him any trouble."

She shrugged. "This is all off the record, Delaney, but that doesn't mean I can't do some behind-the-scenes research."

"The police have a clue."

"You buried the lede! What is it?"

"Inspector Winters wouldn't tell me, but he did tell me they had one."

"Shoot. Well, I have contacts in the police much less scrupulous than your Inspector Winters. Maybe I can find out."

"If you do, will you tell me?"

She smiled slyly. "Maybe."

I attempted a withering look, but she only laughed. "Of course, I'll tell you, if you'll answer my call, that is."

"I am truly sorry," I said. "I really have been busy."

"We're all busy." She downed the dregs of her drink and set the glass back on the table. "But we need to make time for friends, and for some silly reason, I enjoy your nutty American friendship."

"Thank you?"

"It was a compliment."

"I enjoy you too, Bridget. I really do."

"Oh, I know. What's not to enjoy?"

I smiled again, and as happened now and then, briefly considered the surprising path my life had taken.

It's worth remembering that it is often the small steps, not the giant leaps, that bring about the most lasting change.

It was the queen again. Tears filled my eyes. The queen had now become a bookish voice. I didn't need a radio at all. I was sure it wouldn't last, but I did like hearing her voice in my head. I liked all the steps I'd taken to get to this point. I would do better with Bridget.

"Delaney, what's wrong? Are you okay?" Bridget asked.

I sniffed and quickly blinked them away. "I'm fine, just . . . well, despite everything it turned out to be a good day."

"See what I mean—you are my nutty American friend—and I'm glad for it." Bridget stood and waved toward the bar. "Thanks for the drink. Good to see you all, particularly Artair."

They returned her salutations. We promised to let each other know whatever we came across and she gave me another genuine hug. I was definitely going to have to answer her calls. As my time in Edinburgh had gone on, my friends had become my family. If I thought about it, it was odd that Bridget might feel like family, but there was no doubt that she did.

I regathered my emotions before I picked up both glasses and took them back to the bar, my handsome husband smiling as I made my way.

CHAPTER TWENTY

When my phone rang the next morning, at least Tom and I were already awake, and almost finished with breakfast. I didn't recognize the number, but something told me to answer.

"Hello."

"Delaney, hello! This is Jolie."

"I recognize your voice. Good morning." I wanted to remain friendly to Jolie, but I still wondered if she'd somehow agreed with Cramer Donnell to tell the police that Edwin stole the sword.

"Lass, do you have time to come out to Rosebud this morning? I would like to chat with you a little. Perhaps by yourself."

"Why by myself?"

"Edwin and I are old friends. I don't want to let those old feelings influence my words."

"What about my friend Elias?"

"Well, I suppose that would be fine, but, really, I would like to chat without anyone else in our way. I will even send Trudie to another room."

I thought a moment. I didn't sense I would be unsafe, but there was more to her wanting me there alone than just the fact that we wouldn't be interrupted.

"Hang on a second." I covered the phone's microphone and looked at Tom. "Care if I take the car to Roslin?"

His eyes got wide a moment, but I assumed it wasn't because he thought I couldn't handle it. It was my first drive-alone request that would take me outside of our everyday routes.

"Of course," he said a beat later.

I put the phone back in place. "I need to stop by the bookshop first, but I'll head out after that."

"Oh, lovely, Delaney. I look forward to seeing you."

We disconnected the call and I looked at Tom. "I wonder what's up."

"Do you think there's any danger?"

I shook my head immediately. "No. I was with Jolie and Trudie when Alban was killed. They are harmless."

"Homer?"

"The police let him go." Bridget's words rang through my mind: *That doesn't mean he's not guilty.* "No, I'm not concerned. I am curious, though."

"Do you want me to drive you?"

I smiled. "No, it's not a difficult trip, even if it will be on the wrong side of the road."

Tom smiled too. "I wouldn't mind some text updates."

I leaned toward him for a kiss. "Happy to oblige."

I would never admit to anyone that I white-knuckled the entire drive to Rosebud House. I had to dig deep for the fortitude. But once I was in the circular drive, I relaxed and decided that now that I'd gotten it out of way, maybe I could drive anywhere.

Maybe. But not today.

Jolie opened the door as I reached for the knocker.

"You made it!" Today she was dressed in a black velvet gown, making it appear that she was in mourning. Perhaps it was her way of respecting Alban, or maybe she knew him better than she'd let on so far. The article I'd read had percolated and I began to wonder about their true relationship. Maybe I'd ask, but I wasn't sure.

"I did." I smiled satisfactorily.

"Come in. Trudie has already put out the tea." She pulled the door wide and set out toward the library.

I took a step to follow her but was stunned into place right inside the entryway. It was completely cleared. There were no stacks of anything in sight.

It was even more beautiful than I could have known before. A pointed star-like and colorful design, very much like the stained-glass window above, was the center of the floor tiles.

"Jolie!" I said.

She stopped and turned to face me again. It was her turn to smile satisfactorily. "Do you like it?"

"I . . . I can't believe it, but I love it. It's so pretty."

"Thank you. It's a start. Homer, Trudie, and I worked hard yesterday evening. We were all exhausted by the end of it."

"How are you doing with it?" I asked.

"I think I'm okay. I'm not upset, but I'm not relieved either."

She was halfway down the hall, but I could see her eyes fill with tears. I hurried toward her.

"Jolie?"

She wiped her eyes. "I'm being silly, Delaney, but I don't know what this cleanup or my lack of feelings about it means. Am I okay?"

I put my hands on her arms. Though I wasn't sure I trusted

her all the way yet, I didn't think her hoarding was an affliction she couldn't beat.

"I would vouch for you being okay any day of the week. I don't know much about . . . your need to keep things, but I can't imagine that this cleanup isn't a great thing, particularly if it stays that way."

"I hope so. I wonder if this was Bowie's goal—to threaten me enough to get me to clean it up."

"Maybe she really does have your best interests in mind." I didn't know what I believed when it came to Bowie Berry, but I hoped.

"I know she used to, but I can't say I'm not concerned that's somehow changed." She shook her head. "Anyway, come along."

The library hadn't seen the same attention as the front of the house, but neither Jolie nor I commented about it as we followed the path to the green velvet table and sat. My eyes glanced over the portrait behind the desk. I'd now seen many pictures of Vivian, but this one was still by far the most glorious.

Jolie had been correct—Trudie had outfitted a tray with all sorts of wonderful snacks and a pot of tea.

Coffee was easily accessible throughout Scotland, but I'd been offered more tea here than I ever had in Kansas. I wasn't a fan, but I would never turn it away—I'd found there was a certain insult somehow attached to saying "no thank you" to tea.

I was all about adding plenty of cream and sugar, though. The tray held both.

As we each attended to our mugs and snacks, I said, "What's going on, Jolie? What did you want to talk about?"

After taking a sip of her tea, she said, "Aye."

"I'm listening."

"Well, I feel you might be my only friend after all of this. Well, you and Trudie and Homer, but they are family, so they have to be my friends. But I must tell someone, and you are the someone."

"Okay."

"Well." She clicked her tongue. "I did tell Cramer Donnell that Edwin took the sword. I lied to the police, though, and told them I didn't say that to Cramer."

"Why would you do that?"

"Because Mr. Donnell scared me. He frightened me and he made me angry. I felt I had no choice."

"I'm sorry he scared you. How did he manage that?"

"He told me I would be arrested for not calling him immediately, first thing. He wasn't wrong, Delaney. There are laws."

Already, I wasn't a fan of Cramer Donnell's, but Jolie's lie to the police wasn't good. "You should tell the police exactly what you're telling me."

She shook her head. "Not yet. I might. I have a deal I want to make with you, though."

"Why with me?"

"Hear me out."

I'd taken a bite from a sugar cookie but set the rest of it on a napkin. "I'm still listening."

"You are the only one I trust regarding the sword."

I was baffled. "Why?"

"You have no interest in it. You are an American, so it can't mean the same thing to you that it would to a Scot. I trust Edwin, but even he might have ulterior motives. I have no doubt that Cramer does. You are the objective party here."

"I have an appreciation for it that maybe even some Scots don't. I've worked with historical artifacts for years."

"Okay, okay, but the police have an agenda, and Cramer had one too. Even Edwin has a multifaceted agenda. Yours is simple and honorable."

She was correct about my motives—I wanted to understand the sword, but I had no intentions or notions regarding what to do with it. Everyone else did, though I would never call Edwin's intentions dishonorable.

"What do you want me to do, Jolie?"

"I just want you to be the one to research the sword and tell me the details about it first."

I thought about whether to tell her what Inspector Winters had said. I made the quick decision to fill her in. "I think the police are negotiating with the museum to allow me access to their equipment so that I may do that, or at least be a part of it."

"Well, that's not a terrible plan, but I wish . . . well, I wish I'd done things differently. Nevertheless, will you tell me first what you conclude about the sword before you tell anyone?"

"I don't know. I can't make any promises, but I will keep your request in mind."

Jolie frowned again. "I would like more of a promise from you, but I understand your position and I accept your terms."

Terms didn't feel quite right regarding our discussion, but I decided not to fight it. "Great. Okay then." I picked up the cookie. "I'll do what I can to stay involved, but Cramer Donnell shouldn't have threatened you. You need to tell the police you misspoke to him. You know you need to do that."

Jolie's shoulders relaxed as she sighed. "Aye, and I will."

I chewed the cookie, swallowed, and took a sip of tea. "Jolie, may I ask you some personal questions?"

Her eyebrows raised. "Aye, dear."

"They are about Edward VIII."

"Oh. I see. Well, that's an old story, but one that I'm willing to revisit, at least a little bit, I suppose."

I nodded. "Did you know him?"

"No. Once my mother made her claim, apparently he and Wallis stayed far away."

"Do you still think he was your biological father?"

She shrugged. "The queen's death, of course, brought back . . . things." She thought a moment. "Aye, I suppose I still believe my mother; however, I have long let go of the idea that I should fight for any flimsy right I might have to the throne." She laughed. "Maybe that's because I'm old and too tired to consider any sort of life of duty, but, no, I'm not sure I ever truly thought I should be queen."

"That was probably for the best."

"Aye. The path of least resistance, no doubt."

"Did your mother talk about him much?"

"When I was a wee girl, she talked a little bit, but she stopped when I turned thirteen or so, though I don't know why."

"How about your father? Was he bothered by her story?"

Jolie laughed again. "Not that I ever saw, though he would never talk to me about it. He was a lovely man, a good father, if not thought of as a kind man. I think he was unable to father children."

"That would lend some credibility to your mother's story."

"Well, it would lend some credibility to the fact that another man was involved in the creation of little old me, but though I will stand by her story forever, I do wonder if my mother shot for the moon, so to speak, when she said Edward was my father, maybe making her infidelity appear less awful. I don't know. I do know that Edward denied her claims, and never once veered from that."

"Did you know the queen at all—ever meet her?"

"No, never, and when she passed, I wished I had. I would have only greeted her, not ever accosted her with my mother's claims. Of course, the royals are well protected, as they should be, but because of that I was convinced they would make sure I was never in her proximity."

"Probably. I'm sorry, Jolie . . . if . . . well, it's quite a story."

"Isn't it, though? No need to be sorry. Things work out the way they're supposed to." She shrugged. "Or that's what we tell ourselves, at least."

"Jolie, did you ever know anything about any of Edward's personal secretaries?"

"I don't think so. Why?"

I shook my head. I wasn't going to offer a name. Not yet. I'd asked the question mostly to gauge her reaction. Her answer seemed honest.

"Just curious," I said.

The knocker sounded, echoing with a low thud all the way to the library.

"Who in the world?" Jolie said.

"Shall we go look?" I said.

"No, no, you sit. I'll be right back."

I nodded.

I strained to hear but didn't have to work too hard. I recognized both speakers, though I couldn't immediately distinguish the words.

I hurried to the hallway. A few steps and the entryway was in sight. Bowie and Jolie were there, still by the front door.

"It's great, Jolie, but it's only a temporary. You won't be able to keep this up." Bowie's words were critical, but her tone wasn't. I would have called it patronizing, and it irritated me.

"I suppose time will tell. Are you just here to check on me?"

"Aye, but not in a bad way. I just wonder how you're doing. I heard about the sword. On top of the terrible murder, you must be stressed. Are you okay?"

I cleared my throat. The two women looked in my direction, surprise and irritation showing on Bowie's face.

"Well, Delaney, aren't you like a bad penny." Bowie stuck her hands on her hips.

I could have said the same about her, but I didn't. "Bowie. Hello." I made my way toward them. "I was so pleasantly surprised by the changes Jolie made in here. It's beautiful."

"Aye, it is." She smiled at Jolie. "If she can keep it up."

"Are you a betting woman, Bowie?" I asked.

"Excuse me?"

"Are you a betting woman? Because if you are, I'd like to bet you, oh, 20p—my dad always says that if you do bet you should only ever wager a quarter, and 20p is close enough. I would bet that Jolie will not only keep her house straightened up, but she will enjoy it that way too."

Bowie cocked her head at me. "Did you not just meet each other a few days ago?"

"Some friendships form quickly," I said.

Bowie had a point, but my gut told me that Jolie could use someone on her team, and as she'd just mentioned a few minutes earlier, I might somehow be one of her only team members.

"Why are you here, Bowie?" Jolie asked.

"It's just like I said, I was worried about you, and I just wanted to check in."

"I'm fine. Thank you."

"Bowie, did you see Alban traveling down the walking path the day he was killed?" The question jumped out of me—surprising everyone in the room. I worked hard not to clear my throat or retract the words. It wasn't easy to keep my steady gaze on her.

"I did not. I drove away before Gilles and . . . Alban separated. In fact, that's why I stopped by his auction house yesterday, to ask him what happened. You're not the only curious one, Delaney."

"What did he say?" I asked.

"Did you not ask him?"

"I didn't," I lied.

Bowie nodded. "He said that Alban just wanted to get out of the car and walk, that he was anxious. That's all he said."

I nodded. That checked out with what Gilles had said to Elias and me. "Thanks for sharing."

"You're welcome." She looked at Jolie and then back at me. "Well, I'll be on my way then. I'm glad to see all is well. And," she winked at me, "I hope I lose that bet. I would love nothing more than for Jolie to . . . be okay."

"I think she's great," I said.

"Well, I suppose we'll see." Bowie looked at Jolie. "Did I leave my gloves here? Maybe in the library?"

"Not that I've noticed."

"I'll look," I said, knowing Jolie wouldn't want Bowie to see the mess still in the library. In fact, I thought Bowie was only asking about the gloves so she had a reason to take a look.

"No, no," Jolie said. "I'll do it."

Once Jolie passed by me and then made her way into the library, Bowie stepped right into my space.

"I am watching you, Delaney. I don't know what it is you want from Jolie, but it is my job to watch over her."

I stood my ground. "Maybe you could quit talking down to her."

Her eyes widened quickly, and I could feel the anger coming off her. I kept my eyes locked on hers. She would have to look away first. She did.

"No, Bowie, not there," Jolie said as she came out of the library. "Where else should we look?"

Bowie stepped out of my space and normalized her expression. "It's fine. I'm sure they are at home then. I'll find them. Thank you, Jolie."

"You are welcome." Jolie frowned. "Thank you for stopping by. I appreciate your concern."

"You are welcome too." She looked at me again. "Delaney, always a pleasure."

"Same."

Bowie opened the door and stepped through. When I'd parked Tom's car, I'd moved all the way to the end of the circular drive. Bowie had parked behind me. There would be enough space for her to get around, but I was surprised when I saw the vehicle she'd driven. After meeting everyone, I thought it had been Gilles who'd driven the old van, but that had been Bowie's vehicle.

When the door closed, I asked Jolie, "How many kids does she have?"

"None. Why?"

"The van . . . I assumed."

"She's driven that old thing since I saw her about a year ago, but no kids or spouse that I'm aware of."

"I shouldn't have assumed."

Jolie sighed. I could hear her weariness. "Thank you for supporting me. See, I knew you were a friend."

I smiled. "Of course."

Shall we finish our tea?" Jolie said.

"Yes, of course." But I'd make it quick.

I had plenty of other things to do.

CHAPTER TWENTY-ONE

I didn't stay with Jolie for much longer and we kept the conversation light. I didn't want to be patronizing like Bowie, and it was clear that Jolie needed some rest. I couldn't promise she'd be the first to hear what we found out about the sword, and she understood the situation, or at least had become tired enough not to want to fight me any longer.

As I pulled Tom's car out of the driveway, I looked in my rearview mirror. Jolie was standing in the doorway waving. I returned the wave, then pulled out and onto the road.

Another glance in the mirror and I saw that she'd closed the door.

I took a sharp right turn onto an old road that ran a berm's distance away from the walking path. It wasn't a smooth ride, but it was somewhat smoother than the driveway. I couldn't deny the urge to explore some.

The road wasn't wide enough for two vehicles, so I hoped no one would come from the other direction, but it didn't appear to be frequently traveled.

"Stay on the left side," I muttered to myself, just in case someone did come in my direction.

The road was almost parallel to the walking path along the border of Jolie's property, and I was gifted with yet a different view. This one was expansive—from the side property all the way to a thick tree line. I wasn't sure if the trees marked the end of the property or not. Homer had mentioned there was a lot of land that didn't need tending to, so maybe Jolie's property went on farther than the eye could see.

I drove about ten more minutes, knowing I couldn't get lost. Just when I was about to turn around, I spotted a small house. A cabin would be an apt description, though it wasn't made of logs like a mountain cabin, and it wasn't nearly as small as the shed where the sword had been kept.

"That yours, Homer?" I asked aloud.

I pulled the car as far off the road as I could without sending it into a ditch and stepped out. I stood, my hands on my hips, and looked around. There was no sign of Homer, or anyone else. The edge of the village of Roslin that had been in view just off the driveway wasn't in sight either.

I cupped my hands around my mouth. "Homer!"

There was no answer.

I had to step carefully over uneven terrain to get to the walking path, and then even more carefully over a rock bed. Jolie had said it was meant to be a deterrent, but it could be easily navigated if taken slowly. It wasn't a difficult trip.

On the other side of the rocks, I hurried toward the cabin, continuing to look around for signs of life as I went.

I took a moment to consider the location where Alban had been found. He hadn't *happened* to veer off the walking path. He must have walked off it purposefully. There was no accident in getting to where he was discovered.

Once at the cabin door, I knocked. "Homer, it's Delaney."

After a moment, I tried the doorknob, not surprised to find it unlocked. It didn't seem like trespassing, or that's what I told myself as the door swung wide.

"Homer?"

The space inside was small and tidy, somewhat austere with what seemed like only the necessary furnishings. One couch, one end table, one lamp. A kitchen table with two chairs tucked underneath. Small kitchen appliances—the size of those in many of the apartments I'd visited throughout Edinburgh.

I assumed the doorway in the back led to a bedroom and bathroom, but I didn't explore; I couldn't bring myself to step over the threshold uninvited.

I expected Homer to walk around the corner of the cabin at any moment. But he didn't. I gazed over the space again, seeing nothing suspicious, nothing off at all. I pulled the door closed.

I made my way to the car, hopped in, and turned it around.

CHAPTER TWENTY-TWO

As I pulled into Tom's parking spot in Grassmarket, my cell pinged with a text.

Can you come to the museum? It was from Joshua.

A mix of excitement and trepidation ran through me. I wanted to ask why, but that didn't feel quite right. I went for coolheaded.

In an hour? I texted back.

Sure, he responded.

I was only minutes away from the museum, but I needed to check in with . . . everyone. I was pretty proud of myself for my driving. I'd first let Tom know I was back.

I hurried up to the pub, the car keys in my hand.

The afternoon crowd was bigger than I expected. There was no football on the television, and it wasn't the weekend, but the pub was busy.

My eyes caught Tom's as he worked behind the bar. I would never tire of the way his eyes lit up when he saw me, and today they were even brighter than usual. Of course, he was glad I'd made it back safe and sound, but he'd be pleased the car made it back too, not a new scratch on it.

"Hey," I said as we each leaned over the bar for a quick kiss.

"Lass, how'd it go?" he asked.

"Great. No problems at all."

"You'll be driving up to Loch Ness next."

"Uh, okay. We'll negotiate that later."

"Jolie?"

"She was fine too, getting things cleaned up. I wonder if she just wanted me to see her progress on the house."

"Interesting. Are you heading to the bookshop?"

"No. Yes, but only so I can call everyone and see if it's okay to go to the museum. Joshua texted me and asked me to come over."

"Are you worried?"

I thought a moment, condensing my reaction to Joshua's text. "I'm curious."

"Sounds about right."

Rodger moved next to Tom. "You got a call here, Delaney."

"Here?" Both Tom and I looked at him.

"Aye. Bridget rang to see if you were here."

"She has my mobile."

Rodger shrugged. "I don't know. I told her you weren't here, but I'd give you a message if I saw you. The message is— call her."

"Thanks, Rodger."

I called Bridget as I stepped out of the pub. It went to her voicemail, so I sent a text:

Returning your call.

There was no immediate response, so I continued to the bookshop. It was just about closing time, but it appeared that Rosie wasn't in a hurry to leave. She and Hector were at the front desk, with Hector on her lap as though they were both reading the book in front of them.

I smiled and watched a second through the window. I'd had several moments like this since I'd moved to Edinburgh, moments I wanted to memorize. I was so glad Rosie and Hector were in my life.

I opened the door.

"Lass, you're back." Rosie closed the book, and Hector jumped off her lap and ran to me.

I picked him up for our usual greeting.

"I am, and I'm sorry I didn't check in earlier."

"I didnae expect you to." Rosie smiled. "I got roped into this book and I havnae been able to tear myself away long enough to turn the sign."

"The best kind of book."

"That is correct. Oh, Bridget rang earlier, looking for you."

"She did? She called the pub too. I wonder if . . . oh, I wonder if there's shaky cell coverage in Roslin."

"Might be. I told her I'd pass on the message."

"To call her."

"Aye. That was it."

"I left a message with her. What else have I missed?"

"Let's see. Edwin had to go talk to the police again."

"Oh no." I told her what Jolie had told Cramer Donnell.

I thought Rosie might be angry at Jolie, but she just shook her head and frowned.

"Who is this man, Cramer Donnell? Poor Jolie. According to Edwin, the police are convinced that he didn't steal the sword. He had to deliver it to the museum, though, and he wasn't happy about that turn of events."

"I imagine he wasn't. I'm sorry I wasn't here to go with him."

"I'm afraid that wasn't the only bit of drama. Joshua stopped by and he and Hamlet had a bit of a tiff in the bookshop. Thankfully, there were no customers at the time."

"Oh no."

"Aye. It wasnae pretty. I've never seen that side of Hamlet before."

"What were they arguing about?"

"The silly sword, of course. Well, I'm not sure it was the item so much as it was the fact that Edwin took it from Jolie's and, according to Joshua, it should have been a Treasure Trove responsibility."

"Oh no," I repeated.

"The argument didnae last long, and it appeared they mended their differences or at least came to some sort of truce, but, lass, I must insert my opinion here."

"I'm listening."

"Jolie. I'm sorry she was threatened, but you need to know, she's only trouble. Always has been."

"You don't think those days, days of her being trouble, are in the past?" I asked, a hopeful tone to my voice.

"No. Some people arenae capable of letting go of causing trouble. Jolie was one of those types of people a long time ago. I have seen nothing to think that has changed."

"Rosie, do you think there's any chance she was involved in Alban's murder?"

"I don't want to think that, but, aye, I wouldnae be surprised in the least. Have you researched her past?"

"A little."

"Well, did you read anything about her mother's death?"

"No. There were so many links to explore, I probably only scratched the surface."

"Give it a look. She was poisoned by one of her own mixtures, but . . . well, I suppose there's not much more to say except that either she took it on her own or Jolie put it in some of her food."

"You think Jolie killed her own mother?"

Rosie frowned. "I really don't know, but like I said, I don't even like to think about it. I worry about Edwin, and now you too, since she's in both your lives. I wish she'd never rang about the sword, but she did. And Edwin would never be able to turn away from the possibility of a Crusader sword."

"I think that would be difficult for me too."

"Aye, but when Jolie is involved . . . Believe it or not, my heart goes out to her, but I wish everyone would just ignore her."

"Rosie, I . . ."

"I ken. It's too late at this point, but I'm glad for the time to talk to you, share my concerns. Be on the alert. I ken you were out there today, and I've been worrit about you since I heard. I'm glad to see you're fine."

"Goodness, you really are worried."

"Aye."

"I hear you, and I will be careful."

"Ta. That's all I need to ken."

"I'm . . . heading over to the museum. Joshua texted me."

Rosie's eyes lit. "Edwin is already there. I imagine everyone is waiting for you. You'd better hurry."

"Oh. I didn't know they were waiting . . ."

"Let them wait, lass."

"But Hamlet and Joshua?"

"I believe they both said their piece, and if they didnae, they will figure it out. I dinnae ken why Mr. Dunning was killed, but it appears a sword, a silly sword, might be more trouble than it's worth. Your job is your job, but things are always much less important than people. Edwin kens this too, but sometimes he forgets."

I walked around the desk and hugged her. "Thank you for reminding us."

She patted my back. "Always, lass, always."

It wasn't because of the compelling book on the desk. Rosie hadn't closed the bookshop because she knew I would stop by, and she could say what she thought needed to be said.

I left the bookshop, my priorities back in their proper place, and headed to the museum.

CHAPTER TWENTY-THREE

The museum was locked by the time I climbed the stairs up to the front doors. I texted Joshua to let him know I was there. I thought about texting Edwin, but I wondered if he was inside waiting for me like Rosie had said.

Shortly after Joshua responded to the text, one of the doors opened and a familiar security guard—Victor—peered out.

"Lass. Welcome. I'm here to escort you down." He pushed the door wide.

I loved an empty museum, and tonight was no exception, though after what Rosie told me about the argument between Joshua and Hamlet, I wondered if this might end up being one of my last visits.

I just wanted us all to get along.

Victor and I made our way to the elevators in the middle of the building, passing by displays on the history of aviation, including an entire old plane, the kind that always made me think of kites more than anything that used an engine to propel itself.

"It's quite a thing, isn't it?" Victor asked conspiratorially. "The sword everyone is here for."

"I think it must be," I said, though Rosie's common sense was still fresh in my mind. "We'll see. Is everyone being silly over it?"

"Aye."

"Well, I'm not sure anything is worth that, but I'll give it a good long look."

"Aye."

"Who's here?"

"Mr. Donnell, our new Treasure Trove Unit director, Joshua, and Edwin MacAlister."

"How are they getting along?"

Victor thought a moment. "Quietly."

"I see."

Victor laughed. "Lass, I'm old enough to enjoy a few minutes of awkwardness. It's entertaining."

I had a question for him, but it felt impertinent to ask. Nevertheless, I said, "Is Mr. Donnell liked around here?"

"He hasn't been here long enough for anyone to have any sort of consensus, but he and I have yet to have one conversation."

"Oh? That doesn't sound normal. You talk to everyone."

"Aye, but not everyone talks to me."

"Hmm," I said.

"Hmm, indeed."

The elevator took us to the basement level. I'd been there a few times before and had once used a centrifuge in one of the labs.

The basement contained both archives—protected shelves filled with cataloged items—and a two scientific labs.

Though the lights were extra bright down here, I always found them soothing. I felt like I could spot a tattoo on a gnat if I looked hard enough.

Victor bid me goodbye as we reached windowed walls of the lab where the three men were waiting.

Joshua was reading something on a laptop screen, Edwin was perusing a hardbound book that he'd probably grabbed from the bookshop's shelves before making his way to the museum.

Cramer Donnell appeared to be inspecting some shelves, his back to me, his hands on his hips.

"Hello," I said.

They all turned, and Edwin and Joshua stood, smiling.

Cramer pushed his way around a lab table. "You must be Delaney." He extended his hand.

"Nice to meet you, Mr. Donnell."

"Oh, Cramer, please. I look forward to working together."

"Me too." I looked at Joshua. "Hey."

"Hey," he said with a smile that I thought held a tiny apology of sorts, at least some sort of regret.

I walked around Cramer and toward my boss. I didn't hesitate to pull him into a hug.

"Hello, lass," he said. "Are you all right?"

"Great." I looked at him. "You?"

"I'm doing very well." The twinkle in his eye told me my earlier thoughts about him enjoying all the ruckus had been correct.

We parted and I put my hands on my hips. "Okay, so what's the deal here?"

"What do you mean?" Cramer asked.

"First of all, where's the sword?" I asked.

"Right here." Cramer walked back around the lab table and put his hands on a long box. He lifted the lid.

I made my way around and peered down. The sword appeared to be in the same condition it had been when I'd first seen it.

I looked up at them all again. "I appreciate having the opportunity to study this and do the work to figure out if it's what we all hope it is, but I won't be able to begin tonight, and I won't be able to work with anyone else in the room."

"No, no, we can't let you work alone," Cramer said.

"Why not?"

"We have to protect our interests."

"I'm not sure what that means, Cramer, but if you want me to do the job you want me to do"—I looked at Edwin, wondering if maybe he didn't want me to make such a demand but he voiced no protest—"I need to work alone. I need to focus. Any sort of distraction could cause me to make an error."

"Well . . ."

"There are other archivists in the city," I said, risking the position it seemed most everyone wanted me to be in. But I knew I would not be able to work if Cramer Donnell was looking over my shoulder, and I needed to establish that up front.

Cramer appeared to consider my words.

"There's no one better than Delaney," Joshua interjected.

Cramer frowned.

"I just thought of something. I would be happy to have my father-in-law, Artair, assist me. He works at the University of Edinburgh Library. He would be not only helpful, but more educated about such things than most people. If he's agreeable, how about that?" I looked at Cramer.

"I was thinking someone from the museum. I should be here."

"I'm afraid that won't work," I said. I didn't even want Joshua there, for reasons I could only think of as some sort of conflict of interest.

Cramer appeared to wait for me to continue, to explain why I didn't want him there. I decided silence was better than telling him that I didn't trust him enough to want to work with him.

Cramer sighed. "What about Joshua?"

"No," Joshua interjected again. "I know Artair. He would be the best."

Cramer rubbed his hand over his chin. "We would need to check on you a few times throughout your review. And all of your work will be recorded." He pointed at the video camera that hung from the ceiling.

I nodded. "Twice per day, at designated times. It won't take me long to determine what we have here. After that, you'll need to hire someone else to clean it up completely." I looked at Edwin again. I knew he wanted me involved, but as I'd made my way to the museum, I realized that I should truly do only the parts I felt best qualified for.

Edwin nodded.

I looked at Cramer. "Well?"

"You can't work tonight?"

I shook my head. "I'm tired and it's been a long day."

"Shoot."

I smiled. Cramer Donnell's disappointment made him seem younger than he was. I'd come to this meeting expecting to not like him at all, but in that moment, with his genuine disappointment, I wondered if maybe I would. Still, though, I wasn't ready to work with him.

But then I caught Joshua's expression—he didn't like Cramer Donnell. Neither did Edwin, or that's what I deciphered. They both glared at the new director. There was plenty to unpack here before I could know if Cramer Donnell and I would get along.

"I'm not happy about any of it, but I trust that you are qualified, and I don't want to wait any longer than we have to.

Looking for someone else would be time consuming," Cramer finally said.

I smiled. "Thanks. We'll be here first thing tomorrow morning."

Edwin and I left Cramer and Joshua in the lab. In the elevator, he offered me a ride. I accepted a lift to the pub. The trip was short but long enough for me to tell him about my visit to Jolie, and then for him to tell me about his visit with the police and how he further convinced them that he wasn't a thief.

Like Rosie, Edwin seemed to be forgiving of Jolie's lie to Cramer.

"I don't understand why you're not angry," I said.

"At Jolie?" Edwin sighed. "She's been known to fib a time or two, but she always clears it up eventually."

I nodded but still couldn't quite grasp his casual attitude. "She said she would."

"Aye, she will, and the police do believe me." Edwin frowned. "At least I think so."

"I hope so."

"You and Artair tomorrow?"

"Yes. He seems like the perfect unbiased party."

"I agree. I wish you luck."

"I'll keep you up to date."

"Ta, lass."

My heart went out to him as I watched him drive away. Yes, he enjoyed the "ruckus," but everyone had a tipping point. I'd never witnessed Edwin's, but I wondered if we were close to reaching it. I'd have to worry about it later.

Tonight, I needed to call Artair and convince him to join me.

CHAPTER TWENTY-FOUR

"Lass, have you ever done anything like this before?" Artair asked me through my cell phone.

I'd taken a seat on a stool next to the bar to do some research and call my father-in-law.

"I've seen it done. Edwin knows my level of experience, but he really wants me to be involved. He knows I'll do right by it."

"But . . . it's not just something you can google, and if the sword is a Crusader . . ."

"Well. Actually, I did do a little helpful googling, and I've sent an email to a friend back in the States who might be able to give some valuable input. I think we'll be fine." I crossed my fingers as I looked at Tom over the bar. He crossed his fingers in solidarity. "Please, Artair. I promise it won't take long. Everyone knows you and I have real jobs."

"Aye?"

"Yes. Please, Artair. You know, even if you don't want to do the work with me, you could just keep me company—if your project isn't demanding you be there early every day."

"It's not, and I have plenty of time . . ."

"Great!"

"Well, all right. I suppose it can't hurt."

"I think it'll be wonderful."

"Aye," he said doubtfully.

"Thank you, Artair. I can't tell you how much I appreciate it."

"Well, thank you for asking this old man to be a part of something new. I shall do some research myself tonight and meet you tomorrow morning."

"Perfect. See you then."

We ended the call and I smiled at Tom. "Success."

"I had no doubt, and don't let him fool you. I bet he's thrilled."

"I hope so, Tom," I said.

"Aye?"

"Do I get too carried away?"

For a moment, he appeared to freeze in place. "Is this a trick question, lass?"

I smiled. "Well, I suppose that's the answer. Do you ever feel like you should rein me in?"

This time he laughed. "I would never dream of doing anything remotely like that. I love you just the way you are."

"Well, that's mutual, but the way you are," I waved my hand toward him, "is pretty spectacular."

"Glad you think so."

"Delaney!" a voice called from the front of the pub.

I knew that voice.

"Bridget," I said as she approached. "I tried to call you."

"I know." She scooted up and onto a stool. "Tom, are you buying again tonight?"

"Of course. What can I get for you?"

"I'll just have a Coke. I still have work to do."

"Lass?" he said to me.

"Same, thanks."

"Coming right up."

The pub wasn't big enough to keep many things a secret, but Tom had become well practiced in appearing as if he wasn't listening in on conversations. He fell into that mode as he grabbed our sodas.

"You have been busy," Bridget said to me.

"I have. I'm sorry."

"It's okay. I just had some juicy news for you . . ."

Tom set the drinks in front of us and then turned away again to busy himself with some of the bottles on the back mirrored wall.

"I'm listening," I said.

"Well, I guess I owe you. I'm sure I would have eventually put the pieces together, but you nudged them close together sooner."

"You're welcome."

Bridget lifted her glass. "Aye, thank you."

We clinked.

"Alban Dunning and Jolie Lannister knew each other."

"Oh, from when? What were the circumstances?" I remembered Jolie's denial when I'd asked that question. Some sour betrayal bit at the back of my throat.

Bridget reached into her bag and pulled out a manila folder, setting it on the bar and sliding it in my direction.

Inside was a copy of an article that had run in Bridget's small alternative newspaper three years earlier, though she hadn't written this one.

I read the headline aloud. "Edinburgh Man Honors His Grandfather in a Surprising Way."

"You can read it, but in short, Alban Dunning broke into Jolie Lannister's house about three years ago. He was searching for some papers that his grandfather had once had but which had allegedly been given to Jolie's mother by Edward VIII."

"Papers?"

"A journal."

"Uh-oh. Journals tend to spill the beans."

"As this one purportedly does. Allegedly, Jolie has a journal that was kept by Alban's grandfather, wherein he talks about Edward and Vivian's relationship."

"Interesting."

"Well, it would be if the journal was real. There's no evidence that it is or was, and the only thing Alban got out of that house with was an arrest—one, by the way, that Jolie fought, telling the police that the 'dear man' hadn't meant any harm."

"I see."

"No one was hurt. Jolie's companion came upon Alban in the library, and he simply put up his hands."

"I would think he could have asked Jolie to search the library. She might have just let him."

"Jolie is an odd one, Delaney."

"Right."

"You don't think so?"

"Oh, I think so. I just wish I had a handle on her quirks."

"I get that. I rang the police with this information, but I did try to reach you first."

"I appreciate that."

"What's wrong?" Bridget asked when I fell into thought.

"It's all very sad, as well as scary, obviously. There's a killer on the loose."

She lifted her soda. "My money is on the sword."

"Someone wanted the sword?"

"Aye. Somehow the information about the sword got out and someone killed Alban Dunning for it."

"There's no indication that Alban knew about the sword. There are so many questions. How and why? I don't get how you're reaching your conclusions."

"Isn't it our job to figure that out?"

"It is the police's job."

Bridget laughed. "No, Delaney, it's our job too, just as long as we stay safe ourselves. They can use our help, and though they can't say it aloud, I think they like it."

I didn't disagree completely, and if there was anyone who might cross lines even more easily than I would, it would be Bridget. "Thanks for sharing this with me."

"You are welcome. Also, I got a lead on the evidence they found."

"I'm listening."

"Part of a red knit scarf, or some other knit item that didn't seem to belong to Alban was found on him, as if it had been torn off a bigger piece."

"That's it?"

"That's it." Bridget shrugged.

"Huh." I looked at the folder. "I wish I knew why this wasn't part of the story. The police would have put together that Alban had broken into Jolie's house. Why didn't Jolie tell the police?" What I really wondered, though, was why she hadn't told me. She'd lied about knowing him at all.

"We don't know that she didn't tell the police."

I looked at her. "You have a point." Though I didn't think she'd said a word to anyone about it. Neither had Trudie, if I were to speculate.

"Of course I do." She smiled and winked at me. She downed her soda. "I need to go, but watch your phone for my calls. Read the article at your leisure."

"I will. Thank you."

Bridget nodded at me then turned to Tom. "Thanks, again." She sidled off the stool and turned to leave, her blond curls bobbing as she went.

"She is a force, but I like her," I said.

"Aye?"

I laughed. "What?"

"Oh, lass, that one word feels like another trick question. I don't think I should say anything else."

Despite everything, Tom and I managed a laugh.

CHAPTER TWENTY-FIVE

Artair and I were geared up, wearing protective clothing that included white coveralls, face masks, and gloves. We could have been investigating a crime scene.

The equipment all around us was more intimidating this morning than it had been the night before. I'd triple-checked that the red recording light on the camera above was illuminated. I didn't want anything off the record.

I'd already decided the best we could do regarding the item's time of origin was a general dating. Without looking at the site where it had been found, we would only get an idea of the date the sword had been created, as well as how it had come to be in Roslin. The dates would indicate battles in which it was potentially used.

Several methods are used to establish absolute chronology, which is a list or timeline of specific events: radiocarbon dating, obsidian hydration, thermoluminescence, dendrochronology, historical records, mean ceramic dating, and pipe stem dating.

Frankly, the options were overwhelming. I'd heard back from Gwen, my former coworker, at the museum in Wichita, Kansas, and she'd told me that our best bet for this item was researching historical records, but cleaning the sword was my first concern. Gwen had said that a steel brush was the appropriate tool for getting off some of the grime.

Artair stood next to me and observed as I took a brush to all parts of the sword. I started gently, but when it appeared that the brush would do the trick better if a little more pressure was applied, I gave it more elbow grease.

Artair and I took turns.

Unfortunately, the brush would remove only the topmost layer. The rest of the grime was going to need something more aggressive.

"We need to do some work on the hilt," I said as I held a hooked pick in my left hand and handed Artair one with my right hand. "That will confirm my suspicions."

Artair nodded. We were both having more fun than expected.

We'd planned on a good three hours of work this morning so we could make some big strides on the first day. This sort of thing was never quick work, but it didn't take long to realize how fruitful it was going to end up being. The sword was actually cleaning up.

About two hours into the process, we were at the pommel and had managed to chip away enough to determine that the pommel was indeed wheel-shaped. There was no enamel, no family crest like might have been included if it was one of the "newer" swords.

"Artair, I think it's one of the first versions ever made," I said.

"And the condition it's in. Gracious." Artair removed his face mask and scratched his cheek. "This might be . . . something that hasn't been found before."

I sighed. "I agree, and I do think we're close to out of our league now."

Artair nodded. "The real experts need to be brought in."

I bit my bottom lip. "I don't think anyone wants us to stop. Everyone's in a hurry."

"You could just refuse to go on," he said.

I shook my head. "I don't think I can. I mean, I could. I have every right to, but I think Edwin would be mightily disappointed and worried if one of his people weren't involved. Let me think about the best way to go about all of this."

"He might just need to get over it." Artair continued quickly, "I'm sorry. I mean no disrespect."

I smiled. "Rosie said something similar last night, but Edwin has never pushed me to do something I was uncomfortable doing. Sure, he might have asked me to blur some lines, but I'd done so willingly. And had fun while at it. This might be different, though."

"I understand that. Breaking rules can be fun."

"Until they're not, I suppose."

I was shocked by how much progress a steel brush and a couple of picks had made so quickly. This was unquestionably a Crusader sword. A Crusader sword!

Precisely at the time we'd decided upon, Edwin, Cramer, and Joshua entered the room.

"Well?" Cramer said.

I nodded. "It's a Crusader."

"That was fast," Edwin said.

Joshua didn't say anything but kept a serious and concerned expression on his face.

"The wheel-shaped pommel, along with the condition of the pommel and hilt tells me what I need to know to call it a Crusader. Somehow it was well preserved, though it's hard to believe it was just buried all those years. It still needs to be further cleaned. We were careful." I looked at Edwin, but his concentration was on the sword.

Joshua stayed by the door as Edwin and Cramer came around the table to take a closer look.

"Look at that," Edwin said.

I couldn't fault him for the awe I heard in his voice. This was a pretty big deal.

Cramer reached for the sword.

"Sir, I wouldn't do that if I were you," Artair said. "We've been careful as we worked on it, but we need to keep it as sa . . ."

Artair couldn't finish the word by the time Cramer had the sword in the air, wielding it as if he were a thirteenth-century warrior. He slashed at the air as Edwin gasped. I would think back to that moment and remember Joshua turning green, though that might have been my imagination. We all might have turned that shade had we foreseen what was going to happen.

Cramer Donnell, a man who was now the director of the Treasure Trove Unit, one of Scotland's most respected positions, was playing with a priceless item.

We couldn't have known how fragile it might be, but our brushing off the first layer of grime would only loosen any parts that might have been weakened over time. The gunk and grime also served as a safety net of sorts. We knew that. Everyone knew that. Didn't they? It was imperative to be even more careful with it than we had before, until we had it fully cleaned and someone with proper training could test its viability.

For some reason, Cramer Donnell didn't know this, or else he was reckless. As the sword waved through the air and the rest of us tried to discourage him, the sword broke, right where the blade and hilt came together.

The blade came off and clanked over the concrete floor.

For a long moment, none of us knew what to do. We all froze in place. I thought maybe I'd stopped breathing.

Cramer looked at the hilt in his hand, at the blade resting near Edwin's feet, at the hilt again, and then at Joshua.

He said, "Well, that's not good." His knees buckled and his face turned distinctly gray. "Oh, that's not good at all."

CHAPTER TWENTY-SIX

Despite what Rosie had reminded me of the night before, I'd never witnessed such mourning for a thing as I did with the sword.

Sickening dread followed our collective disbelief. Then came some numbness, which led to unpredictable waves of emotion.

It was just a silly sword. Also, though, it was a rare item that meant much to Scottish history.

I admit, I felt a little like an interloper. As Edwin, Artair, Joshua, and Cramer took turns gasping, being aghast, and being upset and angry (no punches were thrown, thank goodness—I *was* concerned), I felt my own sorrow but wasn't sure it should have as big a place as the others'.

Though he wasn't the Treasure Trove Unit director, Joshua had worked at the museum much longer than Cramer. After those first few moments of chaos, he took over and started giving firm orders regarding what each person in the room needed to do.

Mostly, we needed to calm down and step out of his way as he gathered the pieces of the sword and placed them back onto the table.

"What did you do to it?" Cramer asked me and Artair.

"We didnae do a thing to damage it," Artair answered before I could gather my thoughts or words. "We werenae the ones to throw it around."

"Artair is correct," Joshua interjected as he looked at Cramer. "You will not accuse anyone of anything, Cramer. We all witnessed your behavior."

"But it's a sword! It's meant—"

"Enough," Joshua said, his voice raised and firm. "You will not say another word. In fact," he looked around the room, "no one will until I get this sorted. Let me put this to you all another way, sit down and shut up until I tell you that you may speak."

Even Edwin, who wasn't accustomed to taking orders from anyone, did as Joshua said.

Once the sword was back in its spot, Joshua called Victor down to the room again.

"Joshua?" Victor asked as he came through the doorway. "You sounded upset."

"I'm fine. Thank you for hurrying to get here. I need to tell you the situation and then I need you to call the police."

"The police!?" Cramer said as he stood and stomped his foot.

Victor stepped in between the director and the man who'd taken charge.

"No, Mr. Donnell. We will all remain calm. Please take your seat again."

Cramer's face was now splotchy and his breathing fast. I didn't like the man, but I was suddenly worried about his health.

"Cramer," I interjected, "please take some deep breaths. Your coloring is off. Let's none of us get sick, okay?"

I looked at the others in the room. No one appeared to be having the difficulties that Cramer was.

"Call for medics too," I said to Victor.

"Aye," he said.

Joshua nodded. "Aye."

I texted Inspector Winters. He arrived right after the other police and medics did, which wasn't long after Victor made the call. By the time they got there, Cramer did look a little better, but I overheard one of the paramedics read his blood pressure aloud. It was high enough to concern them, but Cramer told them he'd be fine. He just needed some time to calm down.

No one stopped Inspector Winters from making a beeline in my direction.

"Lass?" he said, probably not knowing exactly where to begin.

Quietly, I told Inspector Winters what had happened.

He had a pretty good poker face, but even his eyes widened as I told him about Cramer picking up and swinging the sword.

"Unbelievable," he muttered when I finished.

"I don't disagree," I said.

He sighed. "All right. Sit tight. I'm sure the other officers will want statements from everyone." He shook his head. "Beyond that, I just don't know, but I will keep you up to date if I'm able. Should I get ahold of Ms. Lannister?"

"I don't know. I think Cramer should speak to her, but that might just be my anger speaking." I paused. "I'm rattled, Inspector Winters. Maybe no one should listen to my suggestions right now."

Inspector Winters's eyes were sympathetic. "It'll be okay. It's just a thing, after all."

Sure. Kind of.

Edwin had taken a chair by the door. Inspector Winters spoke to him and Artair next, seeming to make sure they were fine as well. They were. Edwin sent me a thumbs-up, and Artair rolled his eyes at Cramer and then shook his head.

Once Joshua spoke to the police, he found his way to me too.

"I'm so sorry," he said.

"Me too," I said.

"You did nothing wrong. I should have pushed the museum to take a closer look at Cramer. He's been . . . not quite right ever since he was hired. We all thought it was charming at first, but it's become clear that he's not fit for this job. I'm sorry I put you through having to deal with him."

"Thanks, Joshua," I said. Tears filled my eyes, but I blinked them away. I knew I'd done nothing wrong, but I couldn't deny the guilt in my gut.

He frowned and nodded and went to attend to the others.

Ultimately, we were all separated and had to give statements. It wasn't painless—very nerve-racking—but it wasn't terrible. I was pleased that everything Artair and I had done had been recorded.

It felt like days had passed by the time we were released, but as Edwin, Artair, and I made our way outside to the museum's steps, I looked at the time; only four hours had gone by since Artair and I had begun the cleaning.

"Are you two okay?" I asked the men.

"Fine, Delaney, other than angry at that complete buffoon," Edwin said.

"That's a perfect word for that man," Artair added.

"I'm sorry I got you into this," I said to my father-in-law.

Artair shook his head. "In fact, I'm glad you did, lass. I

would have hated for you to have been there alone. I don't . . . I simply don't understand how that could have happened."

"May I buy you both some lunch?" Edwin asked. "Please."

"Ta, Edwin, but I think I'm going to get to work." Artair sighed. "I have no appetite. I will see you both later?"

We watched Artair make his way down the street.

"Lass, how about some fish and chips from the takeaway. Let's take them to Tom's pub and luncheon there?"

"That's a great idea."

CHAPTER TWENTY-SEVEN

"That's the craziest thing I've ever heard." Tom had taken one bite of his fish and chips, then turned his focus to the story Edwin and I had told him.

We'd brought food for Rodger too. He'd eaten already and was now attending to customers as Edwin, Tom, and I sat around a table. The pub was beginning to get busy again, so we wouldn't be able to keep Tom on this side of the bar for long. We managed to get the whole story told, though.

"Isn't it?" I wiped my fingers on my napkin. "Given a little time, I'm now wondering if he didn't break it on purpose. No one in their right mind, particularly someone who has worked with valuable museum items, would be so accidentally careless. Right?"

"Aye, but why?" Edwin asked.

"I couldn't even begin to guess," I said.

"What else did Jolie tell Cramer?" Tom asked.

"Why?" I asked.

"Maybe she told him Edwin would reap whatever benefits the sword would produce and this was his way of getting back at everyone."

"That's pretty unprofessional," I said, somewhat disappointed in myself that I hadn't thought something like that could have happened.

Edwin shrugged. "I don't know. I might bet that he showed his true colors in Glasgow. I will make some calls today and ask around. It just might be who he is."

I could be angry enough to spit nails and I would never have behaved as Cramer had. If it was purposeful, it was beyond immaturity; it was sociopathic, and though I couldn't tie Cramer Donnell to Alban Dunning at all, didn't everyone know that one trait of a killer was a lack of empathy?

"We need to see if we can tie Cramer to Alban Dunning." I grabbed another chip.

"Aye?" Tom said, but then he nodded a moment later. "Aye. I understand what you're thinking."

"I see what you're saying too, but it's difficult to believe that they even knew each other," Edwin added.

I thought back to that first day, when I met Jolie. "Someone told someone other than you about that sword. I really do think that Berry, Gilles, and Alban were there because of it, even if there's no proof yet."

"But didn't Gilles tell you that he didn't know about it?" Edwin asked.

"I didn't mention it specifically, but he said he hadn't been asked by Bowie to go out to Jolie's for any specific item. Yet Bowie did get him there. Maybe they were cover for her?"

I still felt overwhelmed and out of sorts, and a gigantic headache was laying a foundation at the back of my neck. I hadn't had a doozy headache for a long time, but I knew what was about to happen and I didn't look forward to it. Apparently, so did Tom.

"Lass . . ." Tom put his hand on mine.

I nodded.

"Headache?" he asked.

"Coming on."

"I'll get you home, Delaney." Edwin took my paper boat plate and stacked it on his. He looked at Tom. "I'll make sure she's taken care of."

I didn't want to go. I wanted to go to work, but I let Edwin take me home instead. After I downed some paracetamol, I ended up under the covers, fast asleep. When I awakened three hours later, I realized that I'd done just what the doctor would have ordered. I felt much better. I found my way downstairs and discovered some chicken soup in the fridge ready to be warmed. Edwin had also left me a chocolate bar. He and Tom must have discussed my favorite cures.

The headache was almost gone—and even more so after the soup and chocolate.

I texted Tom that I was better and would see him when he was done for the day. It was only four in the afternoon, which was much earlier than I liked to be finished with work. As much as I enjoyed curling up with a good book and glancing out at the ocean view in front of our house, I felt too restless to do that. I needed something else to occupy an hour or two.

I made my way up to the attic. Tom had transformed the space into a library I'd never dared even imagine. Cozy and comfortable, I opened the laptop I kept up there.

I found my favorite news site, still populated with links that led to things about the queen's life throughout the years. I skimmed the articles and inspected the pictures, this time looking for some specific photographs of Elizabeth with her uncle, Edward VIII.

At first, I couldn't find even one. I dug deeper.

Elizabeth was only ten years old when Edward abdicated. Her father then took over the throne, and she didn't become queen until she was twenty-five. There did not appear to be many (or perhaps any) happy reunions between the royals and the abdicated relative. Most accounts mentioned that Edward's abdication didn't wear well with anyone. Tensions were inevitable.

There was, however, pictorial evidence of them both attending the 1967 centenary celebration of the birth of Edward's mother, Queen Mary.

It was reported that Elizabeth did meet with Edward as he was on his deathbed and they reconciled, for whatever that was worth. It seemed that Wallis Simpson was never well thought of by maybe anyone other than Edward.

Though I found it all interesting, I turned my search into something that might tell me more about Edward and Alban Dunning's grandfather, Otto Dunning.

In that regard, I found absolutely nothing. Not one mention anywhere, though there were records of other men who'd attended to or worked for Edward over the years. Had Bridget really uncovered something, or was she mistaken?

I needed to talk to Jolie, but I wasn't ready to do that today.

I continued to search the names I'd learned over the last few days.

Gilles Haig was up next. There seemed to be no surprises with Mr. Haig. He was exactly who he appeared to be, and he did remind me of what I'd learned about Alban Dunning—a loner who worked hard. I found mostly positive reviews of his business.

My next search was Bowie Berry. It didn't take long for me to realize I should have looked closer at the attorney earlier. Other people and things had grabbed my attention, but I was beginning to think that maybe she should have been my priority.

Bowie might have been aptly described as a hot mess.

She had represented clients in quite a few civil trials, cases she'd mostly lost, and had been publicly criticized for her handling of them.

"Oh, Bowie, you're not the best at what you do, are you?" I said to my laptop screen.

It was when I tried to find her office address that I began to feel deep suspicion replace the annoyance I had previously felt toward the lawyer. There was no address to be found.

She hadn't had a card the day I'd asked her for one, but I did have her phone number.

Did she have an office address? It felt like a valid question. It's possible she worked from home, but I didn't quite buy that. I grabbed my phone and dialed the number.

"This is Bowie. Leave a number and I'll ring you back. Cheers," the message said.

I hadn't thought I'd want to leave a message, but I changed my mind. "Hey, Bowie. It's Delaney Nichols. Give me a call when you can."

I ended the call and hoped to hear from her soon. She must have an office somewhere. I was just missing it. I couldn't let my dislike for her cloud my judgment here. I would need to keep an open mind.

CHAPTER TWENTY-EIGHT

My phone didn't ring until the next morning, just after Tom dropped me off in front of the bookshop. I reached in my bag and hoped it was Bowie.

It wasn't. As I stood outside the bookshop, I answered the call. "Jolie?"

"Aye, lass, it's me." She was clearly distraught.

I quickly assumed it was because of the sword. "Oh, Jolie, I'm so sorry . . ."

"For what, lass?"

I hesitated. "You sound upset."

"I am, but it has nothing to do with you. At least I don't think it does."

"What's going on?" I asked.

"Someone broke into the house last night. They stole . . . they stole my proof."

"I don't understand, Jolie, but if someone broke in, you need to call the police."

"I have. They've already been here. Can you please come out? Bring Edwin if it's at all possible."

I stood there a long moment, knowing I could not completely

trust the woman on the other end of the phone but feeling sorry for her anyway. And curious.

"Delaney?" she asked.

"I'm here. I . . . give me an hour or so, Jolie. I need to round up Edwin. Okay?"

"Aye, lass. Ta." I heard her disappointment that I couldn't rush over immediately, but I wasn't willing to let that bother me.

We disconnected the call and I hurried into the bookshop.

Edwin couldn't go with me to Jolie's. He also didn't want me to go by myself. Elias had promised Aggie that he would take her shopping this morning, but he would be available in the afternoon.

Tom said I could take his car, but he couldn't leave the pub and he wasn't thrilled with me going alone either.

"I'll go with you," Rosie volunteered. "Hamlet can watch the bookshop."

"Aye. It would be no problem at all. I don't have any classes today," Hamlet piped up.

I thought about Rosie and Jolie together and realized their meeting might turn uncomfortable, but decided they'd be able to handle themselves.

I did not want to decline Rosie's offer.

"I'd like to have a word with her anyway," Rosie said as we made our way toward the bookshop's door.

Hamlet and I shared a look. The question in Hamlet's eyes didn't assuage my initial concerns. We might be living dangerously.

I was otherwise thrilled to have Rosie along. This time, I

didn't need to work too hard to focus on staying on the correct side of the road.

"The feeling like you're on the wrong side," Rosie said, "goes away in about five years, or so I've been told by some other friends who moved here from the States. Then, when you go back to visit, it starts to feel like the wrong side over there."

"I do like to drive. I'm still nervous but I'm glad I'm finally doing it."

"No need to feel nervous," Rosie said. "Statistically, I think we're fine."

That didn't make me feel much better, but I didn't argue. "I hope so."

As was Rosie's way, she changed the subject.

"I'm going to be a failure," she said.

"How's that?" I asked.

"I'm going to foster a baby kitten until a home can be found for it."

"Oh, no, that will never work. You might as well just sign the adoption papers now."

"I know."

"How will Hector react?"

"I had a cat when I first got Hector. They got along, mostly because they ignored each other very well. I suppose we'll see."

"I'm glad you already know you will be a failure. Those sorts of surprises aren't always good."

"Aye, I'm ready. I hear Jolie's house is in bad shape," Rosie said. "It used to be beautiful."

"I can only imagine," I said. "Let's hope she's still working on cleaning up the inside."

"She's old and she's seen a lot," Rosie said.

"Is that sympathy?" I paused. "Everyone seems to forgive her for things that some might find unforgivable."

"A wee bit. I'm hard on her because I remember how she used to be. Sometimes I forget that we all just turn into more of who we really are as we get older."

"How did she used to be?"

"A character to be sure, but generous to a fault. She worked hard to erase her father's reputation. He was a vicious businessman but also a loving father."

"He wasn't upset about Vivian's claim of an affair and a different father?"

"By the time I met Jolie, her parents were gone, but I could never understand those dynamics."

"Edwin and she were . . . involved?"

"Oh, yes. Very much so." Rosie sighed. "They were good together, until they weren't."

"What happened?"

Rosie shrugged. "Timing, I guess. She's the one who broke it off. And it ruined him."

"I can't imagine Edwin ruined."

"He was, lass. It was rough."

"That's sad."

"'Twas a long time ago, but aye, it was sad."

"You're okay seeing her?"

Rosie nodded. "Not to worry, lass, I willnae be mean to her."

I smiled. "Well, that never crossed my mind."

I steered the car onto the circular drive. There wasn't another vehicle in sight.

"I just don't want you to be bothered," I said.

"Not much bothers me like that anymore." Rosie scanned the house. I could see question and concern in her eyes, but she didn't say more about its condition.

"Okay then." I turned the car key.

We made our way to the front door, and I lifted the knocker.

"Same one," Rosie said as she nodded toward the dragon's head.

Jolie opened the door with a dramatic flourish after the boom sounded. Her eyes were rimmed in red. Her posture was proud as if she wanted to put out a brave stance, but when she saw Rosie, her composure melted.

"Rosie, is that you?" she said.

"Aye, Jolie. Hello, dear." Rosie extended her arms.

Jolie hesitated as if to be sure that Rosie would truly accept a hug.

"Go on then," Rosie said.

The two women embraced like old friends, which is probably exactly what they were, despite their differences from those long-ago days.

The histories of the lives of so many of the people I'd come to know were, of course, a mystery to me. Except that in these moments, when I saw their genuine emotion mix with their memories, I was sure I could almost replay what they'd been through—well, the spirit of it anyway.

When they disengaged, they smiled at each other and Rosie said, "Now, what's this bad news about someone breaking in?"

"Come in," Jolie said. "I'll tell you everything."

I was happy to see that the entryway was still clear. The hallway seemed less junked up too. And the library had been half cleared.

"Jolie," I said. "Everything is looking so much better."

"Aye, lass. Ta. I wish I'd done it all sooner, but here we are."

Once again, we made our way to the green velvet table, where a tray of refreshments had already been placed.

"Is Trudie here?" I asked.

"No, Homer took her into town for a doctor's appointment."

"I hope everything is okay."

"All is well. Just a checkup, she said. Sit. Please."

Instead of beginning with the break-in, Jolie turned to me. "I know about the sword."

"I . . . I'm so sorry," I said.

"I know what happened and it wasn't your fault, lass."

Rosie paid attention to everything. In fact, I suspected that though she was more an observer than a participant, she picked up on things the rest of us might have missed. I was surprised by her immediate jump from their happy greeting to a sensitive question, but I wasn't surprised that she was the one to ask it.

"Jolie, dear, did you call Cramer and Edwin at the same time? Did you tell them both about the sword *on the same* day? Were you attempting some sort of race?"

Jolie's face fell. "It turned out that way, but that wasn't my intention." She paused and turned her unfocused gaze out the window a moment. She looked at Rosie. "I was torn. I knew what the right procedure was, but I also knew that Edwin was the best man to call. It seems ridiculous now, but put yourself in my place. I wanted Edwin to know about the sword because he's the one person in my life that appreciates such things. Cramer had just been hired on as the Treasure Trove director, and he needed to be filled in. It's our duty as Scottish citizens. I didn't think through the challenges that might come of it. I didn't expect Cramer to be like he is. I wish I'd only rang Edwin, but it's too late now, and it's . . . well, it's destroyed so it's worthless."

"It's not worthless," I said. "It just might not be worth what it would be in one piece. And I've given it some thought. Though Cramer should not have done what he did, there might have been a weak spot that would have shown itself eventually anyway. Artair and I were careful, but it could have just as easily have broken on us."

Rosie made harrumph noise. "No, Delaney, it wouldnae ever have happened to you, I'm sure of that." She turned to Jolie. "What's going to happen with the sword?"

"I don't know. It's out of my hands." Jolie shrugged. "I asked the police to somehow put it to good use, but they don't have to do anything I ask."

Inspector Winters had told me he was going to work to keep the sword in Jolie's possession for now, but I didn't want to be the one to share that with her in case he hadn't been able to pull it off.

"I'm so sorry," I said again.

"It's the way it is. It's the way it would be if I'd called the authorities first, and . . ." She trailed off.

"What, love?" Rosie asked.

"Of course I've been wondering—what if the sword is the reason Alban Dunning was killed? If so, he was killed for a thing—one that is now destroyed! It's all a tragic waste."

A sense of familiarity pinged in my gut. I'd wondered the same thing, of course. "What are the connections?"

Jolie sighed. "I don't know, but I've lied to everyone."

Rosie and I shared a look.

"Jolie?" Rosie prompted.

She nodded. "Aye." She signaled over her shoulder toward the desk. "I didn't want to get him in trouble. I didn't want him to be seen in a bad light."

"Who?" I asked, though I thought I knew who she meant.

"Alban Dunning. I knew the lad, recognized him the moment he and Mr. Haig walked into my house with Bowie."

Rosie and I were silent as Jolie gathered her words.

"He tried to steal from me a few years back."

"A journal, aye?" Rosie said.

"You know?" Jolie asked.

I nodded. "Tell me."

"Alban's grandfather allegedly worked for my presumed biological father, Edward," Jolie said. "Otto Dunning kept a journal. He wrote of Edward and my mother's affair—"

"Wait," I said. "Allegedly?"

Jolie nodded. "There's no written record of his employ except *that* journal. A few years ago, Alban found out that I had it and tried to steal it. This morning, someone finished the job. I found the front door open, and the locked desk drawer where I kept the journal had been broken into. The journal is gone."

"No one heard anything? No one was hurt?" Rosie asked.

"No." Jolie shook her head.

I stood and made my way to the desk, crouching to peer at the drawers.

"Top left one," Jolie said.

The desk wasn't as old and historically valuable as the one I worked on in the warehouse, but it was beautiful—stained light-colored wood with inlaid purple flowers, the craftsmanship not something found these days.

The top-left drawer's keyhole had scratches around it, as if someone had, indeed, attempted to break in. I pulled the drawer—it was completely empty. And there was no fingerprint powder anywhere.

"Did they try for prints?" I asked.

"No," Jolie said. "There were too many possible prints to find something accurate. They tried the front door but weren't optimistic about finding anything. I'm afraid . . . well, I'm afraid Trudie and I don't always remember to lock the front door. We did after the break-in years ago, but we sometimes just don't think about it."

I made my way back to Jolie and Rosie. "If the journal was written by Alban's grandfather, I can imagine why he might want it, but why would anyone other than him or you want it?"

"I have no idea." Jolie lifted and dropped her hands.

"What else did it say?" I sat again.

"It has been ages since I read it, but I remember most of it. There was one small entry where Otto Dunning said that Edward and my mother met and sparks flew. It then turned salacious."

"How did you come to have it?" Rosie asked.

"I don't know. My mother had it." She paused. "She left it for me. A few years back, I rang Alban to see if he wanted to read it, but then he broke in and tried to take it. I felt so bad for him. In fact, the day he was killed"—she looked at me—"he walked by right out there, remember?"

"Of course," I said.

"I thought maybe he'd stayed around to see if he could see the journal, if maybe I'd give it to him now. He could have asked, and I might have just handed it over."

"Did he seem upset?" I asked, remembering what I thought was discomfort because of the contention.

"Immediately. When he walked into the house, he and I looked right at each other. I tried to tell him with my eyes not to worry. I . . . I was going to ring him later . . . I hadn't thought about it for so long, then when I saw him . . ."

"Who else would want that journal?" I asked. "Was there anything about a sword in it? Could there be any tie that way?"

"No, nothing about a sword at all. The journal only had about ten pages of writing. It was brief."

"And you didnae photocopy it?" Rosie asked.

"Never even considered doing that. I might attempt to re-write the words, but that doesn't feel . . . authentic in any way."

I needed to call the police and confirm her story. This felt strange, and I didn't trust that Jolie was telling the truth about any of it. Still, Alban had been killed, and a sword had been found on her property.

"Jolie, do you think Alban, Gilles, or Bowie knew about the sword before you called either Edwin or Cramer?"

"As I've said, I wonder, but I don't know how."

"If it wasn't from you, it only makes sense that Trudie or Homer told someone. Do you think that was possible?"

"I don't, and I hope not, but briefly I wondered the same thing. Bowie showing up that day with Mr. Haig and Alban Dunning . . . it was all such a shock, but I don't know."

Gilles Haig or Bowie Berry knew. I could not believe it was a coincidence that Bowie had brought Gilles and Alban out on that specific day. Had Bowie been the one to orchestrate the "ambush?" Alban might have just come along because it was his job.

"They met on holiday," Jolie continued. We looked at her. "My parents were on holiday in France, where Edward and Wallis lived. That meeting is in the journal, but only that they met, no other specifics. Though the subsequent entries purport that the four of them got along well, sparks apparently flew between Mother and Edward. Sparks that weren't meant to be ignored. The two of them stole away, after hours, the nighttime beach and ocean . . . well, here I am."

"That's it?" Rosie asked.

"Well, the journal does have a wee bit more detail, as

though they were all being spied upon. I can tell you that my father and Wallis weren't stupid. They cut their holiday short, and all returned home, not to meet again until I was a child." She nodded. "There's a picture of that meeting in Paris in the hallway. My mother said to me that she never told either Edward or Wallis, but when they met me, they suspected it."

"What about your father?" I asked.

Jolie laughed. "He pretended not to know, but he must have. In his later years, with his mind age-muddled, he told me he was sorry he hadn't been my true father, that it was impossible for him to ever have been." Tears came to her eyes. "I told him he always would be. No one else. I don't know if he understood me. It wasn't until after Edward died in 1972 that my mother thought I should have my rightful place in the royal family. Even if Edward was my biological father, I still wouldn't have had a legitimate right to any throne. Still, my mother . . . My father and I tried to dissuade her, but she was determined. Then our reputations became so tainted, and we were ordered to stop."

"Ordered?" I asked.

"Legal people, solicitors came to the house and told us that legal actions would be taken if we didn't stop making such false claims. My parents weren't as worried about legal actions as they were *illegal* actions. They became concerned for all our lives, so we stopped talking about it. I brought it up later in my life, but perhaps I was just seeking attention. I'm not sure anymore."

"Even your father admitted he wasn't able . . . so, you think the story is true?"

"Lass, I don't know."

"If there wasn't an Otto Dunning, did someone make up the journal?" I asked.

"It wasn't written in my mother's hand. My father's either. Edward had many assistants, secretaries, butlers, footmen. Those were different days. I can't imagine many of them were considered important enough to make record of. If Otto Dunning wasnae a private secretary, I don't know how the journal got written."

"Did Alban ever tell you anything about knowing about his grandfather?" Rosie asked.

"We never had that conversation."

After a long pause, I said, "Even with all of that, someone told someone about the sword. That's the best conclusion I can come to."

"It wasn't me," Jolie said.

I thought she was being honest, but those lines were blurry for her.

We heard the front door open and the rumble of conversation.

Jolie stood up. "Well, I suppose we can ask Homer and Trudie right this minute. I'll bring them both in here and you'll question them, Delaney. You'll get to the bottom of it."

"Me?"

"Aye. You. No one else will be able to get it done. I feel as if you will. Wait here."

Jolie left the room and her voice mixed with the rumbles of the others.

I kept my own voice low. "Rosie, I don't think I should—"

"She's right, lass. You're the only one. I ken it as well as I ken anything. You'll get to the bottom of it."

"I—"

I didn't understand why they thought I could handle such a task, but I could hear the three of them coming in this direction. If I knew anything, I knew I needed to at least appear confident.

I cleared my throat and sat up as straight as I could.

CHAPTER TWENTY-NINE

"We've been having the same discussion," Trudie said. "I've been blaming Homer, he's been blaming me. I didn't tell a soul, and though I cannae speak for Homer, he insists he didn't either. I believe him."

Though tiny and soft-spoken, Trudie was no shrinking violet. As we gathered around that same table again, I'd asked if there was any chance that either of them had, even accidentally, told someone about the sword. I hadn't felt confident in my position as interrogator, but, while they didn't appear scared of me, they seemed genuine in their answers.

"I didnae," Homer said.

We'd gone around a few times, but their stories, their adamancy hadn't changed.

"I believe you," I said.

Jolie nodded agreeably. So did Rosie, but not until she'd given it another long moment of thought.

I took a deep breath. "Okay, so let's talk about the break-in last night."

They both nodded eagerly.

"I didn't know about it until this morning," Homer said.

"Trudie told me on the way to the doctor's office." He looked at Jolie. "I wish someone had rung me last night."

"I didn't notice until this morning. I called the police."

"I heard noises when the police arrived, but I didn't hear the break-in." Trudie shrugged and tapped her ears. "I dinnae have my ears in when I sleep."

I looked at Jolie. "You didn't hear a thing overnight?"

"No. I even came downstairs for a cuppa. I couldn't sleep. Might as well have some tea. I didn't look in the library, but I think, I would have noticed if the front door was open. I don't know, though. I did notice it this morning when I came down. I closed the front door, at first thinking nothing was wrong, but my intuition told me to look around. I found the desk broken into and called the police."

I sat back and bit my bottom lip.

It's all to do with the training: you can do a lot if you're properly trained.

The queen's voice rang through my head. What was she—my intuition—telling me?

I stood and walked to the window, looked at the places hands might touch if someone was opening it from the inside. Of course, it would have had to be opened from the outside if someone were breaking in.

I opened it anyway. It slid up easily, would have from either side, I thought.

I looked at the others. "Are you sure they came through the front door?"

"It was open." Jolie's eyes were wide as she stood. "Why? What do you see?"

"Did the police check this area around the window?"

"Not that I saw."

I peered outside, on the ground beneath the window. "Are those footprints?"

"They could be," Jolie said.

She was right. There might be footprints there or not. If there were prints, they weren't distinct, more just disrupted dirt. I turned my attention back inside.

"If someone came, though, their hands would have landed here." I crouched and studied the floor more closely. I didn't see any fingerprints or handprints, but thought I saw something against the wall, right next to the baseboard. It was small and dark.

"Let me grab my phone." I went back to the table to retrieve it. I crouched next to Jolie again.

"Aye?" she asked.

I illuminated the light and shined it at the object. "I think it's just a rock."

Homer stood and moved to a spot behind me. "Let's have a look."

I leaned out of his way, but I couldn't imagine that a rock would be important.

Homer put his hands on his knees and inspected the whole area. "I think it's . . ." He looked back at Jolie. "I think it's from the bridge."

"You do?" Jolie said.

"I do."

"The bridge?" Rosie and I asked together.

"The area where I found the sword," Homer said.

I looked at him. "The rocks are distinct?"

"Aye." He nodded.

"Take me. Take us all if the walk is easy enough."

"We don't have to walk," Jolie said.

"I'll grab the machine," Homer said as he hurried out of the room.

I looked out the window again. It was still cloudy, but it wasn't raining. It still wasn't too cold, but I wasn't sure Rosie should be out in the weather.

As if she knew what I was thinking about, she said, "I'll be fine, lass. I dinnae want to miss this."

We all loaded onto a vehicle similar to one my dad used on his Kansas farm. It was a big four-wheel off-road vehicle. Seeing it made me realize better how Homer covered so much ground on the large estate, when it was necessary.

Though the driver had a dedicated seat, the rest of us had to find a spot on a long middle bench. It wasn't completely safe, but it wasn't too precarious, particularly since Homer took the trip relatively slowly.

Judging by the smile on her face, Rosie was not only fine, she was having fun.

We first took the path that Alban had walked, but we didn't go as far as Homer's cabin. I felt a twinge of guilt as I thought about opening his door and almost entering his place. I swallowed it away and focused on today's explorations.

Homer steered the four-wheeler over three hills before we spotted a small pond. These grounds were the gift that just kept giving.

Short trees and groomed grass bordered the pond. A redwood bridge curved over the water. Each end of the bridge was set into a bed of dark red rocks.

I saw why Homer thought the pebble from inside might have come from this area—they were distinctly different. However, these rocks looked much bigger—though it was plausible that smaller pebbles were in there too.

He stopped the vehicle next to one of the rock beds. "This is where I found the sword."

"Where? In the rock bed?" I asked.

"No, but where the rock bed is now. Before I found it, there was only dirt, but I'd decided to add the rocks. I was shaping the earth, preparing it for the rocks when I came upon the sword."

We all stared at the rocks for a long few long moments.

"When did you put the bridge in?" I asked.

"I put both the pond and the bridge in about five years ago."

"The pond wasnae here?" Rosie asked.

"No, but the land dipped enough. It was an easy add."

"But you had to do some digging back then? Some shaping?" I asked.

"Aye."

"Did you come across anything back then?"

"Old, valuable, you mean?"

"Yes."

"No, nothing."

I cocked my head at the rock bed. "Homer, who knew you were going to add these rock beds?"

"Jolie and I discussed it. I doubt I mentioned it to anyone else."

"Jolie?" I said.

She nodded. "I guess Trudie knew about it."

"I did," Trudie confirmed.

"Anyone else?"

"Oh. Aye. Bowie Berry, I suppose. I was talking to her on the phone back then. She had been going on and on about something or other. I told her I had to talk to Homer, that he was planning the rock beds by the pond. I used it only as an excuse to get off the phone with her. If you hadn't asked me, I wouldn't have remembered. I'm surprised I did now."

I nodded. "Jolie, I have her phone number, but where is Bowie's office?"

"Edinburgh. Off Princes Street Gardens."

"I'm going to need that address."

"Aye. Of course."

With Homer's permission, I took one of the smaller rocks from the bed with me. Inside the house, we fetched the pebble. It seemed possible that it had come from that rock bed, but maybe not. It was just a pebble, after all.

I don't know why I thought the open front door was a ruse, but I did, and I wanted to explore the idea that the window had been used as the entryway. I still wasn't sure why that might mean something, except that there might be evidence by the window that the police had missed. I would tell Inspector Winters as soon as I could.

Convinced that neither Trudie nor Homer had told anyone about the sword, Rosie and I left, leaving Jolie in better shape than we'd found her and Homer and Trudie more perplexed than they'd been before.

I told them all would be fine, but I didn't know that. None of us knew. I was emphatic, though, about them locking the doors and windows. Even with a killer on the loose, they appeared surprised by the idea. But they promised they'd do as I asked.

Rosie and I made our way back to Edinburgh.

CHAPTER THIRTY

I dropped Rosie off at the bookshop and parked Tom's car in his space. The drive each way had gone just fine, but I was glad to resume my travels using Edinburgh public transportation. I texted Inspector Winters my suspicion about the window being used as an entry for the journal thief. He texted back that he wasn't in on that investigation, but he'd touch base with those inspectors and officers.

I knew the bus schedule so well that I was confident enough to help anyone who seemed confused as to which bus to board. After leaving the bookshop, I hurried toward a stop and was at the address Jolie had written down in only fifteen minutes.

"Harris Bosworth," I read the sign above the glass doors of the two-story modern building. It was a legitimate solicitors' office, which was immediately disappointing.

I thought I'd caught Bowie in a lie when I hadn't been able to find her office location. Now, I wondered why I hadn't been able to track it down—this should only have required a simple internet search. I wondered if I'd misspelled something.

I pulled open the door and was greeted by a young woman behind a sleek counter.

"Welcome to Harris Bosworth. How can I help you?" she asked with a friendly smile.

"Hi. Thanks. I'm here to see Bowie Berry."

For the briefest instant, something like shock skimmed over her eyes, but she was a professional. "I'm sorry. Ms. Berry doesn't work here any longer."

"Since when? This is the address I have for her."

The woman sighed and bit her bottom lip. "Oh, about a year now, I think."

"Can you tell me where she went?"

She shook her head. "I'm afraid I don't know."

I thought as quickly as I could. "Well, shoot. I really need some help. Are there any attorneys available?"

"I think so. What do you need help with?"

"Family stuff," I said.

She nodded. "Have a seat. I'll be right back."

She had a full phone and intercom system on her desk, but she chose to search in person. There was something about mentioning Bowie Berry's name that had set off alarm bells.

This was getting even more interesting.

And, I needed a story, quickly.

I heard approaching voices before I noticed the woman and a man were on their way back to the lobby. I smiled in their direction.

The woman veered to her spot back behind the podium as the man walked to me. He was probably in his forties, with a little salt but mostly pepper short hair. His brown eyes were immediately intelligent, and, I thought, a little suspicious.

"Daken Miller." He extended a hand.

"Delaney Nichols."

"From the States?"

"Yes."

"I'm your man then. I studied both here and there. I can help with any legal issues you might have. Shall we go to my office?"

"Thank you."

As we made our way, I wondered how much trouble I was going to be in. I hadn't lied to Mr. Miller yet, but if I told a story, even an innocuous one, was it illegal to lie to an attorney? I didn't think so, but still . . . The walk down the hallway was long enough to convince me to go with the truth instead and hope for the best.

"Coffee, tea?" he asked as we entered his glass-walled office after passing a bunch of others, all with serious-looking people working on computers.

"No, thank you."

Daken sat behind his desk as I took the other chair.

"I think I know you," he said.

Uh-oh. "You do?"

"Aye. You're Tom's wife."

I had become slightly recognizable because of my position at the bookshop. Edwin was somewhat famous; those who worked with him were bound to garner a little extra attention in the right crowds. But it was rare that I was recognized as Tom's wife—well, by a man. His previous girlfriends—long- and short-term—were in every corner of Edinburgh. Bridget was the only one I'd formed a friendship with.

"How do you know Tom?"

"The pub. I've seen you in there with him a time or two."

"I'm sorry I didn't recognize you."

Daken laughed. "Well, I'm just another bloke in a bar. You're the redhead from the States who caught Tom." He cleared his throat. "I don't think that sounded very polite. I'm sorry."

I laughed. "I know what you mean. I've heard something like that many times before. It's working out well."

"Oh good. When I saw you out there, I wondered if maybe you were here to discuss divorce."

"No, not at all."

"Good. All right, so what can I do for you?"

"Mr. Miller—"

"Daken."

"Okay, well, I'm here under false pretenses."

"Oh. Well, that's interesting, which is something I might not say if I was super busy, but I just finished up a big case with nothing pressing right now, so you have my attention." He sat back in his chair, his expression telling me that his patience might not last long, but he liked Tom's pub so he'd try to remain polite.

"I've had some recent dealings with an attorney who used to work here." I thought maybe the receptionist had mentioned who I'd originally asked about, but when he didn't prompt me to continue, I did anyway. "Her name is Bowie Berry."

At once his eyebrows rose as one corner of his mouth quirked as if he was working not to frown too deeply.

I went on. "This is the address I have for her, but she's not here."

He finally spoke. "No, she's not."

I nodded. "Can you or anyone tell me where she's gone?"

"No."

"That was a quick answer."

"It's the only answer I'm allowed."

I thought I understood what might be between the lines.

"Daken, did she leave here on bad terms, and you all have signed something that said you wouldn't talk about it?"

"I can neither confirm nor deny."

"Boy, that must have been a doozy of an exit," I said.

Daken kept his gaze level. I realized he wasn't upset. In fact, there was something about the set of his shoulders that made me think he wished he *could* talk.

"Can you tell me anything at all?" I asked. "If it helps, I'm trying to assist a friend—someone Ms. Berry might be taking advantage of."

Daken pinched his mouth even tighter. "I'm sorry. No. I still can't share the details of Ms. Berry's departure."

I thought about promising him I wouldn't tell anyone his name, but that sounded too cliché. He was a person of the law. If he was also ethical, which I had no reason to think he wasn't, he knew that if he was asked about our meeting, he would be obliged to tell the truth.

Just my luck to find an ethical attorney.

"So, she must have gone to another office?" I said, pushing it, I knew.

"That's a possible scenario," he said.

He wasn't rushing me out of there. I took it as encouragement to keep going.

"It's a possible scenario? Okay, so what're the other possible scenarios? She's no longer a working attorney? She was disbarred, or whatever the Scottish equivalent is?"

"That's also a possible scenario," he said with a tone that made me think I might be onto something.

"Really?"

He shrugged.

"Wow. Wow, that *really* must have been an exit."

He shrugged again.

I bit my bottom lip. "One more question and then I'll get out of your way. Do you know where she lives?"

"No, I truly don't know that, but," he paused as if he was thinking through his next words, probably weighing them against the things he shouldn't say, "well, I live in a flat just around the corner, The Piccadilly Flats. She and I *used* to be neighbors."

"Oh? That's a great lead. Maybe I'll stop by there and ask for a forwarding address."

He shrugged yet again. "That's up to you."

"Thank you, Daken."

He stood. "It's a pleasure to meet you, lass. I hope you and Tom will be well."

"I look forward to seeing you in the pub. Next one's on me. Well, on Tom."

Daken laughed. "I'll take you up on that."

He saw me to the door, both of us getting a wide-eyed questioning stare from the receptionist.

CHAPTER THIRTY-ONE

The Piccadilly Flats were housed in an old building on the outside, but slick, modern, and ritzy on the inside.

The doorman wasn't thrilled to open the doors for me when I said I hoped to talk to management, but maybe he thought this naïve American, who surely couldn't afford the rent here, needed to learn a tough lesson, and the manager was the person to dole it out.

I found my way to the office in the back of the chandelier-topped lobby, knocking on the door with as much confidence as I could muster.

"Come in," the cheery voice from inside said.

The woman inside was older, with wild gray hair and eyeglasses on her head, a pair on a chain around her neck, and another pair on the tip of her nose. The smile disappeared as I went inside.

"We've no flats available," she said.

"Oh, gosh, I couldn't afford this place anyway. Too rich for my blood." I closed the door behind me.

The nameplate on her desk said "Gretta." Gretta sighed. "What are you selling?"

"Nothing, I promise."

She eyed me up and down. "You're looking for a rich husband and want me to tell you who the single men in the building are?"

"Nope, I'm happily married. Good idea, though."

"No, it's a terrible idea, and not mine. You'd be surprised how many women and men come asking. And," she glared out toward the front of the building, "the doorman dislikes me enough to keep sending them in here. All right then, so what can I do for you?"

"I need a forwarding address."

Gretta frowned. "Whose?"

"A woman named Bowie Berry."

Gretta laughed. "That piece of work?"

I smiled. "That's the one."

"Well, all I have is a restaurant."

"I'll take it."

"Aye." Gretta typed onto the keyboard on her desk, squinting through the glasses on her nose and at the screen. "Here it is. Roger Rabbit on Sprey."

I typed a note into my phone. "It's a restaurant?"

"She called one day asking about mail. I had a small stack here. That's where she asked me to forward things, so that's what I've been doing."

"Any chance you know the kind of mail she's gotten?"

"Sounds like you expect me to do something illegal like check others' mail."

"Sorry. I take it back. But thank you for this." I waved my phone.

"You're welcome. I have work to do now, so be on your way." She pushed up the glasses on her nose. "Good luck with Ms. Berry. She's . . ."

"A piece of work?"

"Aye. Exactly."

Armed with this new information, I set off for the nearest bus stop.

On the way to the restaurant, I texted Tom with an update as to where I was going. I'd learned the hard way that it wasn't wise to keep my locations to myself. You never knew what danger might be found at any turn.

Before the bus came to a stop, I spotted the restaurant. It was cute, but also a little rough around the edges, as everything was in this neighborhood. There were no ritzy apartment buildings in sight.

The restaurant reminded me of the country places back in Kansas that served big, delicious, greasy breakfasts as well as the "best pie or cobbler in America," as my father would award such desserts. His sweet tooth had been the divining rod to discover all the best places, in Kansas at least. I smiled as I took in the aromas and the atmosphere, decorated with vinyl booths and confetti-patterned tabletops.

"Take a seat anywhere," a waitress dressed all in pink said.

I was thrown off by her Scottish accent. It should have been distinctly Midwestern to fit with the rest of the place.

I took a seat on a swivel stool at the counter. There were three other customers in the place, but no sign of Bowie Berry.

The waitress stopped in front of me. "Just coffee, please."

She hurried to grab a generic white mug and filled it with the good stuff. Along with the pies and cobblers, this sort of place could only serve the greatest coffee.

As she set it down, I said, "I have a question, when you have a minute."

She studied me before she said, "In a second." She took care of serving one of the customers in a booth before she returned to me. "What's your question?"

"I guess I have a couple. First of all, I bet an American opened this place. Am I right?"

She laughed. "No, but the owner based it on a place he visited back in Iowa. Or was it Ohio. One of those. Maybe Idaho."

"I knew it. I'm from Kansas, and I feel right at home."

"Welcome. What's the other question?"

"I know that a woman named Bowie Berry has her mail forwarded here."

"Aye. She's not on today. Maybe not tomorrow either. Do you want me to check her schedule?"

"Oh." I had to work very hard to hide my surprise. Though waitressing was a noble profession, I could never picture the brassy Bowie in any sort of customer service position. "Yes, please."

"I'll be right back."

I didn't know why I hadn't considered that Bowie worked in the restaurant. Maybe it was as simple as I couldn't see her as anything but the lawyer she'd portrayed herself to be.

The waitress returned a moment later. "Aye. She's in tomorrow. Afternoon shift. Starts at two o'clock."

"Thank you."

"Need anything else?"

"No, I'm good."

I set an alarm on my phone to remind me of the time Bowie would be at the diner and finished the coffee, set a good tip next to it, and eyed the dessert turntable. I thought about exposing Tom to what were probably the best pies in Scotland someday soon.

I stood outside the restaurant and looked around. This is where Bowie Berry worked? I'd confirmed that she'd been an attorney at one time, but I didn't think she was anymore. I concluded that she must have been disbarred. I'd researched her enough to think that those sorts of admonitions must not be public record, but I sure wanted to confirm my suspicions.

As I hopped on a bus for home, I realized that something that Bridget had said did make sense. We *were* helping the police.

Though with their resources, they would have surely been able to track down Bowie much more quickly than I would, they probably wouldn't have thought to go down this path in the first place.

It might be a waste of time, but it was better to waste my time than theirs. Right?

I hoped so.

CHAPTER THIRTY-TWO

I started the next morning by checking my phone, but to my dismay, no one had called, texted, or emailed. I'd left another message for Bowie last night, and then one for Jolie, Edwin, even Joshua.

"Lass?" Tom asked as I walked into the kitchen, my focus on my phone. I hadn't even started the coffee machine.

I looked up. "Good morning."

"Morning. Toast, coffee?"

"Yes, please. Kiss first, though."

"I can accommodate."

Once the important stuff was attended to, we sat down to eat breakfast. I'd shared most of my discoveries with Tom the night before, but he'd asked for a recap to make sure he hadn't missed something important.

He rubbed his chin. "Okay, so you think that Bowie knew about the sword?"

"I do. It was a fleeting thought at first, but it's more solid now. I still can't figure out the logistics or the motives, though."

"Do you think the sword is the reason Alban was killed?"

"I don't know," I said. "It feels like it should be, but I can't tie them together either. I can tie Alban to Jolie now—"

"But you don't think Jolie or her group to be killers?"

"I do not."

"Where are you going to begin the day?"

"The bookshop."

Tom smiled. "Well, there's a murder to be solved, love, I doubt you'll stick around there for long."

"You're probably right."

"Ring Inspector Winters. He might know more he could share now."

"Good idea."

"Thank you."

"If you ever get tired of the pub life, we could do this together, with Elias, of course."

"What? Investigate murders?"

"Yeah."

Tom laughed. "I'll keep that in mind."

"Want to really live dangerously?" I asked.

"Aye, why not?"

"I'll drive in."

Tom laughed again and handed me the keys.

I didn't pull into the wrong lane once.

"Time to get you your own auto?" Tom asked as I handed back the keys when we parked.

"I don't think so. Not yet."

"Let me know."

"Will do."

As Tom walked toward the pub, I turned in the other direction toward the bookshop. Finally, my phone rang.

"Joshua, hello?" I said as I answered.

"I'm sorry I missed your call. What can I do for you?" Joshua asked.

I was only halfway to the bookshop, but I stopped walking. It was a beautiful day—in that it wasn't too cold and it wasn't raining, but it was cloudy.

"Joshua?" I said.

"Aye?"

"I don't like your formal tone. I want us to go back to the way it was. That's what you can do for me."

A pause went on almost too long. Finally, he cracked. "I'm sorry, lass. I was afraid you were angry at me. That was me readying for a fight."

"I could never be angry with you," I said.

"That's so good to hear. I'm so sorry for . . ."

"You didn't hire him."

"No, I didn't, but I should have protested more. Okay, then, so what's up, my friend?"

"How are you? How's the museum? What's going on with Cramer Donnell?"

"You don't want to know about the sword?" I heard a smile in his voice.

I laughed as I resumed walking. "I know what happened to the sword, and, honestly, it's the least of my worries, but before I get into all that, how about my other questions?"

"I'm fine, angry but trying to channel that positively. The museum is fine. We all acknowledge that Cramer shouldn't have been hired. Hindsight and all. We will get it sorted. Mr. Donnell has been dismissed." Joshua sighed. "There's talk of charging him with a crime, but as much of a mess as that man is, I hope it doesn't come to that. Why add salt to the wound? He truly does feel terrible."

"Hmm."

"You doubt that?"

"I don't know, Joshua. It was all so bizarre."

"Yes. All right, what is your question regarding the sword?"

"I'm beginning to wonder if it really came from Jolie Lannister's property," I said.

"She lied?"

"I don't know if she lied or has been lied to, but it's an avenue that hasn't been explored enough, I think. I don't understand it all, but I think someone might have planted it there."

"Again, why?"

"That's the part I don't know. With your resources, is there a way to see if someone's old Crusader sword has gone missing?"

"Really?"

"Maybe? Yesterday I saw the place where it was supposedly found, and something doesn't sit right. It's that plus other things."

"Why would someone plant the sword there?"

"Love or money—aren't those always the reasons?"

"I suppose." He paused. "I'll do some research."

"Thanks, Joshua. And if you do find something, I suggest you call the police first, although I would love to be the second call."

"It's a deal." Joshua paused again but I could tell he had more to say. "Thank you, Delaney. The last thing I want is for our friendship to be jeopardized."

"That will never happen."

"Good to hear. I'll get back to you."

I hit the end button and then pulled open the bookshop door, ever grateful for Hector's happy greeting. I lifted him to my cheek.

"I am so happy to see you," I said to him. "Never change."

I thought about the cat Rosie was fostering and smiled at the thought of Hector as a sibling.

He wiggled that he was fine with it.

"I'll be right around," Rosie called from the back.

"It's just me," I called back.

"Och, lass," Rosie said when she saw me. She smiled. "Thank you for the adventure yesterday." She smiled big. "I've uncovered something you might find interesting."

My curiosity piqued and, still holding Hector, I followed Rosie to the back.

"See." She pointed at a notebook opened on the table.

It was a thin photo album, maybe only five double-sided pages at the most. It was filled with pictures of Edwin and Jolie.

They were caught in time on a boat, on a bridge, in formal attire, at a restaurant table.

"Oh my goodness, they were lovely together," I said.

"Aye," Rosie said sadly. "I'm trying verra hard to give Jolie the benefit of the doubt, lass, so I tracked this down last night to remind me of that time."

"Did it help?"

"Only a wee bit. Pictures were then like they are now, brief moments. I know they don't give the full story. Jolie was a challenge, though that's not to say that Edwin wasn't. He wasn't a—what's the word—playboy, but he certainly never wanted to settle down. He made that clear, though there came a point when Jolie no longer wanted to accept that. What had started as fun, turned strained, and then sad. Edwin missed Jolie but couldnae be what she wanted. She broke it all off."

"I see." I looked at the pictures again. I liked getting more of the story. "Thank you for sharing these. I love them."

"Well, dinnae tell Edwin. He doesnae ken I kept them."

I sat and settled Hector onto my lap. I wanted to study each picture. Their youth, their eyes, the mere air around them shone brightly from the now fading black and whites. I felt like I was looking at early Hollywood stars. I thought about the old movies I used to watch in the middle of the night when I visited my grandparents. It was a short but delightful escape.

Until my eyes saw something that stopped me in my tracks.

"No, that can't be," I said.

On my lap, Hector whined, and Rosie came back around.

"What, lass?"

I handed Hector to Rosie and then picked up the album, bringing it close to my eyes.

I still couldn't make out what I was seeing, so I stood and turned toward Hamlet's file cabinets. I knew the one to open to find a magnifying glass. I grabbed it and took it back to the table, holding it over the picture.

It was a shot of Jolie on her own—taken, I presumed, by Edwin as she stood in her library, in the spot where I thought a desk was now located. The portrait of her mother that was there now wasn't anywhere to be seen. On the wall behind her was a short, pointed blade. The entire weapon, if that's what I was seeing, was not in view.

"Rosie, does that look like the blade of a sword?" I pointed.

She handed Hector back to me and then took the magnifying glass.

"Maybe. It's covered in dirt."

"Yes, it is." I frowned. "Very much like the dirt that covered the sword that Artair and I worked on, the one we got from Jolie's shed."

"You think it's the same one?"

"I think it could be."

"Lass, what would that mean?"

"I have no idea." Still holding Hector, I grabbed my phone and called Edwin.

I had to leave a message. Edwin, I need to talk to you ASAP. I was going to have to go against Rosie's request not to share the album. She'd be fine with it. I hoped.

CHAPTER THIRTY-THREE

"I don't remember," Edwin said.

He'd received my urgent message and hurried to the book-shop, no questions asked.

"You don't remember the sword or the photograph?" I asked him.

"Neither." He reached over and picked up Hector, setting the dog on his lap. "Delaney, this was forty years ago. Time does fly, but this was a very long time ago."

I was struck directionless. If Edwin didn't remember seeing a sword in Jolie's library, there was no way to force him to.

"Lass, they didnae care about such things back then," Rosie said. "They were young. Why don't you just ring Jolie and ask her?"

"Because if that is the sword that has caused all the ruckus, she and maybe Homer and Trudie have been lying this whole time."

"It makes no sense, lass. I think you're just going to have to ask her," Edwin said. "Or call Inspector Winters and ask him."

I nodded. "The other problem is that it could be something else, not a sword or not *the* sword."

"Oh, no, lass," Rosie said. "I think it's a blade of some sort. It might not be the one you have been working with, but it's a blade."

"I agree with Rosie. Do you want me to call Jolie?" Edwin asked.

I bit my bottom lip. "Not yet. Let me . . ."

I caught Edwin glancing at the pictures, smiling. He didn't appear to be sad.

"Good memories?" I asked.

He looked up at me. "Mostly. Well, I can remember the good things and work to forget the bad things. At some point, you must decide which you want to hold on to. I made the choice long ago to focus on the good."

Edwin and his current lady love, Vanessa, were without drama. They adored each other, still lived their own lives, but enjoyed vacations together. They would never consider marriage—it wasn't their thing—but they were also completely devoted to their relationship.

The emotion I saw on Edwin's face now wasn't a wish for what used to be, but probably as simple as what he said—a memory of the good things.

"Seems smart," I said.

"To be honest with you, lass, I'm not sure I would give myself enough credit to call myself smart, but old can sometimes be a decent substitute." He scratched behind Hector's ears. "What are you going to do?"

Before I spoke the words, I hadn't decided, but as I said them aloud, I knew it was somehow the right thing. "I'm going to start by talking to Gilles Haig."

"Great. Want company?"

"I would love it."

I led the way as we pushed through Gilles's warehouse door. The place was much more cleared out than it had been before. I'd thought about attending one of the auctions but hadn't asked for a schedule. Helen was in the back of the space, on a stool, next to a table that still contained some items.

"Can I help you?" she called.

"We're here to see Gilles."

"He left."

I shared a look with Edwin. We set out walking toward Helen.

"Left? For the day?" I said.

"For a while," Helen said. "We had an auction two days ago, and then he said he had to go. Needed some time away. I think he took a brief holiday."

"Because of Alban?" I said.

"I suppose." Helen was sad too, but here she was still working.

"We met the other day. I'm Delaney, this is Edwin."

"Pleasure. Aye, I remember you." She continued her inspection of some small porcelain figures on the table she sat next to.

"Do you have his mobile number?" Edwin asked. "I've an estate I need to speak with him about."

"Just call the office number and leave a message. He'll get back with you."

"I'm afraid it's more urgent than that. The property owner is in financial trouble. It could be a big win for Gilles as well as an offer of much-needed assistance to my friend."

"Aye?"

"Aye."

Edwin was the best liar I'd ever met. I think it was Joshua who once told me I should pay close attention to that trait and not let it catch me off guard one day.

"I'll take your number and give him a message to call you."

It was going to have to be good enough.

Once that was done, I asked, "Helen, are you okay?"

"Aye. Well, I miss Alban. He was a friend."

"I'm so sorry."

"It'll be all right. In time."

"Is there anything we can do for you?" I asked.

"Och, lass, no, ta though. I'm just an old woman. When younger people pass, it makes me extra sad. I do have my daughter. I'm verra fortunate that way." She glanced at her watch. "She'll be here shortly to pick me up."

"Can we help until she gets here?" Edwin said. "I'm very good at lifting and moving things."

It might have only been my imagination, but there was something in the air that made me wonder if Gilles was ever coming back. I shook off a weird sense of foreboding that I wanted to blame on Helen's seeming sadness, the dim lighting, and the culmination of the last week's events.

Before Helen could agree to let us help her, though, the door opened. We all looked in that direction.

"I'll be right there, sweetheart," Helen called. She turned back to us. "Thank you for the offer, but I think it's time to be done for the day."

The young woman waved. "I'll be out in the car."

Edwin and I dawdled with Helen as she gathered her bag from a shelf by the office and then locked the door.

Edwin opened the passenger side door of her daughter's car and then shut it as Helen got herself situated.

We thought the car would take off, but Helen's daughter exited it a moment later instead. She inspected me. "Hey, I know you."

I hadn't really looked at her before, but now I did. "Yes, just yesterday! You're the receptionist at the law firm."

"Goodness, what a small world," she said.

I thought about it a moment. "Or we were meant to run into each other again. Do you have a few minutes?"

"Your questions are about Bowie Berry, right?"

I didn't want her to leave yet. "Not necessarily."

From inside the car, Helen said, "What's going on?"

Though he didn't understand the specifics of what was happening, Edwin said, "Could we buy you a coffee?"

Finally, she looked at me. "It's so frustrating not to get answers you need."

"That's true."

She sighed. "They didn't ask me to sign anything, so sure, we can talk. A little." She looked at Edwin. "Coffee could be lovely. There's a place up around the corner."

"We'll meet you there," I said.

She hopped back into the car and took off as Edwin and I hurried to his.

"And that's who?" he asked.

"The receptionist at the attorneys' office where Bowie Berry once worked but left under circumstances that caused some of them to have to sign something so they wouldn't speak about the seemingly ugly exit."

"This is fortuitous."

"Or it's the connection," I said.

"How?"

"I have no idea."

"I guess we'll find out soon enough."

Mere moments later, we parked and hurried to meet the two women inside the coffee shop.

CHAPTER THIRTY-FOUR

Helen's daughter's name was Stacy. She was smart as a whip, that was easy to see, and not nearly as worried about her words as she'd been inside the offices of Harris Bosworth.

But I didn't want to attack her immediately with the question of why Bowie was dismissed from the law firm.

"Were you the reason Bowie found Gilles's place?" I asked her.

"No, but she asked me about it before she left. I remember it well because she'd never once given me the time of day. She came up front and said something to the effect of 'doesn't your mother work with Gilles Haig?' I told her yes, and then she turned and walked away."

"That was it?" I asked.

"No. The next day she asked specifically if Alban Dunning worked there too. I told her he did, though I was close to telling her to figure it out herself. She wasn't pleasant." Stacy looked at her mother and then back at me. "I do want to keep my job, though, so I sometimes put up with bad attitudes."

I considered how to ask my next question. "Did any of that have anything to do with why she was . . . dismissed?"

Stacy shook her head. "I don't think so. The big problems for her came when she wanted to file a lawsuit, something about someone's right to the throne, though ultimately it was found that Bowie forged some of the paperwork. The person who was allegedly filing the suit didn't even know about it."

I sat up straighter. "Jolie Lannister?"

"Aye. The queen's health appeared to be failing, and Bowie got a bee in her bonnet about how Elizabeth should never have been queen in the first place. Apparently, she got out of control with her claims. The higher ups tried to talk some sense into her, but she kept insisting. If I remember correctly, it was all ridiculous. Ms. Lannister wouldn't have ever been in a position to have a right to the throne."

"So she was fired and disbarred?"

"She was fired and struck off, disbarred, because she misrepresented herself to the courts. Stupid lies on her part, but I heard she thought it would give her more credibility. I'm afraid I don't know the exact timeline."

I nodded. "Why would she want to know anything about Gilles Haig and Alban Dunning?" I still couldn't connect everything.

Stacy took a sip of her coffee as if stalling dramatically. Edwin and I shared a quick glance. I looked at Helen, wondering how she felt about this whole thing. She didn't seem fazed.

"I have a theory on that one," Stacy finally said. "But it's only a theory, and if anyone ever knew I said it, I could get in big trouble."

"We won't give it away, lass," Edwin said, before I could tell her she didn't need to share if she didn't want to.

I looked at Helen again, who seemed to be just fine with all of it, enjoying her coffee along with the rest of us, and kept my lips tightly shut.

Again, Stacy thought about it for a long minute, but she really didn't like Bowie Berry, and that was ultimately going to be why she talked to us.

"She stole something from one of the managing partners. I mean, and I'm just speculating, but I think she stole something, and she needed to find a way to move it. I think she went to Gilles Haig so he could act as her fence. I think she somehow heard about my mum working at an auction house, but I don't know why she mentioned their names when she asked me about them."

I looked at Helen yet again.

She shook her head. "This is all news to me. It's fascinating, though."

"What do you think she stole?" I asked, though I felt like I knew the answer. Or I hoped I knew the answer.

"An old sword. It was in terrible shape, but I heard it was very valuable."

You could feel the air go out of the room. Or, more specifically, Edwin and I could.

Helen simply said, "Ah," and took another sip of her coffee.

I regathered the oxygen I needed to breathe. "One of the partners had a sword stolen from them?"

"Aye, the man you met with. Daken Miller."

"Did he call the police?"

"I don't think so. I don't know. I asked once but was met with a firm enough 'none of your business' so I didn't keep asking. I do figure it was absolutely none of my business and I didn't want it to be by then. If I hadn't happened upon you with Mum today, we never would have spoken about any of it."

I nodded. "Did you ever hear about the value of the sword?"

"That it was a lot. I didn't want to care about it after that."

"Helen, do you know anything about Bowie bringing a sword to Gilles or Alban?"

"Not a thing, lass. Again, this is news to me."

Stacy patted her mother's hand. "I didn't see any reason to worry you. You love your job so much."

"I do, but . . . well, no, I'm fine being left in the dark on this one."

It seemed rude to run off from our new friends, but my heel bounced a little as we remained polite in our conversations.

I invited them both to the pub and the bookshop, and I thought they might both take me up on them at some point.

Once we watched them drive away, and after we were back in Edwin's car, I said, "Daken Miller found or had a priceless item that he should have reported to the Treasure Trove Unit, but Bowie took it—knowing he couldn't call the police without being found out."

"How did it get to Jolie's place?"

"I don't know."

"Where to now?"

"I'm not sure what to do next. I need to think."

"Back to the bookshop?"

"Yes, that's always the best place."

CHAPTER THIRTY-FIVE

I'd called Tom to join the rest of us as we gathered around the back table. Edwin, Rosie, Hamlet, Tom, Hector, and I were all there.

The only one I hadn't called yet, though thought I should, was Inspector Winters. First, I wanted everyone else to know what was going on.

"I know Daken," Tom said. "I've always liked him."

"If we call the police, he might be in trouble," I said.

Tom shrugged. "He's not a close friend. I'd be sad for him, but if he had the sword and hid it from the authorities . . ." Tom stopped talking and looked at Edwin. "Sorry."

There was the problem. What we would be accusing Daken Miller of was something Edwin had done more times than I would ever know, probably would have done with the sword if Jolie's better (or just confused) angels hadn't intervened. I didn't think Edwin had ever done any of it to benefit himself. I didn't know Daken enough to understand his intentions.

"It's all right, lad," Edwin said. "Calling the police is the right thing."

"But how will this lead to Alban's murderer?"

"Maybe Daken killed Alban?" Rosie said. "But from everything you've said, I don't think so. I do think Stacy's job will be in jeopardy if you call the police."

"I thought about that. I wouldn't give them her name."

Rosie shrugged. "Might not matter."

"I have a thought," Hamlet said.

We looked at him.

"Let's call Joshua over. Let's tell him."

None of us asked Hamlet to explain why calling Joshua was a good idea. To me at least, it seemed like a good move, even if I couldn't understand why. Maybe it was as simple as we trusted him.

"I'll get him here." I grabbed my phone.

"I don't know him, and I know nothing about him owning a sword. There are legal ways for people to keep such items. Maybe it was passed down through the family over the years. If so, the Treasure Trove Unit has no right to it."

Joshua had joined us quickly. He stutter-stepped when he saw everyone there waiting for him but kept his composure and then listened intently as I went through everything again, now peppered with others' views and opinions.

"Maybe there's another reason Daken didnae call the police after the sword was stolen," Rosie said.

"Like what?" Edwin asked.

We all looked at Tom, though he'd already admitted to not knowing Daken more than on a friendly customer basis.

"Um. Okay." He shook his head. "I don't know him beyond the fact that he isn't an arse."

I grabbed the photo album and opened it on the table. I pointed. "Joshua, do you think this could be the sword?"

He peered at the picture, his eyebrows coming together. "I have no idea. Maybe?"

"Or maybe you're so focused on it, you're turning it into that," Hamlet said to me.

"I think that's possible." I looked at Edwin.

"Edwin?"

"I still don't remember a sword back there, lass. I'm sorry."

I turned my attention back to Joshua. "What is your responsibility based upon what we've told you today?"

Joshua sighed. "Nothing. I'm just a museum employee at the moment—"

"At the moment?" I said.

Joshua frowned. "It's not something I would normally share, but considering everything, I'll let you all know that I'm being considered for Treasure Trove Unit director."

"As you should have been from the beginning," I said.

"All I'm trying to say is that I have no responsibility to report anything anyone has said here today, but if I was the director right now, I would be compelled." He hesitated. "I'm not saying I would turn anyone in." He paused again. "I'm not sure I'm the right person for the job."

"You are," Hamlet and I said together.

"Do you know where the sword is?" I asked.

"Yes. In the museum. Under lock and key."

"Good. That's probably the safest spot for it."

"Should we call the police?" Rosie asked.

"I'd like to talk to Jolie one more time." I looked down at the picture. "I just have a few more questions for her."

"Do you think the answers will lead to Alban's killer?" Edwin asked.

"I don't know." I looked at Tom. "Have time to come with me?"

Tom smiled. "I do."

In a quick flurry of discussion, we all decided that Tom and I were the best combination to visit Jolie.

"Jolie will like the look of you, lad," Rosie said to Tom. "Use it."

I held back a smile. Rosie wouldn't care that what she'd just said was inappropriate, and no one would point it out to her.

I did admit, silently and to myself, that she might have an excellent point.

"A lovely place," Tom said as he steered the car onto the circular drive.

"It's falling apart."

"I can see its bones, lass. It's stunning."

I nodded. It seemed the driveway was even more dilapidated than it had been the last time I'd been there. It felt like a long time ago that Homer, Jolie, Rosie, and I rode the four-wheeler out to the pond and the bridge. So much had happened.

I lifted the knocker and let it fall twice.

Trudie opened the door a moment later, a brightness to her eyes I hadn't witnessed before. In fact, it was almost bothersome, manic.

"Everything okay?" I asked.

"Delaney, hello." She looked at Tom, widening her eyes.

"This is my husband, Tom."

"Well, hello." She extended a hand.

"A pleasure." They shook.

She looked back at me. "Jolie is making us clean—everything. More than once. We are to make the place spotless."

"That's . . ." I said.

"So much work," Trudie said. "Come in. See if you," she looked at Tom, "or you can talk some sense into her."

"We'll give it a try," I said.

I was first struck by the fresh citrus scent as we stepped into the entryway, and then I was equally struck by the shine. It came from everywhere, off every surface. The wood staircases were rich and freshly polished. The tile floor held no grime anywhere. The expression "you could eat off the floor" ran through my mind.

"Wow," I said.

"What a beautiful home," Tom said.

"Aye, and it's changed a lot over the last week," Trudie said.

"It has," I couldn't help but agree.

There were no stacks of anything anywhere.

"I'm in the kitchen, Trudie, if someone is looking for me," Jolie called.

"Come along." Trudie led the way as Tom and I followed her.

I looked over everything we passed as we went—walls, windows, furniture—it was as close to pristine as anything with some years on it could get.

I was struck speechless as we stepped into the kitchen. Despite the clutter, it had been an attractive space before, but now it was the stuff of celebrity home magazines. The stainless sparkled, and we could see that the countertops were tiled in different colors, giving the whole space a modern Spanish feel even though I knew the design had been created long ago.

"I don't know what to say, Jolie. It's spectacular," I said.

Jolie, wearing an apron and a scarf over her head, stepped back from an antique cooker that I hadn't seen before. It reminded me of going to the antiques shops in Kansas—I always enjoyed lifting the burner plates off and then challenging my-self to set them back without needing adjustment.

"Now that I've decided to clean things up, I can't seem to stop myself."

"Me either," Trudie said, rolling her eyes.

"Who are you?" Jolie asked Tom.

I did the introductions.

"Goodness, you are handsome," she said to Tom.

"Ta."

She looked at me and then back at Tom. I held back a laugh.

"I know, I married up."

She shook her head. "No, you married very well. Are you also a nice man?" she asked Tom.

"I like to think so."

"He's the best," I said.

"You are a lucky lass."

"I am." I cleared my throat and Tom tried not to appear uncomfortable. "Jolie, I've brought something I'd like to show you. Could we go to your library a few moments?"

"Aye. Of course."

She set her cleaning cloth on the counter and then led us all toward the library. Trudie came with us, bringing up the end, and I took the time to show Tom the pictures in the hallway, pointing out Edward VIII and Wallis Simpson.

I noticed the frames and the glass over the photographs had all been cleaned.

As we stepped into the library, tears filled my eyes. I'd loved it before, because every library, even a messy one, held a spe-cial place in my heart. Big, little, messy, or clean, a place with books was always a palace to me.

There could be no denying that this one was a hundred

times more spectacular now. This was a room about books—looking at them, reading them, just sitting with them. Enjoying their scents.

I'd had a teacher once who told me she'd trade the world's best meal, whatever that may be, for a room full of books. I'd thought it was an odd thing to say, even though I'd loved books as a child. But this room made me understand what she meant.

I sniffed away the tears. "I don't really know what to say."

"Gracious," Tom said. He hadn't seen it beforehand. "This would turn anyone into a reader."

"Ta." Jolie smiled. She held her hands together in front of herself and looked all around. "My parents would be very proud of me."

"Yes, they would," I said.

"Can we get you anything? Trudie, gather refreshments," Jolie said.

"No, we're good. We don't want to take up much of your time. I know you want to get back to it."

"What's your question?" Jolie asked.

My gaze went to the spot on the wall where I thought the sword had been hung. Jolie's mother was even more stunning now, with the setting around her cleared away. The portrait was a focal point, and Vivian deserved no less. "I have an old picture I'd like to show you."

"All right."

I'd put the picture into a folder and then into my bag. I grabbed the folder and opened it, extending the picture in her direction over the green table. I'd thought about bringing the whole album, but I didn't want to get distracted or potentially cause Jolie unnecessary melancholy.

"Oh, that's me," she said as if it took her a second to be sure.

"Yes."

"I was a looker," she said.

"You are still beautiful," I said.

"Pshaw."

I smiled and pointed. "This is what I'm wondering about."

She looked at the picture and then back up at me. "What?"

"Does this look like the blade end of a sword?"

"Oh." She adjusted her reading glasses. "Aye, it does." She looked behind her at the spot where it might have once been.

"Jolie," I said, not wanting to immediately sound like I was accusing her of something, but still needing to get an answer. "Is this the same sword that was found out by the bridge?"

Jolie's mouth made an O. She looked at Trudie. "Do you remember a sword there?"

"I don't."

There was no sense that either of them was lying, but I had already begun to wonder if Jolie was just exceptionally talented at the skill.

Jolie's eyebrows came together as she tapped her finger on her lips. "Delaney, if my father had a sword on that wall, I don't remember it. Though when I was the age I am in that picture, there is a very good chance I wouldn't have noticed any swords on the wall. I was out to have fun, that was all."

"I found it in an album with other pictures of you and Edwin."

"Aye?" She smiled. "That would be a fun trip down memory lane."

"I'll bring it out one day, but do you remember who took the picture? Was it Edwin?"

She laughed. "That was so long ago. I don't know, but if it

was included in an album with other pictures of Edwin, then there's a good chance it was."

The reason I'd asked that question was because though I hadn't known him as a young man, I would assume that Edwin would have always been interested in something that might be a Crusader sword.

"Jolie, what about the law firm of Harris Bosworth?"

"Bowie's firm?"

"Yes."

"All I know is that's where Bowie works."

"Jolie, I have some news." I waited until she nodded. "Bowie was . . . struck out. She's no longer an attorney. She's been lying to you."

For a few moments, confusion took over Jolie's features. Her face fell and her color drained, but she recovered quickly. She smiled. Then, her smile transformed into laughter. Though it wasn't maniacal, it was pretty darn close. When her eyes started to water, Trudie stood and made her way to the desk. She grabbed a box of tissues and brought them back to the table.

Jolie took one and dabbed her eyes. "I'm so sorry, but . . . well, all this cleaning is because of her threats, and, though I don't want to admit it, I'm grateful. This is the way I want to live. Gracious, what did she do to be struck out?"

"I believe she lied to the courts, but I don't know for sure. Also, I think she stole a priceless sword from one of her fellow attorneys."

"Oh." Jolie's face didn't fall this time, but she did sober. "You think she planted it on the property?"

"I don't know what I think."

"Why?"

I shook my head. "The only thing I can guess is to hide the fact that she stole it."

"I don't see how all those pieces fit together," Jolie said.

"I don't either."

We heard the front door open. "Jolie? Trudie?" Homer called.

"In the library." Trudie stood and made her way to the hallway.

Homer joined us. I introduced Tom, and Homer asked what we were doing there.

"Do you remember a sword on that wall?" Jolie asked.

"A sword? No," Homer said.

"Show him the picture," Jolie said.

I opened the file again.

"Oh, not a sword. I remember that item. It was a cross."

"A religious item?" Jolie said. "My parents were never religious. We never went to church."

"No, but they were given a cross as a gift. They asked to have it displayed when they planned a party so the person they got it from might see it." Homer smiled back at the memory. "I only remember because they argued about it. One of them kept telling me to keep it there, one of them kept telling me to take it down." Homer paused. "Though I cannae remember which one said what."

"Well, they were polite that way."

Homer laughed. "I know exactly where it was put away."

"Where?" Jolie asked.

"It's in my cabin," he said. "Your mother gave it to me once she and your da agreed it didnae need to stay up. I'm not religious either, but your mother felt it was wrong to throw out such a thing so she asked if I would take it. I did. It's in a drawer in my house. I haven't thought about it in years, but it brings back lovely memories of your parents."

"Do you remember when Jolie and Edwin were close?" I asked Homer.

"Of course, though back in those days, I was more distant from the family."

"Aye," Jolie said. "For my parents, the help was the help. To me, we are all family."

I did not want to suspect Jolie of any wrongdoing. I wanted to like her without reservation. I wanted to solve all the mysteries and then bring the photo album out for her and me to look through. I wanted us to become friends as we enjoyed refreshments on the green velvet table.

But I wasn't quite ready to let down my guard.

"Homer, is there any chance we could see the cross?"

"Aye. Do you want me to go get it?"

"Maybe we could venture out to your place together."

"I'll stay here, keep cleaning. I've had enough adventure for a while," Trudie said.

"I'd like to see it too," Jolie said. "I still don't remember it."

We hopped on the four-wheeler again. Tom was pelleted with questions from Jolie as we made the journey. By the time we arrived at Homer's house, she knew where in Edinburgh he'd grown up, what schools he went to, where his pub was located, and if he'd be working the next Friday when she thought she might stop by.

I pretended I didn't recognize the cabin. "Such a cute place."

"It's been home for a long time. I've been very happy here."

Homer led the way into the house, still neat and sparsely furnished and decorated. There were no pictures on any of the walls and the furniture wasn't covered with sumptuous cushions, but the place still felt homey and comfortable.

"It's in a box in my bedroom. I'll be right back." Homer took off for the area I hadn't already explored. I was glad to be inside the space with permission.

Jolie took a seat on the couch as Tom and I stayed in the entryway, both of us looking around and taking things in, even though there wasn't much to notice.

We heard noises from the back room before Homer emerged, carrying a large cross.

"This is it," he said.

"Gracious, I don't remember that at all. That was on the wall in the library?" Jolie said as she stood.

"Aye. But not for long. Your parents had it up only briefly."

I inspected the item, turning it so it looked like the image in the picture. I could see how the illusion of a blade could happen.

"Huh." Jolie shrugged. "I can see how it could be a match."

I stepped back from the picture. Inadvertently, my attention went to the couch. It was a neutral-colored piece of furniture, but something red was now sticking out from under a cushion. I made my way to it and lifted the cushion. I retrieved a red scarf.

"What is that?" Homer asked.

"I've never once seen you wear a scarf, let alone a red one," Jolie said.

"I don't have one that I remember," Homer said.

"Aye."

I had frozen in place, holding the scarf, staring at it as my mind tumbled. Bridget had told me that the item the police considered evidence was a part of a red scarf. Was this the scarf the scrap came from?

There were many red scarves in Scotland even if Homer had just mentioned that he didn't have one.

I just did the best I could not to behave in any way that might make Homer think the scarf was something important. It might not be, anyway.

"Delaney?" Tom asked. "Are you all right?"

My phone's alarm buzzed. I glanced at it, seeing that Bowie's shift at the diner was about to start. I used those moments to inwardly calm myself and then set the scarf back on the couch.

"I'm sorry. I forgot. I have an appointment." I turned to Homer. "Thank you for showing us the cross."

"Aye. I'll get you back."

By the time we reboarded the four-wheeler, I thought I'd normalized pretty well.

We left them to get back to their cleaning and Homer's non-stop care of the grounds. I wasn't worried for the women's safety because if Homer had killed Alban, I was sure he'd done it to somehow protect Jolie and maybe Trudie too.

Once in the car, I looked at my dashing husband and said, "How'd I do?"

"What do you mean?"

"Did I show my inner freak-out at all?"

"Not bad. I might have picked up on something, but I doubt the others did."

"Okay."

"What's going on?"

"I will tell you, but on the way to somewhere. Do you have any desire to visit an American-like diner?"

"Will they have pancakes like the one in Kansas?"

"If they don't, we will straighten them out."

By the time we were on the road, I called Bridget to confirm what she'd told me about the evidence the police were using. She also confirmed that her source was confidential and, no, I wasn't supposed to tell the police I told her anything.

I did tell her my next call would be to Inspector Winters, but I'd keep her out of it.

"Did you see the scarf?" she asked.

"I saw *a* scarf."

"Tell me where."

I hesitated for so long, she said, "Delaney, you owe me."

She wasn't wrong. "I don't want you to put yourself in danger."

She laughed. "That's pretty rich coming from you."

I looked at Tom, who could hear the whole conversation coming through the mobile speakers. He shrugged noncommittally.

"All right. Yes. I saw a red scarf at the groundskeeper's house at Jolie Lannister's place."

"The man who was originally arrested?"

"I think he was only questioned."

"Thank you."

"Bri—"

But she'd disconnected the call. Immediately I dialed Inspector Winters.

"Delaney?"

In the back of my mind, I was so glad people were answering. "I can't tell you how I know why this is important, but I saw a red scarf at Homer's cabin on the Lannister property."

I could hear the wheels of his mind turning through the cell signals. I was sure some of what he was thinking had to do with not being happy with me.

"Got it. Thank you."

He ended the call just as quickly as Bridget had.

I looked at Tom. "If Homer killed Alban, Elias is going to be so disappointed."

"Aye."

"I hear doubt in your voice."

"It's just a red scarf, lass. It might not be the one the police are looking for. I don't want anyone to be a killer, but I would be sad to see Homer did the deed too."

Homer could have killed *for* them. And Homer had been right there.

Wasn't it true that sometimes the simplest answer was the right one?

I sighed. My stomach was going every which direction. It was rare I wouldn't be able to enjoy a good diner pancake, but the mere thought of food didn't sit right.

Maybe coffee would do.

CHAPTER THIRTY-SIX

"She rang in sick," the waitress said. "Her next shift is in two days."

My heart sank. There were still so many unanswered questions.

"Do you know where she lives?" I asked.

The waitress raised an eyebrow. "No, I'm afraid I don't. Would you like to leave her a message?"

"That's okay. I'll get in touch with her."

"Sorry, love," Tom said as the waitress turned and walked away.

My stomach was unsettled enough as it was. I was probably going to disappoint Tom, but I said, "I'm not hungry. Are you?"

"Not really."

"Some other time?"

"That works."

Tom dropped me at the bookshop before he headed back to the pub. I filled everyone in on everything, including the scarf.

No one wanted Homer to be the killer. I texted Inspector Winters, asking if he'd let me know what came of the scarf.

As we waited to hear from him, we all fell into a glum state, but thankfully, work kept us on our toes.

I texted Bowie, inviting her to the bookshop, lying to her by saying Edwin had some legal questions and was looking for a new attorney. Though she'd been struck off, she seemed gutsy enough to take the bait, if only out of curiosity. However, I didn't hear back from her.

I also didn't hear back from Inspector Winters or Bridget.

I found a little solace in the warehouse, or maybe just distraction. I got to work on a tedious project—returning some stones to their proper setting on a bracelet chain. It required complete focus. Both Edwin and I were perfectionists, particularly when it came to items from his collections.

But sometimes a distraction is just the thing the mind needs to work through a mystery without interference from intellect. I was convinced that my intuition was always chugging away in the background. And no one knew how much I cherished it, loved hearing the bookish "voices in my head."

However, most of the time, the words I heard didn't necessarily mean much of anything beyond, maybe, my intuition needing to stretch a little, peek out to the world and make itself known.

Today was a prime example. When I heard the queen's voice again, with words I'd already heard her say in my head, I knew they were words from a snippet of a speech I might have heard on Elias's radio.

It's all to do with the training: you can do a lot if you're properly trained.

"Okay," I said. "Anything more specific?"

No other words came to my head. Typical ambiguity, but I didn't think my intuition was talking to me about my training.

There might be something else to this one.

I set down the tweezers and leaned back from the project on my desk.

As circuitous as the route might have been, I was pretty sure my intuition was keying in on Bowie Berry. Of course, there might be many other reasons I was suspicious of her.

Had she stolen a sword from Daken and then planted it on Jolie's land?

I had another question, but I wasn't even sure why it suddenly seemed important. And, I didn't know who could possibly answer it.

I grabbed my phone and started at the top of my list of possibilities. Bowie herself.

But the phone went to a message again. "This is Bowie Berry. Leave a message and I'll call you right back. Cheers!"

"Bowie," I said. "I need you to call me back as soon as possible. I think you might have been right about Jolie. She might need some help."

I ended the call. It was the third one I'd made to her, but I hoped this one might get her to finally call me back. I couldn't be sure I sounded convincing, but I could hope.

I looked at the phone a long moment, but no one rang back.

"A watched phone and all . . ." I muttered to myself.

I cleaned up my project and did a quick once-over of the warehouse, making sure I hadn't left anything out that shouldn't have been. My eyes glanced over the locked knife bin. I was doubly glad I hadn't shown its contents to Joshua, though I doubted he would ever use any sort of position of power over us at the bookshop.

Once my tasks were done and I was convinced that my bookish voices were going to remain silent, I made my way over to the other side, finding only Rosie and Hector. Rosie was dusting the shelves with one of the feather dusters. I grabbed the other one from the desk and joined her, scratching behind Hector's ears as he rested in the crook of Rosie's elbow.

"What's on your mind, lass?" she asked.

"I need to talk to Jolie's purported lawyer, Bowie Berry."

"Maybe Edwin kens something about her, or maybe one of his attorney friends kens."

"He mentioned he would ask around, but I haven't followed up."

Still dusting, I rang Edwin. At least he was answering my calls.

"Lass?"

"Am I interrupting anything?"

"Not at all. What's going on? I feel a wee bit out of the loop."

"Have you asked any of your friends about Bowie Berry?"

"I have. One said she was a good attorney, one said she wasn't. The third one had never heard of her. I didn't think it was enough to share with you."

"Thanks. No. It sounds like an even three-way split."

"Lass, what's new? Anything?"

I told him about the red scarf, but his response was what I'd already heard and concluded. There were many red scarves in Scotland. He did add, though, that if this one was being *hidden* in a couch, not just somehow left there and maybe got tucked over time, there might be something to it.

I thought he had a good point, but there was no way to know how the scarf had gotten there.

Once the dusting was done (really, though, was it ever?), I asked Rosie if I could leave (yet again).

"Aye, of course. Where are you going?" she asked.

"I'm not exactly sure."

"Aye. Be careful then."

"I will."

"Lass," Rosie said, more sternly than normal.

I blinked and gave her my full attention.

"I mean it. There's no need to put yourself in harm's way."

I nodded. I didn't tell her what I was going to do. It wasn't dangerous, but it seemed a silly waste of time. I couldn't help myself from trying, but I was embarrassed by the compulsion.

As I hurried to the bus stop, I texted Tom that I was going to the candy shop next to Alban's apartment. I would tell him the truth always no matter how silly it might seem.

He texted: Why?

I responded with: I just wonder if someone there saw something.

Tom: Careful, lass.

Me: Will do.

I dialed Jolie's number, thinking I wouldn't get an answer, but was pleasantly surprised when Trudie picked up the phone.

"Lannister's."

"Trudie. It's Delaney."

"Lass, is everything all right?"

"Yeah, why?"

"Ms. Berry rang us a wee bit ago, asking if you were here."

"Did she ask anything else?"

"No, just that. I told her you weren't, of course, and gave her your mobile number. Did she ring?"

"No, but I've been trying to get ahold of her too."

"Why?"

I bit my bottom lip. "Trudie, do you think there's any chance Ms. Berry is living in her van?"

"That's an odd . . . I don't know. Want me to ask Jolie?"

"Yes, please."

I heard the clunks of the phone handset dropping to the counter and then the muffled voices of both women approaching.

"Delaney, what is this about Bowie living in her van?" Jolie said as she picked up.

"I just wonder. She's lost her license to practice law, she moved out of her apartment, she got that van, maybe all about the same time."

"Okay. Well, what would it matter if she lived in the van?"

The reason I thought it might matter was simple: possible evidence inside of it. But I didn't want Jolie to know that. I didn't want anyone to know it. It still seemed too far-fetched.

"Just curious. I'd like to find her, talk to her."

"Aye . . . well, I don't know where she lives, but I know she used to frequent a coffee shop near her old offices. She loved their caramel frappe something or other. The shop is called Bears and Beans. That's where I met her a few months ago."

"Thanks. I'll check it out. And, Jolie . . ."

"Aye?"

"I'm not sure you should trust her right now."

"Oh, lass, I haven't trusted her since she walked into my home and told me she was going to 'force some issues.'"

"Right, but I mean, don't let her into your house, okay?"

After a long pause, Jolie answered. "All right, lass. That seems a wee bit dramatic."

"I know, but maybe don't let anyone in right now."

"Not even you or Edwin?" A smile lined her tone.

"Well, we're okay, but everyone else."

After another long pause, she said, "I hear you, lass. Ta."
She hung up the phone.

I disembarked the bus a half block from the candy shop. My
approach was thwarted when I noticed that the lights inside the
shop were off. Once I made it to the door and saw the posted
hours, I realized I'd missed Luke and any employees by about
twenty minutes. I tapped on the window just in case someone
was still there behind the office door. No one came through.

I took the neighboring doorway and climbed the two flights
of stairs to Alban's flat. There were three other doors on the
floor, but I chose the one directly across from Alban's, based
upon what I thought I remembered Luke telling me about the
person who saw the woman leaving that day.

Classical music came through the door as I rapped my
knuckles briskly.

The door opened with caution. Large, dirty eyeglasses
magnified an older man's eyes. Gray hair stuck up in tufts over
his head.

"Who are you?" His accent was distinctly Irish, not Scottish, and very bothered.

"I'm so sorry to disturb your afternoon. I have a question
about your neighbor, Alban."

"The one who was killed?"

"Yes."

"Who are you?" he asked again.

I sighed. "My name is Delaney Nichols. I work at a bookshop, but I met Alban the day he was killed, and I really want
the police to find his killer."

The man's bushy eyebrows came together tightly. "Huh. Well, what's your question?"

He wasn't going to invite me in, which was good. I nodded.

"Are you the one who saw a woman leaving his flat?"

"How did you know . . . oh, it doesn't matter, I suppose. As a matter of fact, I am, but I'm not sure if the woman came from his place or not. I heard his door slam—"

"You know it was his?"

He nodded. "I know the shut of his door, and that time it was much louder than normal."

"Okay, then what?"

"I opened my door to see if there was a problem. Alban's door was shut tight, but a tall woman was making her way down that flight of stairs, right there." He nodded in that direction.

"Can you describe her?"

His eyebrows lifted. "Tall, wearing a dark coat. She was probably thin, but I couldn't tell for sure."

"Her hair color?"

"I have no idea. A scarf covered her head."

"A scarf? Not a hat?"

"A scarf."

I knew the answer to the next question was maybe the most important thing in all the world right then, or that's what it felt like. Behind my back, I crossed my fingers. "Do you remember the color of the scarf?"

"Certainly, it was red."

"Red?"

"Red. That's what I said."

I nodded, working hard to contain my excitement, but there

was more I hoped to learn. "Could you tell her age? Was she young or old?"

He thought a long moment. "From her back, I could only say that she wasn't old, but she wasn't as young as you, probably."

"This is great, thank you . . ."

"Harvey."

"Thank you, Harvey."

"Is this important? Should I call the police and tell them?"

"I don't think it would hurt. I have a number if you want it."

Harvey took Inspector Winters's phone number. I thanked him before I turned and hurried down the stairway.

I was eager to talk to the police myself, but I would give Harvey a minute or two to make his call first. I burst through the building's front doors with a new excitement. On my phone, I searched for the Bears and Beans Coffee Shop, surprised to see that it wasn't far away—about two blocks from where I was. I set out at a quick pace.

As I approached, I thought I might have somehow finally been gifted with good timing. I was sure Bowie's van was parked right outside the shop. Jolie had mentioned meeting Bowie there. Maybe it was just where she met everyone she called her client. Maybe this is where she spent her days when she wasn't working in the diner, her mobile "office."

Just as I sped up, though, she stepped out of the shop and hurried into the van. I watched her pull out and into traffic. I didn't spot any taxis nearby, so my only option was try to follow on foot.

It seemed the pedestrian traffic was thicker than the vehicles on the road. The van turned right long before I managed to get to that corner, but I could still spot it once I was around.

The left turn blinker went on, sending a jolt of panic through me. I would have to cross the street if I was going to keep up with her. Jaywalking was frowned upon, but I knew that if I went to the corner to cross, it would take too long, and I would probably miss my chance to talk to her.

With a quick glance in each direction up and down the street, I leapt out into a break in the traffic.

But it wasn't a break. In my rush, I'd missed spotting an approaching car. The driver slammed on the brakes, stopping with the front bumper only inches away from my legs. Behind that car, and in weirdly faraway-sounding noises, I heard the screech of other cars stopping. The good news was that no sound of crashing followed.

I apologized to the driver in the car closest to me. The woman's face was drawn and pale, twisting into anger. She sent me a hand gesture that I probably deserved.

I stepped back to the sidewalk and got my breath as I watched the traffic, everyone unharmed, move back into its flow.

I gazed back to where the van had been. Of course, it wasn't there. Carefully, I made my way up to the corner and crossed the street the safe way.

There was no sign of the van. The road curved enough that I might not be able to spot it if it was still on the same course. There were also plenty of streets it could have turned down.

I checked my phone again, but Bowie hadn't called me back. No one had.

My panicked heart rate was slowing. When everyone told me to be careful, they hadn't meant crossing the street, but, nevertheless, I'd been careless and reckless. No harm, no foul, but I knew what I needed to do now.

I pushed the button to call Inspector Winters and left another message.

CHAPTER THIRTY-SEVEN

I watched Tom and Rodger handle drinks and rowdy customers, the largest group of whom was cheering for a football match on the television. There were a lot of goals being scored, from the sound of it.

Usually, I liked watching people enjoy themselves. Tonight, my glee was diluted by . . . everything else. When our eyes met, I forced smiles and tipped my soda in Tom's direction. The questioning frowns he returned told me he wasn't buying my act. When he had a moment, I was sure he'd ask me what was on my mind.

The football match finished, leaving the crowd no further reason to be rowdy, so most of them cleared out, and Tom headed in my direction. Before he could reach me, though, I was greeted by someone I'd met recently.

"Lass?" Daken said as he nodded to the empty stool next to me.

"Hey, hello," I said to Daken.

"May I?" He nodded at the empty stool next to me.

"Of course."

"What can I get you?" Tom asked him.

"Hello, Tom. A pint please."

"Good to see you, Daken. Coming right up."

Daken turned to me. "How's everything? How are you?"

"I'm fine." I studied him, trying to decide what I should reveal. My curiosity won out. "I know you can't talk about Bowie Berry, but I sure have some questions I'd like to ask you."

Daken took a sip of the beer that Tom had quickly delivered, letting him know the drink was on the house. "Why?"

"Why do I have questions?"

"Aye."

"Someone killed Alban Dunning and I think Bowie Berry is up to no good. I hate to even say it, but maybe she had something to do with Alban's death."

"Oh, there's no doubt in my mind that she's up to no good. I don't know about being a killer, though." He thought a moment and shrugged. "Maybe." His hand on the mug handle and his arms resting on the bar, he looked around.

No one was paying us any attention, and though the rowdiest of the customers had left, it would be difficult to hear anything we said to each other.

"What do you mean by you know she's up to no good?" I kept my voice low. "What's her history? Or, just whatever you can tell me?"

"I can't tell you much of anything." Daken took another drink. "She took something of mine."

"A Crusader sword? How do you know she took it?"

His eyebrows lifted. "Aye. I'm impressed that you know. I can't answer your second question, but I will confirm the first. It was a Crusader sword, one that was in my family since my grandfather's days. This next part might answer your second question if you think it through. My grandfather stole it long before Bowie did."

I nodded. I'd already considered something like that. "Okay, but that had to be long enough ago that no one would care. Any statute of limitation would have run out."

"That's true. However . . . well, it's not the only thing he stole, and the sheer amount of treasures might trump statutes. I'm a lawyer and I'm not sure myself, but I certainly don't want to risk it. And I will deny I told you any of this if I'm ever questioned. No one will be able to find the rest of his hidden treasure. I was stupid to show the sword to Bowie, but I'll never be that stupid again."

Daken had surprised me, and finding me at the pub had probably surprised him too. He knew I wasn't recording any of this. No one could reasonably hear. He seemed to relish talking about it as much as I enjoyed getting some answers.

"I see," I said.

Daken's eyebrows lifted. "No, lass, you don't." He looked at Tom, who was at the other end of the bar now. "But your husband is a good lad, and I like you. Believe it or not, I knew I shouldn't trust Bowie Berry from the first moment I met her."

"Why did you show her the sword then?"

"Ego." He bit his bottom lip. "I found her attractive, even though I knew she was wicked. These sorts of things get men in so much trouble." He smiled sadly.

"True. So, she threatened to turn you in for the sword and all the other stuff?"

"That's about right."

I put some pieces together in my head. "She didn't steal the sword. You gave it to her."

"It was the ransom of my freedom."

"Oh. No wonder you didn't tell the police."

"Well, that and I didn't want them to know about the other things."

"She's been struck out?"

"That's public record now, so, aye, I can confirm."

"She doesn't live in the same apartment she used to."

"I would think not. It's a pricey place."

"Could she be living in a van?"

His eyebrows lifted again. "That *would* surprise me. She likes the finer things in life."

"Who doesn't? But she can only afford what she can afford."

"Living in a van. That's too bad if that's true." Daken frowned. "No matter my soured feelings for her, that would be sad."

"I don't feel too sorry for her. I think she used your sword to try to manipulate a former client of hers."

"Who?"

"Jolie Lannister."

"Aye, I know Ms. Lannister. She's a client of the firm's. Bowie has no say in her legal matters anymore."

"She's playing it as if she does."

"You should let the police know."

"I . . ." I was going to say that I had told the police, but I hadn't specifically shared with them that Bowie's impersonation went beyond tricking Jolie, that she was defrauding the law firm too. "Okay, I will."

"I'll call Ms. Lannister tomorrow and tell her not to worry, if that would help."

"I think it would."

"I'll do it first thing tomorrow," he said.

"Thank you."

"Aye."

Daken finished the beer and scooted off the stool. He set some tip bills on the bar and looked at me. "Where would Bowie be parking the van?"

"I don't know. That's a good question."

"My parents roamed around in a caravan for a while. There are a few caravan parks here in the city."

"Where?"

Daken told me where the parks were located. One of them was close to where I'd seen the van only a couple hours earlier.

"She has to park it somewhere. Car parks aren't fond of just letting people stay there overnight. And, if she's truly living in it, the parks have amenities like bathrooms, showers. They are quite nice, in fact."

"That makes sense."

"Maybe. If she's anything, I would say that Bowie is a survivor, even if she's misbehaving along the way."

I nodded, but my mind was now on the caravan park.

"We didn't have this conversation." Daken smiled. "But it was nice talking to you, Delaney. I hope to see you and Tom down the road, under more friendly circumstances." He thanked and waved at Tom before he turned and wove his way out of the pub.

Tom joined me. "That looked like a serious conversation."

"It was interesting."

"Aye?"

I nodded, knowing that Rodger was closing the pub tonight and, barring another popular football match crowd, Tom wasn't going to work much longer. "I'll tell you all about it on the way home."

"I can't wait."

CHAPTER THIRTY-EIGHT

"This way?" Tom asked as he turned the car to the right.

"Yes, the park should be at the end of this road, and this was the way I saw her go."

"Okay."

It was dark and cold outside, and rain was falling lightly on the car's windshield, the wipers on low. I'd told Tom about my conversation with Daken. Tom had been the one to suggest a drive by, though he might have sensed I was going to make the request anyway.

The park's entrance was marked with a sign pointing down a driveway. Trees hid the RVs until about halfway down the drive. Tom stopped at the entrance gate that was manned by an older man in a brown uniform. He stepped out of a small shelter but remained dry under a short awning.

"Hey, folks," he said, giving the car a curious once-over. "You looking for a place to stay tonight?"

"No, we're just hoping to meet up with a friend who might be staying here," Tom said.

The man grabbed a clipboard from inside the shelter. "They must have given me your name then. It's after hours. I can't let you in without approval. What's their name?"

Tom looked at me. I didn't want Bowie to know we might be onto her, so I said, "We'll turn around and get out of the way. We'll give her a call first. We didn't tell her we were coming. We wanted to surprise her, but we'll let her know."

"Good enough. You can park over there." He pointed to a small pullout that was behind us and on the other side of the driveway.

Tom turned around and parked in the spot. "I don't think we're getting in there tonight."

"Me neither. Maybe just drive on the roads around it. I'll see if I can spot the van."

"We'll give it a try."

Tom steered the car on the roads along the perimeter of the park, but there were too many trees blocking the view.

And then, once again, fate intervened. As we came back around toward the park's driveway, Bowie's yellow van pulled out ahead of us.

We were two vehicles behind her, and it was dark and raining—she had no clue we were watching her from Tom's car, my mouth agape.

"There she is," Tom said.

"Follow her?"

"I will as long as it's safe."

I'd decided to keep my near miss to myself. Again, no harm, no foul. "Sounds good."

It didn't take long to figure out where Bowie was going. The van took a direct route to Gilles Haig's auction warehouse. The darkness mixed perfectly with the lightly falling rain. Tom and I were both confident that we weren't recognized.

"That's Haig's?" Tom nodded out the front windshield as he pulled to the side of the road a half block away.

The van had parked by the front doors, and though there

were a couple other cars around, it was much less traveled than the main roads we'd taken to get there.

"It is."

Though it was difficult to make out specifics this far away, we could see a figure exit the van and dash inside.

"I would love to know what she's doing in there. What are she and Gilles doing?"

"We could just walk in. We're together. It would be safer than if you were alone," Tom said.

I swooned a bit. I knew that on his own, Tom would have never been curious about any of this, particularly when a murder was involved. But here he was, joining in because he knew that these were the sorts of things that kept me up at night, kept my mind working.

I smiled. "That sounds great. Let's do it."

But just as he put the car back into drive, Bowie exited the building and hopped back into the van.

"Shoot," I said.

"Follow her or go inside and talk to Gilles?" Tom asked.

It wasn't an easy decision, but I had only a moment to make it. As the van pulled away from the curb, I said, "Follow. He might not even be there. We can come back and try to talk to Gilles later."

The weather continued to camouflage us as we made our way back toward Grassmarket.

"I thought she might head to the diner or a coffee shop," I pondered aloud. "This is the opposite direction."

"Aye," Tom said.

When the van slowed to an unwarranted stop on the road just down from the bookshop, Tom and I shared a surprised glance.

"Is she looking over toward the bookshop?" I asked.

"I can't tell, but there's no reason to stop right here unless she's just looking. It's not a parking spot."

A few seconds later, and after a car directly behind her honked, she pulled away from the curb. When she turned at the corner, I thought I knew where she was headed next.

"The museum?" I asked.

"It could be."

The van stopped in a real parking spot—not in front of the museum, but to the side of it, up the road a little bit. Tom pulled into a spot a few cars away. It was a tight squeeze that required some maneuvering.

Bowie exited the van and then ran toward a door I hadn't noticed before, on the side of the museum building and hidden by a partial wall. As Tom squeezed the car into the spot, Bowie went through the door.

"How . . ."

"Let's go," Tom said without asking if I wanted to. He knew I did.

We hurried out of the car and to the door. I pushed on the handle, but it was locked.

"Hang on," I said as I grabbed my phone. "I know Joshua gave me Victor's phone number."

It took me a second to find it because I'd saved it as Security Victor.

"This is Victor," he said when he answered.

"Hi, Victor, it's Delaney Nichols."

"Hello, lass. What can I do for you? Are you at the door?"

"I'm at a side door, one I hadn't noticed before. It's hidden by a partial wall."

"What are you doing there?"

"I saw someone go inside."

"That's not unusual. Many of the employees enter that way."

"Right, but something's . . . something's not *right*. I don't know but . . . could you open it for me and my husband. I don't think the person we saw works here."

He hesitated, but then said, "Aye. I'll be half a minute."

True to his word, he was there about thirty seconds later.

"You're getting soaked," he said. "Come in."

I hadn't even noticed, but we were drenched.

"Thanks, Victor." Tom and I stepped into a generic hallway, dripping. "Do you know if Joshua is here?"

"I don't, but I can find out."

I nodded. "I think we should make sure the sword is okay."

"The Crusader sword?"

"Yes."

"It's not here any longer."

"Where is it?"

"I heard it was returned to the owner, for now."

I was confused, but Jolie didn't have any sort of obligation to tell me the sword had been returned.

"Okay, well . . . can we check out where it had been kept?"

Victor's eyebrows came together as he studied both of us a long moment. "I'll call Joshua on the way."

We followed Victor as he spoke into his phone to Joshua. Thankfully, Joshua was in the building and said he'd meet us at the lab.

It seemed that Joshua had eased any concerns Victor might have had about us being there, and he sped up after the call ended.

We traveled down the generic hallway with unadorned

doors, and then through one to a stairway. Down two flights, Victor kept himself in front of us as he burst through a door to the familiar basement hallway leading to the labs and storage rooms.

As we approached it, an elevator dinged and Joshua emerged, concern lining his features.

"Who did you see?" he asked.

"Bowie Berry," I said.

"Who?"

"Jolie Lannister's former attorney," I said.

"Right, I remember you telling us about her when we were in the bookshop. Victor, let's get to the lab."

At another time, our sliding stop outside the lab might have been comical. However, today, and considering everything else, it was simply perplexing.

Through the windowed walls, we saw a person inside the lab, but it wasn't Bowie Berry. For a few beats it seemed like maybe we'd gone to the wrong place, or not the same spot the person we'd followed had gone, but then my eyes landed on the raincoat that had been placed on one of the tables.

We hadn't been following Bowie Berry. Somehow and in a way that felt too out of sync to understand, the person we'd been trailing was Cramer Donnell.

Tom and I shared a quick and perplexed look.

"Cramer?" Joshua said too quietly for the man in the lab to hear.

Cramer's attention was on something he was reading, a stack of papers. He had neither seen nor heard us yet.

"He's not supposed to be here," Victor said. "Let me handle this."

I put one hand on Victor's arm and one on Joshua's. "I don't know why or how or what it all means, but he drove here in what I think is Jolie Lannister's attorney's van. And there was a murder . . . I think we should call the police."

None of us were armed, including Victor, but just as we moved to get out of Cramer's view, he looked up. Tears were streaming down his cheeks as he lifted the papers in both his fists.

"What . . . ?" Victor said.

I wasn't sure if Cramer had spotted us through the glass, but if he had, he didn't make a move to leave.

"Stay here," Victor said to us.

Cramer's eyebrows furrowed as he focused on us through the glass. "I thought the answers would all be in here. There's nothing about the sword in these pages!" Cramer yelled the words.

"I'm going too," Joshua said, a no-argument tone to his voice.

"This man . . . he's . . . something's wrong," Victor said. "Stay back some. I will too."

"He was escorted out of the building," Joshua said. "Told not to come back."

"I know, lad. I was the one to walk him out. He kept a key, apparently."

"There's nothing in these pages!" Cramer exclaimed.

He'd seen us, but I couldn't be sure if he was talking to us or himself. Maybe both.

He was upset, but not because he'd been caught somewhere he wasn't supposed to be.

"I'll call Inspector Winters," I said.

"Aye. Ta." Victor stepped to the doorway as I made the call. "Mr. Donnell, you're not supposed to be here."

I took a couple steps back and made the call to Inspector Winters. Thankfully, he answered on the first ring. My attention was so focused on Cramer that I'm not even sure what I said, though I did process his words: "I'll be right over."

When I disconnected the call, I wondered if I'd given him our correct location. I hoped I had.

"Mr. Donnell, come on," Victor said. "Let's go upstairs and talk about this with Joshua."

"Hey, Cramer," Joshua added. "Come on out."

I knew the lab held things that could be used as weapons, and that it was important for us all to keep a safe distance.

"I'm not leaving until I have the sword," Cramer said.

"It's not here," Joshua said. "It's gone."

"Where is it?!"

"In a safe place, but not in this building."

"Why . . . ?"

"It was the right thing to do," Joshua said.

Cramer seemed perplexed as he looked down at the papers. His gaze shot back up a moment later. "It's not in here! The only thing this talks about is some affair between someone named Vivian and Edward. I don't even know who they are. Why isn't it in here? Bowie told me this was full of secrets. Who cares about this drivel?"

"Where did you get those papers?" I piped up. We'd all made our way into the room.

Cramer looked at me, his eyebrows coming together in a most unfriendly manner. "I took them from Bowie."

Victor, Joshua, and Tom all seemed fine with me asking questions, though in one manner or another they'd all put themselves somehow in between Cramer and me.

"How do you even know Bowie Berry?"

"What difference does that make?"

"I'm just curious why you are here with papers that she claimed held some secret. What's going on?"

I didn't think he'd answer, but after a moment it seemed he wanted to speak. "What's going on is that she promised me I would get the sword."

"When, how?" I continued attempting to distract him as well as get some answers.

"When the position of Treasure Trove director opened, she rang me in Glasgow, told me I'd be perfect for the job, said I should work to get it."

I cleared my throat. "Did you know her before that?"

"Aye, she was my solicitor at one time. I was sued by a museum I worked for. She got the whole thing settled with no one the worse off. She is . . . was a very good attorney."

"You heard she'd been struck out?" I said.

Emotion crinkled his face. "She told me just tonight. She rang me to meet her at a caravan park. She confessed everything."

"Everything?" I asked.

"Aye. She told me she'd been struck out. She said she'd stolen the sword and planted it on the grounds of Jolie Lannister's house, meant for Jolie to find it. Bowie was going to go to the courts, say that Ms. Lannister was losing her faculties and that at one time Ms. Lannister had asked Bowie to take care of her things, her life. She was going to convince the courts that she should still have the same power. She was going to steal everything from Ms. Lannister and then let me have the sword. Until tonight, I didn't know she was no longer an attorney—living in a van!"

"You took those papers from her?"

"She said there were secrets in these pages, but there's not one thing about a sword!"

A wave of fear ran though me. "Cramer, where is Bowie? Gilles?"

He looked at me with an expression that I had never seen on his face before. Was it evil? Desperation?

My breath caught and I had to look away, but then my eyes landed on something that made me gasp.

Peeking out from under the discarded, wet raincoat, was a red scarf. I sensed immediately that it wasn't the same one found in Homer's house, nor had it been the one worn by a woman descending the stairs in Alban's apartment building. There were a lot of red scarves in the world. This was the one the police had been looking for, I was sure.

"You killed Alban Dunning!" I said without thinking.

Whatever fugue of frustration Cramer had been in the middle of, he snapped out of it. "You have no idea what I've done."

I was becoming more and more sure I did. We were going to have to stop Cramer Donnell from leaving that room. It was four against one, so we could probably do it, but I didn't want anyone to get hurt.

Then the game changed again. Because he'd been behind one of the lab tables, we hadn't seen that he wore a belt with a sword sheathed at his side. It wasn't the Crusader sword, but something more contemporary, most likely even more deadly.

It was quite the sight, striking me as something both medieval and cosplay, but I knew it was real and I swallowed a gasp.

As he stepped around, he left the papers behind on the table and unsheathed the sword. He held it just like he had the Crusader before he'd swung it in such disregard. But this weapon wasn't going to break. Its blade was securely in place, and it shined with the sheen of something that had only recently been forged.

"Get out of my way," he said.

The four of us did exactly as he asked and gave him a wide berth.

His head swiveling back and forth as he watched us all, he marched his way out of the room. I was the last person he passed by, and he stopped and stared at me.

"Move along, Cramer," Joshua said, as all three of the men moved closer to me.

Cramer waited a moment, then nodded and continued down the hallway. I knew he'd killed Alban Dunning, and a new seed of fear had planted itself inside me. I was pretty sure he'd done something to Bowie Berry and maybe Gilles Haig too. We needed to find them both.

I didn't want Cramer to get away.

When he was ten feet ahead of me, I rose up on my tiptoes and scurried in his direction. I heard the gasps and yells of the men now behind me, but they weren't quick enough to stop me from my mission. It all happened too fast for Cramer to do much of anything either, except begin to turn around to see what the commotion was all about. But I'd gotten there soon enough to do something I'd never done before. However, I'd seen my brother Wyatt slide into home plate enough times to know I needed to fold my left leg under me and extend my right leg as I went down.

My form was darn near perfect, if I said so myself, and Cramer Donnell went down before he could turn all the way around to face or stab me. True to the plan I'd quickly formulated, Cramer was forced to fling himself forward. The sword flew out of his hands and skated and slid down the hallway until it was stopped by Inspector Winters's foot as he appeared from the stairwell and stepped down on the weapon.

The three men who'd been behind me were on top of Cramer

only a beat later, and Inspector Winters finished it off by locking Cramer's arms behind him with handcuffs.

Once that was done, I said, "We need to check the van and maybe the caravan park, Gilles Haig's place. I think Cramer's done something to Bowie Berry, maybe Gilles too."

Inspector Winters was on his radio calling in for assistance, but Joshua and Victor agreed to stay with Cramer until help arrived. Cramer starting yelling about his innocence, his right to the sword, the unfair methods we'd all used to take him down.

We ignored him. Inspector Winters, Tom, and I ran down the hallway and up the stairwell to the building's side door. It was raining even harder now, but we threw ourselves out and into it as we rushed to the van. Inspector Winters opened the side sliding door, where we found the body of Bowie Berry—on her side, her hands tied behind her back.

But then the body moved. She tried to turn her head so she could see us. She made noises from behind a gag that had been made of a sock and an old bandana.

Inspector Winters removed the gag. "Are you all right, Ms. Berry?"

"Aye, I'm fine, but you need to find Cramer Donnell. He's . . . well, he's a killer to be sure, which is probably what he was going to do to me next. I don't know . . . Oh, my goodness." Tears came to her eyes as Inspector Winters removed the ropes around her wrists and ankles. "Thank you." She looked at me and Tom. "Thank you, all."

"You're welcome, but I'd suggest you stop talking until we can get an official statement. I'll get you some water and something to eat, and if you're not hurt, I won't make you go to hospital," Inspector Winters said.

She nodded. "I'm fine. Now."

Inspector Winters sent me and Tom back inside the side doorway, where, for the first time in our marriage, the first time since we'd known each other, my husband showed me his temper.

There's no need to dwell on the tone he used as he spoke to me, but I will say that in no uncertain terms he was as angry as I thought he could ever be at my sliding maneuver. He didn't yell, but he was certainly firm.

When he was done with the lecture, all I could do was wrap my arms around his neck and pull him close as I promised to never, ever again do something so stupid.

His anger faded in the embrace, but he held on to me as if he wasn't sure if he should ever let go again.

For a long few minutes, I returned the sentiment.

CHAPTER THIRTY-NINE

Tom did get over being angry at me, but I knew I hadn't heard the end of his concerns. It had been two days since Cramer Donnell had been arrested—for the murder of Alban Dunning and the kidnapping of Bowie Berry. Gilles hadn't been inside his auction warehouse the night we'd tailed the van, or he might have suffered a similar fate as one or both of the others.

Inspector Winters had allowed me to read Bowie's official statement. I was thrilled for the opportunity. I suspected that it was just easier for him to give me the statement than try to explain it, or try to answer all the questions I was sure to ask.

The tragic events began with Bowie "taking" the sword from Daken, in return for keeping some of his secrets, none of which were specifically outlined in the statement. This had occurred a year or so earlier, about the time her personal and professional lives were unraveling. She'd never behaved completely on the up-and-up in her career, but at the same time Daken was telling her he wasn't interested in a relationship, some of her court hijinks were wearing thin on at least one impatient judge, leading to her being struck out.

She decided to sell the sword to get the money, but the only way the item could be hers to do with whatever she wanted was if someone had given it to her legally or if she happened to find it somewhere and went through the proper Treasure Trove Unit channels.

Thoughts of Jolie's land as well as the condition of her house came to mind. There was history there that it might not make it such a stretch to discover a Crusader sword, either on the vast property or maybe even inside the messy house.

Bowie went about executing her plan. She delivered the sword to the area near the bridge, burying it some but not deeply. Her plan was to visit Jolie and then happen upon the sword on a friendly walk that they would take and Bowie would initiate. She would then threaten Jolie—Bowie would execute the clause in the legal documents that Jolie had signed ten years earlier that gave Bowie power of attorney over Jolie and her things. Bowie was sure that Jolie would protest, so Bowie was going to make a deal with her. Give Bowie the sword legally, and she would go away forever.

Bowie had also set in motion Cramer Donnell's appointment as Treasure Trove Unit director. Bowie had gotten him out of trouble a time or two during his years in Glasgow. He owed her and was on board quickly. Yes, he would analyze the sword and then declare it Bowie's property instead of Scotland's. She would then sell it and give him some hush money.

Originally, it had seemed a simple and non-violent plan in Bowie's mind, not to mention a great way to make some cash. Apparently, she'd even considered trying to sell the sword to Edwin.

However, as the poet Robert Burns said, "The best laid plans do often go aftly." Or as us non-Scots-speaking folks say it, "awry."

The day after Bowie dropped off the sword was the day that Homer decided to add a rock bed near the bridge. He came upon the sword and took it to Jolie immediately.

Two days after that, Bowie, with plans to call on Jolie, first visited the bridge just to make sure the sword was still there. To her astonishment (she told the police that she thought she was losing her mind) the sword wasn't there, a bed of rocks now in its place.

She finally deduced that the groundskeeper must have found the sword and given it to Jolie. She had to think of something else.

She remembered speaking with the receptionist at Harris Bosworth about how much her mother loved her job at an auction house and how trustworthy her boss Gilles Haig was. When Bowie contacted him, demanding that she join him the next morning for an emergency inventory, he agreed and brought Alban along. He hadn't known about Alban's past with Jolie Lannister.

What no one else had known was that Cramer Donnell was in the back of Jolie's van the whole time. He'd insisted upon coming along just in case he could somehow intervene.

In fact, since Cramer came to town, he'd been nothing but a painful thorn in Bowie's side. She'd regretted helping him become the Treasure Trove Unit director but couldn't figure out a way to get rid of him until the sword was sold and monies had been distributed.

Elias's and my first visit to the house had thrown everything off yet again. Once outside the house, as Gilles got into his car, Alban spoke with Bowie, accusing her of ambushing Jolie, though he didn't tell Bowie his reasons for sticking up for Jolie—her looking the other way when he'd broken into her house those years ago.

Inside the van, Cramer had heard the conversation between Bowie and Alban, and he knew Alban would try to stop them. When Alban didn't get into Gilles's car, Cramer hopped out of the van and followed him, ultimately using the rake to kill the person who was going to ruin his and Bowie's plans.

No one had spotted Cramer Donnell on the property that day.

Bowie's statement didn't answer why Cramer behaved the way he had when Artair and I had presented the cleaned-up sword. No one understood why he'd felt the need to wield it. Inspector Winters wasn't allowing me to read his statement.

Bowie had then only wanted to stop the things she'd put in motion. She felt responsible for Alban's death. She just wanted away from Cramer, but Cramer had counted on the money he would get from the sword. He felt he was left with no option but to steal it from the museum.

He confronted Bowie at the caravan park, where she was reading the journal pages that she herself had stolen from Jolie's desk, hoping to find something else she might be able to sell or just give to Cramer so he would leave her alone. She had gone in through Rosebud's front door using her own key.

No one had an explanation as to why we discovered a pebble under the window that matched where the sword had been found. I chalked it up to some twist of fate that we must have needed to push us in the right direction. Maybe a physical manifestation of one of my bookish voices.

When Bowie allowed Cramer into her van the night of the storm, he threatened her. She offered him the pages with the promise of the secrets they held just to get him out of there. He'd hit her and tied her up instead, donning her raincoat and taking her van to finish what they'd started.

He was going to take the sword from the museum and then

drive out of town in her van. He was going to have to kill her at some point, she thought, but thankfully we intervened.

Though Bowie had been the one to set all of it in motion, Cramer was the worst of the bad guys in the tragic turn of events.

Tom and I had witnessed Cramer (though we thought it had been Bowie because of the generic raincoat and the storm blurring our vision just enough) going into the warehouse. He'd gone there to confront Gilles, apparently, force him to help Cramer gather the sword. Thankfully, Gilles hadn't returned from the brief holiday Helen suspected he'd taken. He was back now, though—safe and cooperating in any way he could. We were all grateful that Gilles hadn't been there. Cramer was well off the rails by then.

Gilles said he hadn't reached out to Jolie before Bowie had contacted him. If someone truly had called Jolie to inquire about her home and its furnishings, no one knew who that had been.

The woman in the red scarf that the neighbor spotted was still a mystery. I hoped it had been a friend of Alban's, maybe someone he'd dated. Such a thing would go against his loner ways, but I wanted him to have friends, maybe a girlfriend.

We might never know, but I was going to keep an eye out during Alban's celebration of life.

I'd now read the journal, and it was quite salacious. It was supposedly written by Alban's grandfather, but there was nothing to substantiate anything about its contents. The tone felt fictional to me, but I wasn't going to share that with Jolie.

Bridget had written a story about the recent tragedies as well as the old controversies with Stephen, Vivian, Edward, and Wallis. I predicted that her article might win an award—it was that compelling. I thought maybe the royal family would reach out to Jolie, perhaps offer a DNA test using one of Edward's still-saved old brushes or something, but, according to Edwin, that probably wouldn't happen. Jolie didn't care anyway.

Bowie had been arrested too, but she was free on bond—she knew how to work the system. She faced a trial, but we all predicted she'd figure something out, maybe take a plea deal. She'd never be an attorney again, but she'd use her training to put herself into the best position.

Jolie was happy. Her house was spotless, and she was making plans to reinforce its structure, maybe even bring it back to its previous grandeur.

Today, she'd invited us all out to her very cleaned-up house so we might share a private moment of remembrance for Alban Dunning and make plans to go together tomorrow to the celebration of life gathering being held at the coffee shop he visited every day.

Edwin, Rosie, Hamlet, Joshua, Elias, Aggie, Tom, and I were all enjoying snacks on the back patio with our hosts. Homer, Trudie, and Jolie appeared to relish the company and were taking turns chatting with each of us, expressing their gratitude. Jolie kept apologizing for the mess she felt she'd made of everything. Edwin kept telling her it wasn't her fault.

It wasn't. It was mostly Cramer's fault, some of Bowie's, but we were all victims in a way.

"I invited Mr. Haig, but he said he wouldn't be able to join us today," Jolie said. "I will make arrangements with him to take care of things around here after the three of us are gone. He will do a fine job."

"That won't be for a long time," Edwin said.

"One never knows," Jolie said.

The sun was setting, but it hadn't rained. It had been a beautiful day, and it still was. We were sitting in chairs that had been placed in a circle around a firepit, though a fire hadn't been lit. We'd been there a couple hours, and I could tell it was about time to leave Jolie, Trudie, and Homer to their rest, but even they were fighting their weariness, not wanting their first big get-together in a long time to come to an end.

But we'd see each other tomorrow, and we'd be back to Rosebud, most of us. Even Elias and Aggie. Elias and Homer's friendship had been rekindled, and Aggie and Trudie seemed to hit it off grandly.

Edwin and Jolie might never have a romance again, but their shared history was something they wouldn't be able to deny now. I predicted they would be close friends for the rest of their lives.

Though Rosie was having a good time, she might not feel the need to visit Jolie anytime soon. I could see her patience being tested by Jolie's personality. Still, though, it was clear that they were fond of each other.

"Homer, would you mind?" Jolie said.

"Now?" Homer asked as he stood from the chair he'd moved next to Elias's.

"Please."

Homer went through the back door, returning a moment later with the now familiar tub. He made sure we all took a look inside it, seeing the two parts of the priceless sword. My heart hurt a little as I peered at the broken treasure. Homer set the tub on the unlit fire pit.

There had been a brief, behind-closed-museum-doors controversy regarding who, in fact, was the rightful owner of the priceless item, but Joshua had put a succinct end to any argument by declaring the item to be Jolie's because it had last been on her property. He wasn't to be argued with, apparently. He was going to make a fabulous director.

I thought Daken might have tried to claim ownership, but as far as I knew he'd been silent. I might bring it up to him if I ran into him again at the pub.

"All right," Jolie said. "Joshua, you are the new Treasure Trove Unit director. Edwin, I know you'd do right by it. I want to too, so I'm going to let the two of you fight it out."

Edwin and Joshua smiled at each other.

"It's yours, Edwin. I trust you too," Joshua said.

Edwin frowned and then stood and made his way to the tub. He looked into it and then back at Joshua. "I think you will be the best director the Treasure Trove Unit has seen in a long time. I think you should take it."

Joshua cocked his head as he looked at Edwin. The sun was low in the sky, but suddenly a ray bounced off one of the spotless house windows, its glare illuminating Edwin in an almost magical way. We all saw it and were struck momentarily silent as we watched. It wasn't as if he'd pulled the sword from a stone, but the effect was the same. The sun was somehow coronating him, announcing that he was the rightful owner.

"I imagine that's the queen speaking," Aggie finally said. "God save her soul."

Edwin didn't quite know what was happening, but he did lift his hand to block the glare from his eyes as the rest of us voiced our agreement. That sword was to go to Edwin. There would be no argument from anyone. I sniffed and wiped away a surprise tear.

Grief is the price we pay for love, lass. Remember that.

The queen's words rang through my mind—maybe her

most famous quote, though she'd personalized it just for me. Or, maybe I'd done that to myself.

"Are you all right?" Tom asked quietly as he put his hand on my leg.

I looked at him. I looked around at everyone, and watched the sun fall a little lower in the Scottish sky, the illumination of Edwin still there but dimming.

"I'm so good," I said after sniffing again. "So, so good."

ACKNOWLEDGMENTS

I really don't think I've said enough about copy editors. While I must thank all the usual suspects, because I couldn't do anything without my agent, Jessica Faust, my editor, Hannah O'Grady, everyone at Minotaur, and my family, it's the copy editors who really save the day. Thanks to all of you, and on this manuscript in particular, a special thanks to Alda Trabucchi.

There is a Treasure Trove Unit in Scotland, but I made up a whole bunch about it. Apologies if I'm way off the mark.

Also, thank you to my readers. You fill my days with inspiration. Much appreciated.